DAKOTA!

The eleventh stunning novel
in the tales of WAGONS WEST—
original stories of
legendary daring and courage as
pathfinders and pioneers carry
dreams of glory into
dangerous Indian lands.

★★★★★★★★★★★★★★★★★★★★★

WAGONS WEST

DAKOTA!

**A bold new
breed of pioneers rides under
starry prairie skies into a savage,
unmapped land.**

TOBY HOLT
The fearless son of wagonmaster Whip Holt
must carry a flag of truce into warring Indian
lands and is trapped by betrayal . . .
and by desire.

CLARISSA HOLT
A lovely wife left behind to bear her
husband's child, she tastes a bitterness
that may mean a broken heart.

BETH MARTIN
Irresistibly beautiful, her foolish flirtations
are a mockery of her marriage and make her
a prisoner to a man's insatiable lust.

LEON GRAHAM
Behind his gentlemanly manners lies an
unscrupulous heart that will bend a woman to
his will by kisses or by force.

★★★★★★★★★★★★★★★★★★★★★

★★★★★★★★★★★★★★★★★★★★★★★

HANK PURCELL
Young and shy, his superb skill with a rifle
may save a maiden's virtue . . .
and win him a tender love.

KALE SALTON
A honey-skinned octoroon, she sells her
favors to rich men, but she has sworn
vengeance on a shameless libertine.

MA HASTINGS
Cold-blooded and unforgiving, she leads a
band of vicious outlaws and schemes to
lure Toby Holt into certain death.

RALPH HASTINGS
A slave to drink and his mother's greed,
only an innocent love could give him
the courage to act like a man.

TALL STONE
A vicious and cruel Sioux warrior, his burning
hatreds mean death not only for the white man,
but for the woman who spurns his love.

GENTLE DOE
An alluring Indian girl, cruelly abandoned
by her tribe, she is saved by a man who
married another, but couldn't resist her
strong-willed desires.

Bantam Books by Dana Fuller Ross
Ask your bookseller for the books you have missed

WAGONS WEST
★
VOLUME 11

DAKOTA!

DANA FULLER ROSS

 BCI Created by the producers of
Wagons West, Children of the Lion,
Saga of the Southwest, and
The Kent Family Chronicles Series.
Executive Producer: Lyle Kenyon Engel

BANTAM BOOKS
TORONTO • NEW YORK • LONDON • SYDNEY • AUCKLAND

DAKOTA!

*A Bantam Book / published by arrangement with
Book Creations Inc.*

*Bantam edition / August 1983
2nd printing ... August 1983   3rd printing . November 1983
4th printing ... October 1984*

*Produced by Book Creations Inc.
Chairman of the Board: Lyle Kenyon Engel*

ISBN 0-553-23572-9

Published simultaneously in the United States and Canada

Bantam Books are published by Bantam Books, Inc. Its trademark, consisting of the words "Bantam Books" and the por-
trayal of a rooster, is Registered in U.S. Patent and Trademark
Office and in other countries. Marca Registrada. Bantam
Books, Inc., 666 Fifth Avenue, New York, New York 10103.

PRINTED IN THE UNITED STATES OF AMERICA

H   13 12 11 10 9 8 7 6 5

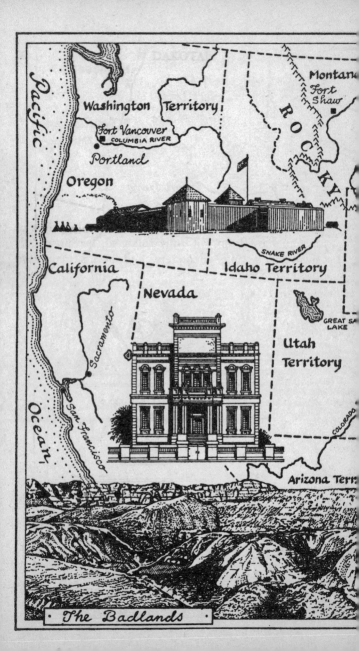

Pacific

Washington Territory

Fort Vancouver
COLUMBIA RIVER

Portland

Oregon

Montana

Fort Shaw

ROCKY

SNAKE RIVER

California

Idaho Territory

Nevada

GREAT SALT LAKE

Sacramento

Utah Territory

Ocean

San Francisco

COLORADO

Arizona Terr:

· The Badlands ·

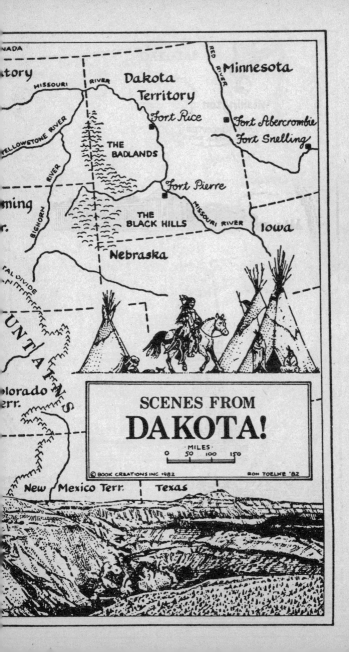

I

Red Elk, chief of the mighty Blackfoot Indians, stood at the edge of a high cliff and watched the snakelike column of a wagon train far below. His expression was fierce as he tried to contain his fury and frustration at the presence of white intruders in the lands that had once belonged to the Indians. Stretching out his arms, he looked up to the heavens, and in a voice bursting with emotion, he cried out:

"By the gods above and by my ancestors, I swear we will destroy the white men who intrude upon our lands! Soon bloody scalps will hang from the belts of all red men. I, Red Elk of the Blackfoot, have been called by Thunder Cloud of the Sioux to meet with him in Dakota. There we will also meet with Big Knife of the Cheyenne to plan ways to work together in trampling the white man into the dust."

With great agility, Red Elk leaped onto his horse and galloped away, followed by his war chiefs and braves, whose faces mirrored the feelings of their chief. The wagon train they had seen heading west would be the last to pass through unharmed. After the meeting of the chiefs in the Dakota Territory, white men would be eliminated from Indian lands once and for all.

The wagon train that moved slowly across the rugged Rocky Mountains, en route from Fort Shaw in the Montana Territory to Fort Vancouver in the Washington Territory, bore a strong resemblance to the trains that had made similar journeys more than two decades earlier. For one thing, the canvas-covered wagons, filled with food supplies and household goods, were similar, as were the teams of sturdy workhorses that pulled them. Also, the men and women who drove the wagons, most of them young and self-reliant, bore a striking resemblance to the earlier pioneers, and the rate of travel in the mountains—approximately ten to fifteen miles each day—was about the same.

But the big difference of this wagon train was the presence of the blue-uniformed troop of one hundred horsemen, members of the Eleventh U.S. Cavalry, who escorted the train. The troops, supplied by Colonel Andrew Brentwood, commander of Fort Shaw, were veterans of the recently ended Civil War, as well as the conflict in Montana the previous month with the Sioux Indians. The soldiers carried rifles and cavalry sabers, and they acted as deterrents to those who otherwise might have found the wagon train a tempting target.

Members of the wagon train included army personnel and their families, as well as a few immigrants from the East, who had traveled to Fort Shaw in Montana by way of steamboat on the Missouri River. Without the army escort, these wagon train members would have faced raids by the Indian tribes of the mountains as well as by bands of outlaws, who preyed on so many immigrants traveling west.

Clarissa Holt, a scarf tied over her red hair to protect it from the sun, was on the seat of her wagon. She was tall and statuesque, qualities that couldn't conceal the fact that she was a few months' pregnant. As she drove the vehicle with practiced ease, she reflected that she was enjoying herself enormously. She had made a journey like this just a few years earlier, when, as a widow in Philadelphia whose husband died fighting in the Civil War, she had traveled to the Washington Territory in what came to be called "the cargo of brides." Her friends on that journey had found new lives and husbands for themselves in the West, and she had found happiness when she had fallen in love with and married Toby Holt, son of the legendary Whip Holt, the mountain man and guide whose name was synonymous with the opening of the West.

Clarissa knew that in years past, when Whip Holt had led the wagon train across the Rockies, the pioneers had only themselves to rely on, and she had heard corroborating stories from Toby's mother, Eulalia, about the adventure-packed, dangerous travel that the settlers on the first wagon train to Oregon had endured. Now, in the 1860s, the trails were well traveled, many army posts were established, and wagon trains frequently moved in the company of army troops. Thus, overland travel in the West held fewer dangers, though it was no less arduous, especially in the mountains. Only the establishing of the transcontinental railroad, which Toby Holt was working on, would make travel through the mountains seem easy.

Forthright and blunt, Clarissa told herself that her happiness would be complete if only Toby were with her right now, sharing the pleasures of this wagon train journey in the pleasant autumn weather. But Toby, whose exploits were winning him a measure of fame almost as great as that of his late father, had been summoned to Washington City to confer with General Ulysses S. Grant, the chief of staff of the United States Army. The exact nature of the meeting was secret, but Clarissa knew it had something to do with the growing problems with the Indians.

Before heading east, Toby had insisted that his wife leave Fort Shaw, where she had stayed while he worked on the survey of the railroad in Montana. She was to travel with the small wagon train of army men and their families and join Toby's mother and stepfather, General Leland Blake, at Fort Vancouver in the Washington Territory, where General Blake made his headquarters as commander of the Army of the West. Clarissa was carrying their child, and Fort Shaw, Toby had decreed, was too much of a frontier post for a new Holt to begin life there.

Clarissa and Toby had been married only a scant six months, and in that time they had experienced a number of trials. Toby's proposal to Clarissa the previous spring had been sudden, and she was conscious that he had made it not so much out of love for her as out of a sense of bewilderment and distress at events in his own life. First, there had been the violent death of his estranged former wife. Then he had lost his father in a tragic rockslide in the Washington Territory. They had been close as few fathers and sons are, and Toby was thrown completely off balance. To further complicate his life, he had been infatuated with Beth Blake, who married his best friend. And to top it off, Toby's mother, Eulalia, married again. Of all the men who could have become his stepfather, Toby couldn't have wished for anyone more worthy than

General Lee Blake, but nevertheless, he had had difficulty accepting his mother's remarriage.

Now, however, all this unhappiness seemed to be fading. Toby had come close to losing Clarissa in the recent battle with the Sioux in the Montana Territory, and this made him realize how much he loved her, that she was the one person in his life who really mattered. Clarissa fervently believed that now their love could shield them from all difficulties—past and future.

A move on the seat next to her aroused Clarissa from her reverie, and blinking, she diverted her attention to Hank Purcell, the sixteen-year-old orphan she and Toby had informally adopted in Montana. Tall for his age, Hank was thin, with sun-streaked hair and freckles on his nose. At the moment he was petting Mr. Blake, Toby's German shepherd, who sat beside him and was accompanying Clarissa and Hank to Washington, acting as their protector.

Hank's accuracy as a marksman with rifle and pistol was remarkable, and the Holts had placed him under their wing to prevent him from becoming a professional gunslinger. Indeed, he was such an expert shot that he had already become the wagon train's principal hunter.

Clarissa was horrified when suddenly she saw that Hank had his rifle raised to his shoulder and was squinting down the barrel.

"Hank!" she exclaimed. "What on earth do you think you're doing? You know very well that the cavalry escort has forbidden anyone to shoot a gun from the wagons. Put down that rifle this instant!"

Hank gave a deep sigh, the reaction of an adolescent to the restrictions of adults. He lowered his rifle, then furiously brushed the bridge of his nose, as though trying to rid it of the freckles that dusted it. "I had the heftiest bighorn sheep you ever saw lined up in my sights," he said regretfully. "In another half-minute, I would have squeezed the trigger, and we'd have had a real treat for supper tonight."

Clarissa averted her face so he wouldn't see the humor that welled up in her green eyes. Toby had been right when he had told her, "That boy is a natural with a gun. He'd rather shoot than eat or sleep."

He was sensitive, too, and inclined to brood over grievances—probably because he was so conscious of being alone in the world. He now looked very unhappy, having been denied his sport, and Clarissa felt she had to distract him.

"I'm sure I'd have enjoyed the mutton," she said. "But to tell you the truth, I'm looking forward to that antelope you shot yesterday." Actually, she had never eaten antelope meat, which she had heard was tough and stringy, and she wasn't looking forward to it at all.

Hank was self-disparaging. "Shooting an antelope," he said scornfully, "ain't what I call fancy shooting."

Clarissa, a former schoolteacher in Philadelphia, had spent months at Fort Shaw teaching Hank correct English. Occasionally, however, especially when he was excited or irritable, he forgot his grammar, which was one reason Clarissa was anxious to enroll him in school once they reached Fort Vancouver. But for the moment she had other matters on her mind. "You brought down three animals in less time than it takes to tell it. I'd call that very fancy shooting, indeed," she said with finality. "Besides, I've been anxious to try out my father-in-law's recipe for antelope meat."

The boy was excited. "One of Whip Holt's own recipes? Golly! If it ain't—I mean, isn't—a secret, maybe you could tell it to me."

As Clarissa had hoped, his failure to shoot the bighorn sheep was forgotten. "You may watch when I make the dish," Clarissa replied sweetly. "I learned the recipe from my mother-in-law." As a matter of fact, she had indeed been told the recipe by Eulalia, who had laughingly explained at the time that she had no intention of ever preparing the dish, having eaten enough antelope steak on the original wagon train journey to the West.

"The only secret of preparing antelope," she said, "is that you cut the meat into small pieces and put them into a pot with some bones and a little water. You don't add the vegetables until later. Then you cook the meat very slowly over a low fire, and you let it bubble away for at least twice as long as you'd cook beef. Antelope is tough unless it's cooked for a very long time, even longer than buffalo meat."

Hank looked grateful. "I'll remember that," he said.

The atmosphere was far less tranquil on the seat of the next wagon in the line. Holding the reins of the team of four horses was Rob Martin, Toby Holt's closest friend and partner in laying out the Northern Pacific's route for a transcontinental railroad. Tall and solidly built, with a strong, square jaw and thick red hair, Rob was the son of Dr. Robert and Tonie Martin, who had traveled to Oregon in the original wagon train. Rob had grown up in the Portland area, and he and Toby had known each other all their lives. Now, however, Toby was en route to Washington City and an unknown destiny, while Rob was heading for Fort Vancouver and then on to California. He had agreed to oversee the construction there of the Central Pacific Railroad, which was scheduled to meet the tracks being laid by the Union Pacific somewhere in Utah.

Seated beside him on the wagon seat, her long blond

hair tousled, her blue eyes icy, was Rob's wife, Beth, the daughter of Lee and Cathy Blake. Many old friends of her parents claimed that she bore a startling resemblance to her mother, but few people had ever seen Cathy be as moody and temperamental as Beth. Indeed, the young woman had suffered terribly when her mother had died with Whip Holt in the rockslide. Missing Cathy so much, Beth had become nearly hysterical when her father had married Eulalia Holt, and Beth's attitude—toward life in general and Eulalia in particular—had grown worse and worse.

"Did you actually tell me," she suddenly demanded, "or did I just dream about that gold mine you and Toby found in Montana? Weren't we supposed to be financially independent for the rest of our lives?"

"All I know," Rob said patiently, used to her sarcasm, "is that when Chet Harris and Wong Ke took over the management of the mine for us, they told Toby and me that we'd be comfortable for as long as we lived. What they mean by comfortable, and what you mean by financial independence, I don't know. I'm inclined to accept the estimates of Chet and Ke because they made their own fortunes during the big strike in California back in forty-nine, and they obviously know what they're talking about."

"If we have the money to do what we please, then I see no reason to hold back," Beth said flatly. "We can buy a house in San Francisco, and I can live there while you're out in the Sierra Nevada, overseeing the construction of the railroad."

He sighed heavily. "Yes, I'm sure we could afford to buy a house there, but why you'd want to live in San Francisco, where you don't know a soul, is beyond me. I think you'd be much better off living with your family in Fort Vancouver until I finish my assignment."

Beth replied in a low, intense voice. "Nothing on earth will force me to live under the same roof with that woman!"

Rob arched an eyebrow. "You mean Eulalia?"

"Correct," she replied angrily. "Eulalia *Holt* Blake. You won't believe this, Rob, no matter how many times I tell you, but I saw her expression when my mother and her husband died in that terrible rockslide. She was determined not to be a widow. She wanted my father's rank and social position, and she went after him right then. She played all her cards right, presuming on a life-long friendship and demanding his sympathy. Well, she got him, and she's Mrs. Lee Blake now, but that doesn't mean that I'm going to show approval by spending even a single night under their roof."

Rob looked with unseeing eyes at the rugged, snow-covered peaks on both sides of the narrow valley through which the wagon train was traveling. Tugging his broad-brimmed hat lower on his forehead, he sighed. "By this time," he said heavily, "you know I don't believe that. I've known Eulalia all my life, and in my opinion she's a fine woman—a damned fine woman."

"You like her because you and Toby are so close," she said. "But I know what I know."

The unending argument led them nowhere, and once more Rob tried to sort out the situation. He recognized that his obstinate, independent wife had been badly spoiled as a girl by her parents. But, as he realized all too well, their problem went beyond that. After her father's remarriage, Beth had become increasingly remote, failing to respond to his lovemaking; her indifference had cooled his passion so that he was rarely aroused.

The lack of ardor shown by one was felt by the other, and the vicious cycle was growing increasingly worse.

Rob, who loved his wife, was in a quandary. If necessary, he knew he could exercise his prerogatives as head of the family and insist that she obey him. But such a course was certain to cause more problems than it would solve. Not only would Beth be miserable if she was forced to live with her father and stepmother, she would also cause them great unhappiness. Worst of all, the gulf that separated her from her husband would become wider and deeper, and it might not be possible for them ever to bridge their differences.

He wondered whether he might to wiser to give Beth her head in the hope that the passage of time would soften her opinion of her stepmother. Once she was cured of that strange fixation, he reasoned, all her other troubles might solve themselves.

"Suppose I were to leave this whole matter in your hands?" he said. "What would you do?"

Beth suddenly brightened. The prospect of having her own way improved her mood instantly. Once again she became the lovely, vivacious Beth Blake Rob had known when he first married her. Her smile was radiant, and her eyelashes fluttered as she looked up at him. "First of all," she replied sweetly, "you and I will leave Fort Vancouver as soon as the wagon train gets there. We'll hire a carriage, load up our belongings, and go directly to your family in Portland."

"Hold on," he said, raising a hand. "If you mean that you won't even spend a night or two under your father and stepmother's roof, I've got to draw the line. You have no call to insult them that way. They wouldn't understand what you were doing, any more than I do. I'll compromise with you, Beth, and we'll find someplace where you can stay for the six to twelve months that I'll be off building the Central Pacific lines. But I won't even consider the matter unless you agree to pay at least a token visit to your father and Eulalia."

Beth was faring better than she had anticipated and felt sure a real victory was within sight. Nevertheless, she hated to concede even a minor point and could not help replying between clenched teeth, "Oh, all right. I suppose I can tolerate watching that conniving woman weave her spell around my father for a day or two."

"That's very noble of you, I'm sure," Rob said.

She ignored his comment. "After that, I'll find a place in San Francisco. The Sierra Nevada aren't all that far away, and you could come down from the mountains and join me in the city whenever you've had enough of primitive living."

"I wouldn't say that San Francisco is an ideal place for any lady to settle in," he said. "Yes, we spent our honeymoon there, but that was different. For a woman on her own, it's a wild, wide-open town."

"Those stories are exaggerated," Beth said impatiently. "The vigilante committees and the army garrison at the Presidio keep order. After all, any number of prominent people live in the town with their families—Chet Harris and Wong Ke, just to mention two who come to mind."

He was dubious but began to weaken. "I don't know," he said. "This will require some thought. I must admit, I like the idea of having you fairly close whenever I can get away from my work for a few weeks or so. But I'm not sure you'd be safe living in San Francisco alone."

"What harm could possibly come to me?" she demanded. "After all, I came to know a great many people there when Papa was in command of the Presidio.

What's more, the Harrises and the Wongs can always act as my chaperons."

Chet Harris had crossed America on the original wagon train to Oregon as a boy and had become a multimillionaire, an industrialist and financier responsible for much of the development of cities in California and Oregon. He was also the stepson of a retired United States senator from Oregon, and there were few people anywhere who had his respectability. Wong Ke, who had immigrated to America from China, had met Chet in the gold rush of 1849 in California, and they had become partners and close friends. Ke and his wife, Mei Lo, were also exemplary citizens of San Francisco.

Perhaps, Rob thought, San Francisco was the answer. "When we reach the city," he said, "I've got to see Chet on business relating to our mine. Suppose I sound him out then and get his advice?"

"What a good idea," Beth said demurely. She felt certain that Harris and his charming wife, Clara Lou, would welcome her to San Francisco. She would not be forced to live under her father's roof, with Eulalia Blake as mistress of the house.

A sense of uneasiness pervaded the Dakota Territory, a land of vast prairies and rugged hills, of hunting grounds for buffalo and elk, antelope and deer. A land larger than the Washington Territory and Oregon combined, the sparsely populated Dakota Territory was now to be the meeting place of three of the most fearsome Plains Indian tribes, who were making plans to engage in war against the United States.

The chiefs and warriors of the Sioux, the Blackfoot, and the Cheyenne were gathering for a meeting in the western part of Dakota, in an area known as the Badlands, a region of deep gorges and high buttes, rugged hills and huge rocks with jagged, strange shapes. In spite of the western migration that had brought settlers all the way to the Pacific Coast and to the lands that lay between it and the heavily populated Middle West, there were almost no white men in the Badlands. The soil was as unproductive as the vistas were bleak, and the temperatures, ranging from blistering heat in summer to numbing cold in the winter, did not encourage settlers to sink roots there.

It was toward the Badlands that Thunder Cloud, the distinguished, shrewd leader of the mighty Sioux nation, the most numerous and powerful of the Great Plains tribes, headed after his warriors had suffered a severe defeat in Montana at the hands of the Eleventh U.S. Cavalry, commanded by Colonel Andrew Brentwood. It was also in the Badlands that Thunder Cloud had decided to hold this meeting of the three Indian nations, and he had sent out Sioux couriers to notify the Blackfoot and the Cheyenne.

Thunder Cloud, wearing his distinctive, feathered warbonnet, rode at the front of the Sioux procession. He was a large man of middle age, with a powerful, broad chest and strong arms, and he carried himself with a natural dignity and grace that belied his years. No one seeing this proud, fierce-looking chief for the first time would have guessed that he had at last met his match and had been driven from Montana.

Behind him, some mounted on horses, some treading on foot, were hundreds of warriors, the survivors of what had been the so-called invincible corps of braves. Colonel Brentwood and his cavalrymen had taught the warriors a bitter lesson: He who attacked settlers and destroyed or stole their property would pay the consequences.

Dazed by their defeat, the braves knew only that they retained faith in Thunder Cloud. Where he led, they followed. So they marched deeper and deeper into the Badlands, the atmosphere becoming increasingly eerie. The hunters who had volunteered to go out into the Plains in search of game were glad to have something to get their minds off the unrelieved gloom.

Living up to their proud boasts that they could make themselves at home anywhere, the Sioux set up their tepees of animal skins, made their campfires, and for the first time since they had been forced to flee the Montana battlefields, they enjoyed hot food instead of having to rely on jerked beef and parched corn. They roasted the elk and buffalo the hunters had brought in that day and ate hungrily. Then, sitting around the campfires, they gazed at the vast starlit sky above the Badlands.

Twenty-four hours later, Sioux scouts sat their mounts on the highest hills near their bivouac and watched the approach of another similar force heading into the Badlands from the north. Mounted on horseback, these braves were armed with bows and had quivers of arrows slung over their shoulders.

When the strangers drew nearer, one of the scouts broke the silence. "Blackfoot!" he said.

That identification explained why the new arrivals looked so self-confident and held their heads so high. The Blackfoot were the scourge of the northern Plains, and none of the neighboring tribes dared to stand up to them. As the Blackfoot poured into the area and set up their camps, the Sioux, sensitive to their recent defeat, kept their distance, as Thunder Cloud had instructed them. The chief knew that his warriors were hot-tem-

pered, and because they were unafraid of the Blackfoot,
fights could break out at any signs of condescension or
ridicule on the part of the other Indians.

No hostile incidents, however, marred the meeting of
the two nations, not only because of the common sense
of Thunder Cloud but also because of that of Red Elk,
the chieftain of the Blackfoot. Many years younger than
Thunder Cloud, he was nevertheless just as sensible, and
he, too, instructed his braves to keep to themselves.

As it turned out, the warriors of the two nations got
along very well, and after two days they were hunting
and fishing together, eating their meals with each other,
and even sharing evening campfires. The Sioux and the
Blackfoot, to their mutual astonishment, discovered they
had many attitudes in common, not the least of which
was a burning hatred for the people of the United
States. These intruders who migrated from the more
settled parts of America, bringing their wives, children,
and household belongings with them, were indifferent to
the fate of the Indian nations and settled in the sacred
hunting grounds of the tribes, literally taking food out of
the mouths of the Indians. The braves agreed that this
situation could not be allowed to exist any longer.

Eventually the two groups were joined by a third
tribe, the ferocious and defiant Cheyenne of the south-
ern Plains. Arrogant and proud, the Cheyenne recognized no authority other than their own. They were so
suspicious, even of other Indian tribes, that when their
leader, Big Knife, arrived to confer with Thunder Cloud
and Red Elk, he was escorted by a hundred heavily
armed warriors.

The outraged Sioux refused to admit Big Knife and
his entourage into the encampment, and a heated alter-
cation followed. A fight that would have ruptured the

peace and destroyed the carefully laid plans of Thunder Cloud was averted when the Sioux chieftain heard raised voices and, with Red Elk following him, emerged from his tepee to see what was amiss.

Raising his voice, Thunder Cloud bellowed like a wounded bear. "You are now brothers at this council! He who raises a hand against his brother will die the torture death of the Plains!"

Order was restored with difficulty, and the Cheyenne bodyguard permitted their chieftain to accompany the other leaders only because they were reassured by the presence of the Blackfoot leader in the Sioux camp.

Once Thunder Cloud was alone with his two visitors, he led them to a small fire burning behind a huge boulder that concealed all three of the leaders from their followers. Seating his guests with due ceremony, he lighted a peace pipe, and once it was drawing freely, he passed it to Big Knife, who puffed on it and handed it to Red Elk.

Thunder Cloud made a gracious welcoming speech, and Red Elk replied in kind, but after the way of Indians, his address was longer and more elaborate. Then it was the turn of Big Knife, who spoke interminably.

Thunder Cloud remained outwardly serene, his face and manner in no way indicating his inner tensions. He was an old hand at conferences with chiefs from other tribes. He had been holding such meetings for many years, and aware of the Indians' love of ceremony, he was resigned to wasting a great deal of time before he could get down to business.

Finally, however, the blessings of the gods who guided the destinies of all three nations having been duly invoked, he proceeded to the subject that had impelled him to call the conference. "My brothers," he said, "I will not be satisfied until every river that runs through the Great Plains, the northern Plains, and the mountains is red with the blood of the white settlers."

Red Elk nodded. "I do not blame you for feeling as you do, my brother," he said. "It is not easy to suffer humiliation by the U.S. Cavalry."

Big Knife grinned insolently. "He who has been bitten by the snake with a rattle in its tail," he said, "is forever afraid when he hears a rattle."

Thunder Cloud looked at him calmly. "The Cheyenne are fortunate," he said, a hint of sarcasm in his voice. "They are luckier than their brothers of the Sioux and of the Blackfoot. Unlike the lands of the Sioux and of the Blackfoot, the hunting grounds of the Cheyenne are still filled with game, their rivers are still well stocked with fish, and many beaver, fox, and bear provide coats of warm fur for the warriors, squaws, and children of the Cheyenne when the weather is cold."

Big Knife was vulnerable to the ridicule of the older leader, and his eyes blazed angrily. "Thunder Cloud," he said, "well knows that the Cheyenne have suffered grave injustices at the hands of the white men, just as the Sioux have suffered them."

"Ah," the older man said mildly, "then you are willing to consider joining forces with the Sioux and the Blackfoot to stop these injustices and to right the wrongs that have been done to our nation."

"My warriors and I," Big Knife said stridently, "have marched for many days to explore with you the possibilities of such a union."

"Then hear what I say," Thunder Cloud told him, "and do you likewise, Red Elk. This is a time for truth. The soldiers of the United States Cavalry are superior to our own warriors. They are not better fighting men, but they are better equipped. They are armed with firesticks. Our bows and arrows cannot compete with them, just as our wooden lances are no match for the steel of their sabers. Their horses are big and strong, and although they are not as swift as our mounts, they are less skittish during battle. The armed might of the white men grows stronger with each passing day, and the troops who wear their uniforms are also growing in numbers. The Sioux met their cavalry in battle, and we were vanquished. Only because our gods took pity on us were we able to escape with our lives so that we may fight again."

Red Elk's brow was furrowed. "What must we do, my brother, if the Blackfoot are to avoid the disasters that struck the Sioux?"

"I do not need to have the vision of a medicine man," Thunder Cloud said solemnly, "to foretell the future. I see the day coming when there will be no hunting grounds left for the Indian nations. Already in the eastern portions of what the white men call the Dakota Territory, farmers are growing wheat and corn. They are encroaching more and more on our hunting grounds. The great herds of buffalo, as well as elk and moose, antelope and deer, that have provided food and clothing and tepees for our people for untold time are beginning to vanish. The white man takes skins of beaver to make hats for men and coats for women, and there are no beaver left in our rivers. The white men are like a great plague of locusts who denude our lands."

"The Cheyenne will take action to stop them!" Big Knife cried.

Thunder Cloud shook his head sadly. "The Sioux have already acted and have suffered a terrible defeat," he said. "Are the Cheyenne mightier and stronger than the

Sioux? In your heart of hearts, you know they are not. Are the Blackfoot stronger?"

Red Elk shook his head. "That is what my warriors like to think when they drink much whiskey," he said, "but they know that they are not the equal in battle of the Sioux."

Having established his point, Thunder Cloud drove home his message. "We must lay aside our ancient feuds. The Sioux and the Blackfoot and the Cheyenne must stand together and act as one nation against the white man's soldiers. We will overwhelm them with our numbers, and even though their weapons are superior to ours, they will not be able to stop our warriors. For every brave that falls to the white man's guns, we will be able to send in another one to take his place, until at last we have driven the white man from our lands. But time is short, my brothers. Either we stand together immediately, or the settlers will drive the last of our game from our hunting grounds!"

Big Knife scowled and shook a menacing fist. "Our warriors must form an alliance and together drive the intruders from our lands."

"You are right," Red Elk said. "We must band together against them!"

Thunder Cloud breathed more easily. Each chieftain believed he had originated the idea of forming an alliance of Indian nations, and therefore each would see to it that his braves accepted the plan.

"In order that there be no strife among us," Thunder Cloud said, "let each nation be commanded by its own chief. But we will act together, and we will take a firm stand against the armies of the white men who would rob us of our heritage!"

Now the warriors of the three tribes were summoned

to a meeting, and the chieftains presented the plan to
them, saying that they would go to war the following
summer. In the meantime, the various tribes would return to their villages to wait out the coming winter and
to prepare themselves for war. The men were to make
more arrows and other weapons, and the women were to
make plenty of pemmican and parched corn. In long,
fierce speeches one theme was stressed repeatedly:
Havoc would be created for the white man, and when
the war ended, the hunting grounds of the West once
again would belong to the Indians, who had called them
their own for hundreds of years.

As the chieftains anticipated, the braves voted unani-
mously to fight together. The fate of white men in the
Plains of the West and in the Rocky Mountains appeared to be sealed.

A silence engulfed the assemblage as the chieftains
engaged in the ritual of exchanging wampum, strips of
leather that had been bleached white in the sun and
studded with beads and shells. Now the treaty of alliance was binding, and the Sioux, the Blackfoot, and
the Cheyenne had become blood brothers. When they re-
grouped in the summer, all of them would be dedicated
to the elimination of settlers from the regions they considered their own.

For the first time in history, the three most powerful
and warlike tribes of the American West were at peace
with each other. As the ceremonies were concluded, and
wild, triumphant war whoops rose into the air above the
Dakota Badlands, the future appeared as bleak for the
army and the settlers as the landscape itself.

The United States Army had grown so rapidly during
the Civil War that its headquarters were located in a

number of buildings in Washington City. At the end of
the war, men had been demobilized by the tens of
thousands, but such were the peculiarities of bureau-
cracy that the headquarters remained overcrowded.

Nowhere was this more evident than in the official
building that housed the secretary of war and the chief
of staff. General Ulysses Simpson Grant, the highest-
ranking uniformed officer in the service of his country,
occupied a suite of small, cramped rooms. His private
sanctum, adjoining a tiny conference room, was barely
large enough for his desk and two visitors' chairs. A
gruff, burly man with a dark, full beard, General Grant
showed his usual disregard for army regulations by leaving the top buttons of his tunic unbuttoned. This was
admittedly sloppy, but as the general confided to his in-
timates, at least he was comfortable and was not in danger of choking.

There was a knock on his office door, which the general answered with a loud command to enter. It was
Toby Holt. Lean and angular like his late father, Toby
appeared to be made only of sinew and muscle. His hair
was sandy colored, his eyes were pale blue and penetrating, and his rugged appearance was that of a man who
spent much time in the wilderness. Only his jacket,
necktie, and brown serge trousers suggested he was also
comfortable with civilized ways.

As Toby entered, General Grant grinned, removed an
unlighted cigar stub from his mouth, and stood, extending one hand in greeting. Toby, who had spent nearly
four years in the Union Army during the Civil War, had
to prevent himself from saluting.

"By God, Holt," the general boomed, "you're the spitting image of your father. Anybody who knew Whip
Holt would know at a glance that you're his son."

Toby often had heard the same comment and invariably was pleased by it. "Thanks very much, sir," he said.

Grant waved him to a chair on the far side of his desk and peered at him from beneath bushy eyebrows. "When was the last time we met?" he asked.

Toby started to speak, but General Grant held up a silencing hand. "No," he roared. "Don't tell me. Let me figure this out for myself. I've got it. The Virginia campaign in sixty-four. You were a troop commander in the Eleventh Cavalry, and you led a charge that helped break the back of the Confederate Cavalry."

Toby grinned at him. "You have a remarkably good memory, sir," he said. "You met scores of officers every day."

"Not all of them were cited for valor the way Andy Brentwood cited you, young man," the general said. "I recall you very distinctly. Well!" He picked up his cigar, jammed it into his mouth, and rolled it from one side to the other. "You seem right for the task we have in mind. What do you know about what we have in store for you?"

"A little, sir," Toby told him. "Colonel Brentwood informed me that there was a serious Indian problem in Dakota and that some of my qualifications might be useful. He also mentioned that my experience in laying out a railroad route for the Northern Pacific might come in handy, as well."

The general guffawed. " 'Might be useful!' " he echoed. " 'Might come in handy!' I don't know who's guilty of understatement, you or Brentwood. Maybe it's just Andy's dry sense of humor, which I've always enjoyed, but the fact of the matter is that your qualifications are indispensable and your services are essential."

The general paused. "Now, to take things one at a

time. I suppose you know that the Army Corps of Engineers has already surveyed the routes for railroad lines across the Dakota Territory. They'll join with the routes that you and young Martin have already surveyed in Montana and Washington."

"Yes, sir, I was told that the army was doing the job in Dakota."

Grant nodded. "Obviously," he said, "once the railroad begins to operate, the United States is expecting a great wave of immigration—a veritable tidal wave—into the Dakota, Montana, and Washington territories. It's an exciting prospect. There are thousands and thousands of acres out there of prime land for the establishment of farms. There's equally vast acreage for grazing. Not to mention the minerals available in the mountains and the development of a tremendous lumbering industry that's already under way in Washington."

"Yes, the potential is certainly there," Toby agreed.

The army's chief of staff smiled grimly. "Right now, however, it's only a potential," he said. "So much could still go wrong. But I'm getting ahead of myself." Briskly he continued, "If you agree to come to work for us, one of your first duties will be to travel from one end of Dakota to the other and inspect the engineers' survey routes. You'll be accompanied by a party of army engineers, including officers who've actually worked on the surveys, and they'll be under strict orders to accept your recommendations without question. If there's anything you don't like, just say so. If you want to change the route, that will be your privilege. All this will be spelled out, not only in your orders but in the orders being sent to the commanders in the field."

"You're giving me a tremendous responsibility, General," Toby said. "I hope I can live up to it."

"I'm sure you can—and will," Ulysses Grant told him.
"The routes you and Martin charted in Washington and
Montana have met with extraordinary approval by members of Congress, and this Dakota link, which has already been roughly mapped, should be nothing
compared with those in the other territories. No, it's only
a matter of time now before there's a railroad being built
in the north as well as the central United States, railroads that will span the continent of North America and
bring the Atlantic and Pacific coasts together. But your
survey work is only a minor part of the job you'll be doing for us. The other part is far more grave and urgent.

"Before I discuss the precise nature of the assignment
with you, however," Grant continued, leaning forward
on his desk and lacing his pudgy fingers together, "I
want to emphasize again that you're uniquely qualified
for this post. You're not only the son of Whip Holt, a
man who was a legend in our time, but you're establishing a reputation of your own that is blame near the
equal of his."

Toby was embarrassed. "Hardly that, General," he
protested.

"Don't be modest, young man," said Grant impatiently. "Not only has Andy Brentwood praised you to
the skies, Lee Blake has written that he agrees with everything Andy says about you. Lee is an old associate of
mine, whose judgment and honesty I value. The fact
he's your stepfather would not sway his opinion one
iota."

Toby flushed beneath his tan.

"I'm stressing your reputation, your standing in the
West, so to speak, because it has a direct bearing on the
assignment. The man who performs this task for us will

need the respect—and the admiration—of the Indian tribes of the area."

Toby anticipated what was coming and waited calmly while Ulysses Grant lighted a sulfur match with his thumbnail, then applied the flame to the end of the cigar stub.

Speaking through a thick cloud of smoke, the general continued, "As Andy Brentwood's probably discussed with you, we've received some very unsettling news from our operatives in the field and from military scouting parties. The chieftains of the Sioux, the Blackfoot, and the Cheyenne have met in the Badlands of Dakota and formed an alliance. Its purpose is to drive the settlers out of the West."

Toby had indeed been told of the meeting of the Plains tribes. "This means a major Indian war, General," he said, "the first major war with the Indians since Andrew Jackson's time."

Grant's face was blurred behind cigar smoke. "Exactly, Holt," he said. "This alliance can mean a war in the West the likes of which has never been seen. To win such a war the United States will have to send thousands of troops out to Dakota, and even with those troops, the planning and building of the transcontinental railroad will be sorely disrupted. The immigration to the West will come to an end, and settlements, towns, and forts will be destroyed."

"But you and Colonel Brentwood think it will be possible to avoid a war?" Toby asked.

"We do. I do," Grant asserted, and jabbed a finger across his desk in the direction of the younger man. "There's one way that it can be avoided, and that's through you! You've fought the Nez Percé in the Washington Territory, and you acted as a scout for the Eleventh Cavalry in their campaign against the Sioux. You grew up learning about the Indians from your father and visiting their villages with him, where he was always welcomed and respected. So you've commanded their respect and have consistently proved your fairness and your friendship. They have good cause to like you, not to mention that they still revere the memory of Whip Holt.

"We've developed a strategy here at the War Department, which is contingent on you. This plan has won the approval of President Johnson. In essense it's very simple. You'll be crossing the whole of the Dakota Territory while you're inspecting the railroad routes laid out by the Corps of Engineers. While you're in Dakota, it should be easy enough for you to visit every Indian community of any consequence. Talk to the chiefs and the medicine men and the other leaders. When possible, confer with the warriors themselves. These are just suggestions, mind you. You'll have a free hand to handle these towns and villages as you see fit. Convince them, if you can, that if they go through with their scheme and declare war on the United States next year, they are committing suicide."

Toby nodded thoughtfully. He knew he would be able to travel to the Indian villages without harm. Though he carried no wampum to offer the Indians as a pledge of his honorable and friendly intentions, he could speak their languages and could identify himself as the son of Whip Holt. These things would certainly stand him in good stead.

"You must convince the Indians," Grant went on, his voice rising and hardening, "that this country will do everything in its power to protect the citizens who establish their homesteads on free American soil. We'll tolerate no killing, no senseless destruction and theft of property. We'll protect our people with as many troops as it is necessary to put into the field. General Blake, acting on my orders, will send units of the Eighth Cavalry to the Dakota Territory, and Colonel Brentwood in Montana will send in his units, too. And that's just the beginning. If the Indians persist with this war, we're prepared to augment the Eighth and Eleventh cavalries with two other regiments and bring our forces in the territory up to brigade strength. If that's not sufficient, General Blake is under orders to increase the size of our units to any level he deems necessary, even if he's required to send several full divisions of troops into Dakota and to place the entire area under martial law!"

Toby could understand why Ulysses Grant had been the late President Lincoln's favorite general. He would allow nothing to stand in the way of his goals.

"We have no quarrel with the Indians," Grant continued. "It's our earnest hope that we can live side by side in peace as good neighbors. We're willing to give them large reservations of their own where they can live in peace; they will have ample land for farming, hunting and fishing. The choice is theirs," the general said flatly. "The Sioux, the Blackfoot, and the Cheyenne will determine whether there will be war or peace. We hope that you can present the alternatives to them in terms that they can grasp and that you'll be able to persuade them not to go to war against us and force us to teach them a lesson they'll never forget."

Toby took a deep breath. "All I can do is to promise you that I'll exert every effort to persuade the Plains Indians to keep the peace."

"Fair enough, Holt," the general said. "We're not asking you to perform the impossible. I'm sending immediate instructions to General Blake to cooperate with you in every way that you see fit. On behalf of the people of the United States, I offer you my thanks for what you're doing."

As Toby shook the hand of Ulysses Grant, the thought occurred to him that he was being placed in a strange situation. Lee Blake was required to put his entire command, the Army of the West, at the disposal of his stepson. Well, that was fair enough. By accepting the assignment, Toby was taking on the burden of a great responsibility. War or peace in the West depended on him.

II

Major General and Mrs. Leland Blake were on hand to greet the wagon train when it arrived at Fort Vancouver. The tall, gray-haired general was very distinguished-looking in his uniform; Eulalia's dress of soft, green wool flattered her fair skin and dark hair. As they walked the short distance from their house to the parade ground where the wagon train would come to a halt, Lee noted the surreptitious glances cast at his wife by younger officers, and he chuckled quietly.

"You're amazing," he said. "You sure don't look like a woman about to become a grandmother."

She affectionately squeezed his arm but sobered quickly as she said, "All the same, I *am* going to be a grandmother, and I can't help worrying about Clarissa. I hope this trip wasn't too much for her."

"I'm sure she's just fine," Lee replied soothingly. "You know Toby wouldn't have allowed her on the wagon train if he'd had the slightest doubt about her health."

When the couple reached the parade ground, they were joined by Eulalia's daughter, Cindy Holt, who had

just finished her day's schooling and still carried several
books held together with a leather strap. Just as Toby
Holt was the living image of his father, Whip, Cindy
also bore a resemblance to her father and had the same
sand-colored hair and the same clear, pale blue eyes.
She was a pretty girl, having grown out of a tomboy
stage. Her hair was pulled back in a ponytail, which emphasized her intelligent, animated face, and she was
wearing an attractive white linen dress decorated with
lace.

"I can hardly wait to see Clarissa," the sixteen-year-
old girl said, "and Beth, too."

There was a moment's awkward pause, and Eulalia
deliberately refrained from glancing at her husband.
Both of them were conscious of the strained nature of
their relations with Beth Martin and had taken pains to
avoid talking about her homecoming. But Eulalia, as always, met the situation squarely. "I'm sure they'll both be
equally delighted to see you, dear," she replied.

Ever since the outbreak of the Civil War, most immigrants to Portland and its environs had come to Oregon
by ship after crossing the Isthmus of Panama by rail. So
the arrival of the wagon train was considered a significant event, and many of Portland's citizens had crossed
the Columbia River into Washington and were gathered
at the parade ground.

A fast-riding scout brought word that the train had
been sighted on the road that led to the fort from the
north and was on schedule. The carefully planned recep-
tion began. A full regiment, eight hundred men strong,
the Eighth United States Cavalry, immediately rode out
to escort the wagon train to Fort Vancouver. The horsemen were followed by the post band playing the "Battle
Hymn of the Republic." An infantry regiment, the Sev-

enteenth, formed a hollow square on the parade ground,
while its own band played a medley of patriotic tunes,
including "America" and "Columbia, the Gem of the
Ocean."

At last the approaching wagon train was sighted by
those in the fort, and the howitzers of an artillery unit
boomed a welcome, making the horses start and shy.

Clarissa, still agile in spite of her pregnancy, was the
first to jump from her wagon and break through the
lines of the infantry. At her heels was Toby's shepherd
dog, Mr. Blake, who, with his ears raised, trotted briskly,
apparently enjoying the ceremony. Clarissa enveloped
Eulalia in a hug, then hugged Lee Blake and Cindy
Holt. As she presented Hank Purcell to the general, his
wife, and Cindy, Beth and Rob Martin reached the
group.

There was another flurry of excitement as Beth clung
to her father. In the flurry of exchanged greetings, Beth
managed to avoid embracing her stepmother. She barely
looked at her as she nodded coolly and said, "How do
you do, Eulalia?"

Certainly Eulalia had not expected to be addressed as
"Mother." Beth's mother, Cathy, had been Eulalia's best
friend, and she knew how close she had been to her
daughter. Eulalia realized she could never take the place
of the natural mother in the young woman's affections.
All the same, Beth's aloofness was a deliberate slap in
the face.

Clarissa, who was conscious of the slight, was embarrassed, as was Rob. But Eulalia refused to accept the
snub and proceeded to handle the matter in a typically
blunt, forthright manner. She reached out with both
hands, caught hold of her stepdaughter's slender shoulders, and pulling her closer, planted a kiss firmly on

each cheek. "I'm so glad to see you again, Beth," she said evenly.

Clarissa was pleased. Her mother-in-law, as always, could take care of herself. Rob Martin was delighted, too, but carefully refrained from showing his pleasure. Beth would take it as a sign of disloyalty to her.

General Blake made a short speech, welcoming the wagon train's immigrants to the Pacific Northwest, and then his entire group withdrew and made the short walk to the Blakes' home. Army personnel had already been sent to attend to the wagons and horses, and they would also see that the belongings of Clarissa and Hank, Rob and Beth, were sent along to the commandant's house.

There was something of a commotion among the re-united Blakes, Martins, and Holts, each trying to talk to the other and attempting to catch up on news. Finally Lee said, "We're blocking traffic spread out this way across the whole road. Cindy, why don't you show Hank the way?"

As they walked, Rob explained, as tactfully as possible, that he and Beth could remain only a single night. "We're going on to my folks' house tomorrow for a quick visit," he said, "and then we're going on to San Francisco. I'm wanted for my new job as fast as I can get up into the Sierra Nevada."

Lee raised an eyebrow and turned to his daughter. "What are you intending to do in San Francisco?" he asked.

Her voice was bland, her smile saccharine. "Why, I'm planning to live there, Daddy," she said.

Rob intervened at once. "We've decided it might be wise for Beth to live in San Francisco," he said, "so that I can be with her whenever I can snatch some time off. If she stayed here, she'd be so far away that I might not see her for a whole year. I'd lose too much time traveling."

Everyone appeared to accept the reason, but Eulalia knew better. When Toby had surveyed a route for the railroad in the mountains of Washington, he frequently had found—or had made—the time to return home for visits to his family. The truth was that Beth was avoiding living under the same roof with her stepmother. For the present, however, Eulalia decided not to make an issue of the matter.

Meanwhile, Cindy, bringing up the rear with Hank Purcell trudging beside her, was uncomfortable.

The boy, falling all over himself like so many of the young males she knew at school, was staring at her steadily, unblinkingly, and his scrutiny made her nervous. "Is there a smudge of dirt on my face?" she demanded in exasperation. "Is my dress torn, or is there a hole in it?"

Hank remained blissfully unaware of the reasons for her irritation. "No, ma'am," he said. "Leastwise, I haven't seen any of those things."

The girl became even more annoyed. "Then I wish you'd stop gaping at me! You act as though you've never seen a girl before!"

Hank pushed his big-crowned, broad-brimmed hat to the back of his head and, reaching under it, scratched his scalp. "Blamed if I thought of it that way," he said, "but you're right. I haven't ever seen a lady of your age before, much less met one." He swallowed hard. "If you don't mind my asking, how old are you?"

Cindy thought he was having fun at her expense and sniffed disdainfully. "I'm sixteen."

Hank looked amazed. "I could have sworn that you were close to Clarissa's age."

The assumption that she was an adult mollified the girl somewhat. Then her curiosity got the better of her. "You were just teasing me, weren't you, when you said you've never met any girls?"

Hank shook his head vehemently and swallowed hard. "No, ma'am," he said. "Sure as mares have colts, you're the first one I ever set eyes on!"

She found it impossible to believe him. "How could that be?"

"Pa and me," he said, "had us a little spread on the Montana frontier. We didn't have any neighbors, and we were too busy raising cattle and hunting to socialize much."

Cindy shook her head. "But surely, at school—"

"I never went to school," Hank interjected. "Pa taught me blame near all I know about reading and writing and doing numbers, and after I moved to Fort Shaw, Clarissa and Beth started pestering me with an education."

Cindy concluded that he was an oafish simpleton.

The boy continued to gaze at her steadily. "You're Whip Holt's daughter," he said at last.

Cindy nodded, unwilling to listen to a long-winded, hero-worshipping recital about her father.

"You look like Toby," Hank said.

The girl nodded her head. "We take after our papa," she replied.

"Toby," Hank announced, "is right handy with firearms. I guess he inherited his talent from his pa, just like I inherited mine from my pa."

Cindy, detecting a hint of bragging in his voice, couldn't resist replying, "As I just told you, I have some of my father in me, too. I'm a pretty fair shot myself."

Hank looked at her in openmouthed amazement. "You?" he asked. "You're just a girl!"

Her face flushed with anger. "I may be 'just a girl,' but I'll outshoot you any day of the week! With any firearms you care to use!"

The boy became uncomfortable. He had actually killed a man—his father's murderer—and his skill with a gun was superior. "You shouldn't go challenging me," he told her. "I'm nearly as good a shot as Toby is."

"So am I," Cindy replied spiritedly. "Are you going to have a contest with me, or are you too big a coward?"

Hank drew himself up to his full height and towered above her. "You just talked yourself into a contest, ma'am," he said, "and you're going to be sorry. Come to think of it, let's make this a competition where you'll be double sorry. We'll make it both rifle *and* pistol shooting."

"That suits me just fine," Cindy replied tartly, and swept past him into the Blake house.

Beth had claimed a headache, and Rob had gone with her to their room; the others were gathered in the living room. Cindy hurried into the room ahead of Hank, anxious to tell them about the contest.

Clarissa and Eulalia were deep in conversation with Lee, talking about the assignment that Toby had gone to Washington City to receive from General Grant. What they were eager to learn—and what even Lee didn't know yet—was what role Toby was going to be asked to play in the problems in Dakota. They were still pondering this as Cindy told about the contest. Indeed, the women were so immersed in thought that they failed to hear the tone of belligerence in Cindy's voice, and Clarissa smiled benignly.

"I'm glad you two are getting acquainted," she said.

"Your mother tells me, Cindy, that you'll be glad to show Hank around school and teach him what's what."

Cindy looked reproachfully at her mother. "No, Mama!" she cried. "I'd be mortified half to death to have this dumb galoot of a boy tagging around school after me. What would my friends say?"

Eulalia was sweet-tempered but firm. "Your friends," she said, "will be very pleased to meet Hank. You will indeed take him under your wing and show him around the school."

Cindy knew there was no appeal from her mother's decision, so she heaved a long, deep sigh.

It was Hank's turn to glower as he looked at Clarissa. "It's bad enough that you're sending me to school!" he said. "Do I have to go with girls?"

Clarissa was unyielding. "You're very fortunate, Hank. Since you'll be living here in the commandant's house, you qualify for admission to the Fort Vancouver school, and that's where you're going, beginning first thing tomorrow morning."

Lee Blake knew the boy needed to be convinced about the benefits to be derived from an education, but he realized that this was not an appropriate moment. Both of the adolescents needed to let off steam, so he intervened smoothly. "If you're interested in holding that shooting contest right now," he said, "the officers' practice range isn't occupied, and I can arrange to have you use it."

"The sooner the better," Cindy snapped.

Hank was awed by the tall, gray-haired man who wore the two stars of a major general on each shoulder. "I'm ready right now, sir," he said, "if you'll give me a few minutes to go fetch my rifle and my six-shooter."

"That won't be necessary," Lee told him. "We have

plenty of weapons at the range. In fact, to ensure fairness in a contest of this sort, both of you should use weapons that are unfamiliar to you."

"Let me just run upstairs to change into an old skirt," Cindy called, and she was gone in an instant.

Cindy and Hank avoided each other as they walked across the grounds of Fort Vancouver to the shooting range. However, the girl was conscious that the boy continued to study her, a puzzled expression on his face.

When they arrived at the range, Lee asked the young lieutenant in charge to provide them with identical weapons, two of the six-shooter pistols that had proved their worth so emphatically during the Civil War and two old-fashioned, single-shot rifles. While the lieutenant was fetching the weapons and ammunition, a master sergeant set up the targets a hundred feet away. The life-sized representations of Sioux warriors had been painted by this same sergeant, who was a veteran Indian fighter.

"Rifles or pistols?" Lee asked. "Which do you want to shoot first?"

"Lady's choice," Hank replied laconically.

The three adults sensed the change in the boy's mood. Once the firearms had appeared, he became quietly purposeful, businesslike, and absorbed.

"We'll start with pistols," Cindy said.

"Colt six-shooters," Hank said, "have the kick of an Arapaho mule, and they're likely to fly out of a girl's hand. I wouldn't mind if my opponent wanted to substitute a lighter weapon, say, a twenty-two caliber pistol."

"I'll use exactly the same kind of gun he uses," Cindy said stubbornly.

Lee placed the two six-shooters and a box of cartridges on a wooden table that separated one shooting lane from the next. "Help yourselves," he said.

Cindy took infinite care as she loaded her pistol, inserting the shells into the empty chambers meticulously, one at a time. Hank, however, tested the gun before loading it, holding it up, squinting down the barrel, and pulling the trigger several times to test its resistance. Then he filled all six chambers in virtually a single, continuous motion.

"You may fire when ready," General Blake said.

Cindy promptly raised her pistol to eye level, looked down the barrel at the figure of the Sioux brave, and squeezed the trigger, noting that her bullet had landed in the brave's shoulder. She nodded in satisfaction and fired a second time, again pausing to see where the bullet had gone and to judge her next shot accordingly.

Hank stood very still watching her as she fired her third and fourth shots, and it was apparent that he was impressed. Then he appeared to put his opponent out of his mind. He stared hard at the target for a long moment, raised his pistol, and emptied all six chambers in such rapid succession that they sounded almost like a single shot. He lowered the weapon again and let it dangle at his side as Cindy completed her fifth and sixth shots.

Lee Blake motioned the party toward the targets and led the group toward Cindy's, which he examined first. All six bullets had struck the target. One had landed in a leg, another in a shoulder, and a third in an arm. The remaining three would probably have been fatal; one had penetrated a cheekbone, another had cut into the figure's chin, and the final shot had landed near the waist. "Very nice, Cindy," the general said. "You'd qualify as a marksman in any unit under my command."

The girl flushed at the compliment.

Lee led the way to Hank Purcell's target and stopped

short, staring in astonishment, as did the lieutenant and the sergeant.

Cindy was nonplussed. All six of her opponent's shots had landed within a radius no larger than a silver dollar, all of them centered on the figure's heart.

Hank appeared to take his marksmanship for granted. He accepted the congratulations of General Blake and the soldiers quietly.

They walked back to the table, where the general handed the boy and girl the cumbersome, old-fashioned rifles and opened a box of cartridges. "This," he said, as the sergeant placed fresh targets at the opposite end of the range, "is going to be more difficult. You'll have to reload your rifles after each shot. You'll have exactly two minutes from the time I order you to fire until you hear the cease-fire order. During that time, you're free to fire as many or as few shots as you like at your target. Both accuracy and the number of shots will determine your final score."

The contestants nodded.

Not wanting to waste time after the order to fire was given, Hank raised the rifle to his shoulder, looked down the barrel, and experimentally pulled the trigger several times. Cindy pretended to be unaware of what he was doing.

"Fire at will," General Blake said.

Cindy lost no time and methodically loaded the rifle in the manner that her late father and brother had taught her. She was painstaking, careful, and thorough. She raised the weapon to her shoulder, sighted down the barrel, and squeezed the trigger.

In the meantime, Hank reacted as though devils were pursuing him. He loaded his rifle, then raised and fired it in almost one continuous motion. Not waiting for the smoke to clear or to examine how accurate he had been, he instantly reloaded and fired again.

When two minutes had passed and General Blake called a halt, Cindy had made a creditable showing and had fired her rifle twice. Hank, however, had fired six shots in all, averaging one every twenty seconds. When they approached the targets, with Lee Blake in the lead, they saw that Cindy had done well. One of her shots had clipped an ear of the target, and the other had landed in an arm. Either would have been enough to incapacitate an enemy.

But all six of Hank's shots were lethal: He had shot out the eyes of the target, then had made a small, tight circle in the center of the forehead.

"You've done well, Cindy. I'm proud of you," her stepfather said, then turned to the boy, his hand outstretched. "If you were a few years older, I'd hire you as an instructor right here at the range. Do well in school, and I'll personally recommend you for an appointment to the U.S. Military Academy at West Point."

Hank flushed with pleasure. He had long taken his prowess with firearms for granted, and it was almost inconceivable to him that an officer with the exalted rank of a major general should praise him.

Cindy made a great effort and forced herself to extend her hand. "That was nice shooting, Hank," she said. "You beat me fair and square."

He gripped her hand so hard that she winced. "Heck," he said, reddening even more, "I'd kick myself from here to the Atlantic Ocean and back if I couldn't shoot better than a girl."

The lieutenant and sergeant, who were taking in the scene, smiled; Cindy did not. She wiped her hands on her skirt as though she had touched something unclean.

As they walked back to the house, General Blake, strolling with the boy, enlarged on the theme of the need for Hank to acquire an education. "I can see now," he said, "why Clarissa was so insistent that you come to Fort Vancouver. You have an eye and an instinct for marksmanship that are very rare. Left to your own devices, you'd have found it necessary to earn a living, and it's possible that you'd have become a gunslinger. In no time at all, you'd have found yourself outside the law, and you'd have wound up with your name on wanted posters in every U.S. post office in the West. But you have a far different future in store for you, believe me. I'm going to make certain that you study your fool head off and that you pass the West Point entrance examinations with flying colors."

"You really think I can qualify for the academy, sir? You really think I'm going to be able to go to school there?"

"You attend to your end of the bargain, and I'll guarantee you that you'll become a second lieutenant in the service of your country."

The boy's euphoria was so great that he did not notice Cindy's reaction. She listened to her stepfather in stunned disbelief. Hank Purcell was an oaf, in no way qualified to become an army officer.

When they reached the house, Cindy hastily excused herself and went upstairs to her bedchamber. Her mother and sister-in-law were in the room directly across the hall, where Eulalia was helping Clarissa unpack. They called to Cindy, and she reluctantly joined them.

Eulalia smiled at her teenage daughter. "Who won the shooting match?" she asked innocently.

"Hank, of course," Cindy snapped. "I guess shooting is the stupid boy's one accomplishment."

Clarissa ignored the slur. "He is a remarkable marksman," she said. "According to Toby, Hank's already the equal of any adult, and if he continues to practice, he'll be in a class by himself in a few years."

"How very impressive," Eulalia said.

"Well, I'm glad he's good for something," Cindy said furiously, "because in my opinion he's the most miserable excuse for a human being I've ever seen! I'll show him around school, and I'll introduce him to everybody—because you want me to—but that's where I draw the line. I wouldn't want a single person I know to think that disgusting boy is a friend of mine!" Turning on her heel, she stalked out, went into her bedroom, and slammed the door.

Eulalia smiled painfully, then shook her head. "I was sixteen so many years ago," she said, "that I honestly can't remember it being such a horrendous age."

Clarissa giggled. "Cindy is mistaken," she said, "if she thinks she's going to walk all over Hank. He's tough—because he's had to be. I'll bet they become close friends— if they don't kill each other first."

Rob and Beth left Fort Vancouver the following day to see his parents in Portland. Dr. Martin and Tonie enjoyed the visit of the young people, and the occasion was much livelier than the visit Beth had paid her father and stepmother, for she had kept to her room almost the entire time.

Then the young couple left for California by steamboat, which now made daily trips along the coast between Portland and San Francisco. Putting off a decision to buy a house until Rob finished his work on the railroad, they checked in at the Palace Hotel, where they had spent their honeymoon. While Beth settled in, Rob looked up the Harrises, who said they would be glad to entertain Beth while she stayed in the city.

Rob could not even spend the night in San Francisco, for he was wanted immediately for his work on the railroad line in the Sierra Nevada. The time for leave-taking had come, and seeing that Beth was comfortably installed in a suite in the hotel, he prepared to depart. Looking at her fidgeting in a stuffed armchair, he curbed a desire to sigh. "I hope to goodness you're going to be all right," he said.

There was a note of suspense and excitement in Beth's laugh. "Why shouldn't I be all right?" she demanded. "There's no better or safer place in all of San Francisco than this hotel."

"I know," Rob replied glumly, unable to shake off a strange sense of foreboding. Still reluctant to go, he said, "You have ample funds, and if you need more, you have only to apply to Chet Harris for them. Don't be afraid to spend money. That's why we have it."

"I refuse to be foolish about that," she said, "but I won't argue the point."

He didn't want to argue about anything. "I'll admit to you," he said, "that I'm worried for you. You're young, you're very beautiful, and you're wealthy enough to be a target of the unscrupulous. Be careful of the friendships you make and always keep in mind that the Harrises are nearby if you need real friends."

"I won't forget," she promised, though she really had no desire to accept invitations from the stuffy Harrises. Tired of his lecturing, she slid her arms around his neck and kissed him.

That gesture ended the discussion with finality.

Rob embraced her, then pulled himself away. "I'll come down from the mountains to see you whenever I can. You can bet on that," he said as he hurried toward the door.

A moment later Beth was alone. On sudden impulse she walked to the table. On it stood a half-empty bottle of champagne from which she and Rob had consumed a farewell drink. She refilled her glass, then held it aloft. "Here's to me," she said, "and to my new life as a free woman."

One of the Sioux villages was located on the edge of the Badlands; it was a small community made up of a number of tepees, a corral for horses, and little else. The inhabitants subsisted on the deer and buffalo that the hunters brought back from the woods and prairies; the squaws grew few vegetables because the soil here, like that of the Badlands itself, was too poor to grow good crops.

What made this village noteworthy was the chief who ruled it, Tall Stone, who was named after the odd-shaped figures that dotted the Badlands. Tall Stone was of average height, stocky, with a barrel chest, brawny arms, and thick, stubby fingers. His large stomach indicated his love of food and, when he could get it, the rum and beer of the white man.

Tall Stone was highly regarded by Thunder Cloud and the other leaders of the Sioux; he had fought with distinction in the battle in which the Sioux had confronted the Eleventh United States Cavalry. He was also an acknowledged leader in the movement to form a solid alliance with the Blackfoot and the Cheyenne. More than this, the reputation of Tall Stone, now in early middle age, rested on his undying hatred for all white settlers who dared to invade the lands of his people.

No one knew exactly why Tall Stone's temper was so violent and his nature was so cruel. No one dared ask him. It was rumored, however, that more than three decades earlier, when he had been a very young warrior, he had suffered excruciating embarrassment at the hands of Whip Holt. According to the story, he had accosted the great frontiersman, who had been trapping and trading in Dakota, and the Indian had been deliberately insulting. Holt had refused to duel with him, saying that he didn't believe in senseless killing, and when Tall Stone had persisted, the mountain man had uncoiled his famous whip from his waist and had thrashed the young brave. Ever since that day, Tall Stone had been the sworn enemy of everyone who claimed allegiance to the United States.

Despite Tall Stone's love of food and drink, he was still a warrior to be feared, and his threats against the white man had not been idle. In his time he had taken many scalps—of men, women, and even children—and he proudly wore a necklace of human teeth, taken, he said, from the settlers who had dared to set foot in the Dakota Territory. Even his own people were known to cringe when they saw him coming.

Now the residents of the village were astonished because he was preparing to entertain a party of white people. Ma Hastings, the cutthroat leader of a notorious bandit gang, had, like the Indians, also left the Montana Territory because of the presence of so many troops. In Montana Ma's son and chief lieutenant, Clifford, had been killed by Toby Holt while the gang was about to raid a settler's ranch, and Ma had vowed she would not rest until Toby Holt was dead.

Now a special meeting had been arranged between Ma Hastings and Tall Stone, and several tepees had been erected for the use of the visitors. The chief obtained the services of two squaws as cooks, and he commandeered the nineteen-year-old Gentle Doe to serve his guests and himself.

Everyone in the village knew that the chieftain lusted after Gentle Doe. They also were aware that the aptly named maiden, as lovely as she was shy, wanted no part of Tall Stone, and with good reason. Since earliest childhood she had feared his temper tantrums, his cruelties, and his vicious mistreatment of anyone who crossed his will.

Gentle Doe's parents were no longer alive, however, and as an orphan she was not in a position to determine her own destiny. Under the unwritten laws of the Sioux, she had to accept any man whom the chief instructed her to marry. But not even Tall Stone was going to force her into marriage with him against her will. He was too proud for that, and he contented himself with the belief that she would come to him in her own good time.

Now Gentle Doe went to the pit where an outdoor cooking fire was burning and vigorously stirred the pot containing the stew the older squaws had made. In it were chunks of venison, carrots, kale, dried green peas, pickled sugar beets, and pieces of celery root.

Tall Stone stood nearby, his eyes fixed on Gentle Doe as he observed every move she made. The intensity of his gaze made her nervous, and she said the first thing that came to mind as she went to the stack of gourds that would be used to serve the stew. "How many guests will Tall Stone entertain today?"

"Two will share with me, and you will serve us," Tall

Stone said succinctly. "The others, seven or eight warriors in all, will go and dine with the unmarried warriors. They will be served by the old squaws."

He still scrutinized her, and Gentle Doe felt she had to say something to ease the feeling of being devoured by his eyes. "Your guests are Sioux from another village?"

Tall Stone shook his head. "They are not Sioux," he said. "They have pale skins."

Despite herself, Gentle Doe stared at him in open-mouthed astonishment. Because she kept to herself as much as possible, she was one of the few people in the village who did not know Tall Stone was meeting with whites.

He realized she was shocked, and his thin lips twisted in a lopsided grin that more closely resembled a grimace. "Gentle Doe," he asked, "has heard of the woman who is called Ma Hastings?"

She shook her head.

"Her fellow paleskins are her enemies, just as they are the enemies of Tall Stone. She is the head of a gang of robbers and bandits that preys on settlers and steals their horses and cattle. When they object, she kills them, just as I, too, slaughter them."

The young Indian woman shuddered.

"She had two sons," Tall Stone continued, "but one of them was killed by Toby Holt—may the gods strike him with a bolt of lightning. Now she has only one son, whose mind and will have been softened by the strong drink of the paleskins. It is said that he is useless, but this is something I will judge for myself. Ma Hastings and her son, Ralph, will be my guests at supper."

Gentle Doe wondered what Tall Stone and Ma

Hastings could have in common, but something he had said intrigued her far more. Like all Sioux, she had heard about Toby Holt and was familiar with stories about the valor of his father. "Gentle Doe did not know that Tall Stone was the enemy of Toby Holt," she said softly.

He nodded, his jaw set, his eyes fiery. In the battle that the Sioux had fought with the Eleventh Cavalry, Tall Stone had been bested by Toby Holt, though they had not met face to face. From a place of concealment, Holt—and it definitely was Toby Holt, according to braves who had seen him—had shot Tall Stone's hand. The Sioux chief, finding himself weaponless, was suddenly surrounded by soldiers, who forced him to flee from the Sioux stronghold in the Montana mountains. This defeat, linked to his earlier humiliation by Whip Holt, increased the Sioux chieftain's rage against all white men, but particularly the Holts.

"Tall Stone and Ma Hastings," he said triumphantly, "will sign an alliance in blood and will swear that they will not rest until Toby Holt breathes no more." He laughed coarsely. "Also, we will sign another pact to support each other in raids on the paleskin settlers in Dakota and Montana."

Gentle Doe could not help feeling sorry for the women and children who would be killed. She said nothing, however. She had seen Tall Stone lose his temper with others, and she wanted to take no risks. She hurried back to the fire and tended the stew, stirring it more vigorously than was necessary.

While she busied herself, a party of nine horsemen arrived on the scene, and glancing up at them, she thought them highly disreputable and unkempt. Their hats and coats were covered with dust, and it looked as if they hadn't bathed in a long time. Only their horses seemed well tended and healthy, no doubt because they had been stolen from someone else.

All but two of the newcomers rode off to the opposite end of the village with the braves who were their escorts. The pair who remained behind and dismounted were Tall Stone's guests.

The elder, wearing a faded shirt and worn trousers tucked into shabby boots, removed a broad-brimmed, high-crowned hat, and Gentle Doe saw a mop of gray hair, only slightly longer than a man's. The mouth was thin and stern, and the eyes, like Tall Stone's, were hard.

It was difficult for the Indian woman to believe she was looking at a female. Gentle Doe knew at a glance that Ma Hastings would show no mercy to her victims. Her walk was a rolling swagger, her laugh was husky and guttural, and there was nothing feminine in her manner.

Ralph Hastings, dressed like his mother, had a weak chin and small, bloodshot eyes. He staggered as he made his way toward the fire; it was apparent that he was drunk.

Tall Stone and Ma Hastings wasted no time in getting down to business. They immediately began planning a raid on a village of settlers located in Montana just past the border where the Dakota Badlands ended, and they signed a pact in blood, both cutting their forearms with their knives and letting their blood mix together in a small pool on the ground. They also swore a pact to destroy Toby Holt, but they decided to wait for the right opportunity before putting that plan into operation.

Trying to shut the unpleasant conversation from her

mind, Gentle Doe served gourds filled with venison stew
and smaller containers into which she spooned a Sioux
delicacy of cornmeal, known as soft bread.

All at once the Indian woman realized Ralph Hastings
was gaping at her. The young man was sobering up with
a great effort, and he seemed stunned by what he saw.

Gentle Doe knew that she was a good-looking woman
and that she had a trim, supple figure. But no man had
ever regarded her with such wonder.

It was unfortunate, she thought, that Ralph Hastings
was a drunkard. Had he been a real man of substance
and stature, she might have appealed to him to help her
to escape from the village and the fate that undoubtedly
awaited her there when Tall Stone finally insisted that
she marry him.

Charles Dickens, acclaimed as the greatest novelist in
the English-speaking world, took the United States by
storm on his tour of the country. Every seat was occupied when he gave readings of his works, the cheering
that greeted him in the streets befitted an international
hero, and hostesses competed for the honor of entertaining him at dinner.

Nowhere was his welcome warmer than in San
Francisco. The bawdy, rough gold-rush town was already becoming a literary center in the nation second
only to New York, with Mark Twain and Brett Harte taking up residence there. The first of Dickens's appearances at Metropolitan Hall, one of the largest edifices of
its kind on the Pacific Coast, sold out so quickly that
two additional readings were scheduled. The first was a
very special occasion, a charity event sponsored by Mrs.
Collis Huntington, wife of the wealthy railroad specula-

tor, for the building of a new hospital. All of San Francisco society turned out for the event, the ladies wearing expensive gowns and their best jewelry, the gentlemen wearing white ties and tailcoats.

Prominent in one of the center boxes were two of the leading financiers of California, Chet Harris and his partner, Wong Ke, who escorted their wives, Clara Lou and Mei Lo. Separately and together, the pair owned gold mines, which had been responsible for the start of their fortunes; vast quantities of real estate in the burgeoning city; and interests in newspapers, hotels, shipping lines, and many other businesses. The partners led a quiet social life, entertaining only close friends and business associates, and they went out only on very special occasions, such as this one.

Their wives were equally discreet. Although Clara Lou Harris and Wong Mei Lo could have worn the most expensive gowns of any ladies present and could have glittered with diamonds and pearls, they were dressed quietly and their jewelry was not ostentatious.

Idly, indulgently, the quartet watched the great and near-great, the cream of San Francisco society, arriving and being shown to seats. Suddenly Chet stiffened.

Moving slowly down the center aisle was an attractive young woman with blond hair piled on her head in the fashion of the time. Her face was made up with as much care as that of an actress. She wore a skintight off-the-shoulder gown of black silk, with a cape of white fox thrown carelessly over one shoulder. Her earrings were long, dangling strands of diamonds and matched a diamond necklace and a double cuff of diamonds on her wrist.

Following her were two escorts, one of them a young

shipping magnate, the other, in full-dress uniform, an
army lieutenant colonel stationed at the Presidio.

Chet had last seen Beth when she and Rob had come
to San Francisco for their honeymoon, and at that time
Beth had looked nothing like the way she did tonight.
Since her recent arrival in the city, he and his wife had
invited Beth to dinner—as they had promised Rob—but
she had declined, saying she had a prior engagement.
Now seeing her make such a brazen entrance, Chet muttered, "My God."

"What is it, dear?" Clara Lou asked, turning to him.
Chet's brown-haired, pretty wife was still as composed
and self-confident as she had been when he first met her
in Colorado seven years earlier, though she had put on a
few pounds and had taken on a somewhat matronly appearance.

"Look there," Chet told her. "That's Rob Martin's
wife—Lee and Cathy Blake's girl."

"She's not really a girl anymore, dear," Clara Lou replied dryly.

He failed to appreciate his wife's humor. "Where in
thunderation did she get all those gems, do you suppose?"

"I imagine she bought them, or her husband bought
them for her," Clara Lou replied blithely. "After all, Rob
Martin and Toby Holt own an extremely profitable gold
mine."

"True enough," he replied gloomily, "and that's probably why she has two escorts. The fortune hunters of the
town have sniffed her out."

"Really, Chet, you're exaggerating," Clara Lou said,
but her words were made inaudible by the storm of ap-
plause that greeted Charles Dickens as he came onto the
stage and stepped up to the podium.

For the next hour Chet fidgeted in his seat, unable to concentrate on the readings, which included selections from Dickens's latest book, *Our Mutual Friend*, with the author occasionally interspersing anecdotes about his travels in America and Europe. Then Dickens took an intermission, promising his audience that when he returned, he would be reading to them from his favorite among his books, *David Copperfield*.

Chet turned to Wong Ke and to Mei Lo. "You remember Beth and Rob Martin, the young married couple who were children of people who came to Oregon with me on the wagon train when I was a boy? You met them at our house for dinner when they came down to San Francisco for their honeymoon. Well, that young woman who came waltzing down the aisle in the black silk dress, diamonds, and fox cape is Beth. She's sitting down front now, with an escort on either side of her."

Wong Ke grinned and nodded. "Certainly, we remember," he said. "We saw her when she came in."

"She looks pretty tonight," said the petite, black-haired Mei Lo, who found it impossible to say anything bad about anybody. "She looks very pretty."

"If you ask me," Chet said glumly, "she looks like one of the courtesans for whom San Francisco has become infamous."

His Chinese partner laughed. "Now you exaggerate, Chet," he said.

"Not at all," was the stubborn reply. "She's half-naked, her face is painted, and she's wearing enough jewelry to decorate a Christmas tree. And to top it all off, she waltzed down the aisle with two men, not one. Look at her now, flirting and laughing with them."

"I see your point, dear," Clara Lou said mildly, "but I can't help wondering if you're exaggerating a bit."

"I think not," her husband said firmly. "Remember, Rob told us that Beth was going to be living in San Francisco in the Palace Hotel while he was off in the Sierra Nevada. There's no telling when he'll be coming back here. Meanwhile, her clothes, her cosmetics, everything about her—including her attitude—indicate that she's a rich, spoiled young lady looking for trouble. You know this town as well as I know it, Ke, and you've got to admit there are a lot of unattached men in San Francisco who would be just delighted to provide Beth with that trouble."

"I see what you mean," his partner replied slowly. "I suppose you're right."

"She struck me," Mei Lo said, "at least on the occasion when I met her, as a very . . . inexperienced young lady."

"She doesn't know her way around a city like San Francisco," Chet agreed. "She's had social standing all her life, being the daughter of a high-ranking army officer. She's always been a little spoiled and headstrong. Now she's rich to boot, with a husband who's off on an assignment that will keep them separated for months at a time. Most of all, she's young and could have her head easily turned."

Clara Lou nodded slowly. "I'm afraid I must agree with you on that score, Chet, dear," she said. "She *is* very young and naive."

"I don't know quite what we'll do about it," Chet said, "but I do know that Rob—and Lee and Eulalia Blake—are counting on me to prevent the girl from getting into trouble." Grimly he added, "I intend to live up to my responsibility to them. She may have avoided *us* since she's been here, but I'm not going to avoid *her* any longer. I intend to see that she gets back in line."

III

Chet Harris sat in his handsomely furnished, mahogany-paneled office overlooking San Francisco Bay, but he ignored the spectacular view, just as he paid scant attention to the stream of documents and papers that crossed his desk. He could not get Beth Martin out of his mind.

As he and Clara Lou had discussed the previous night after they had arrived home, Beth did not appear to have gone wrong yet. But the potential for stumbling was very much present, and this was something that Chet was determined to prevent. He owed it to her husband, and even more so, to her father and to her stepmother. Years ago on that first wagon train to Oregon, when Chet had been a teenager traveling with his widowed mother and brothers, Lee and Eulalia had been his good friends. They had remained so after they had settled in their new homes and Chet had gone out to make his own way in the world. Though he had found success and fortune, Chet was still indebted to these people.

The previous evening, he and Clara Lou had concluded that Beth was enjoying the first real freedom she had ever known after living a circumspect life as the daughter of a high-ranking military officer. Thanks to the gold mine her husband shared with Toby Holt, she could afford whatever luxuries she now wanted, as opposed to living frugally on her family's U.S. government salary.

Clara Lou, drawing on her years of experience as a woman who had to live by her wits (she had even operated a successful gambling establishment in Denver's rough-and-tumble earlier days), had understood yet another aspect of the young woman. In spite of Beth's provocative clothes and makeup, not to mention her flirtatiousness, she was not really looking to have an affair. Clara Lou felt certain that Beth was just exercising her high spirits and independence. Clara Lou had seen many women like Beth, who regarded their marriages as shields that enabled them to defy conventions. They thought their wedding rings protected them and that the men who escorted them would respect their marriages. Like Beth, they were naive, perhaps, but not wicked.

Despite what Clara Lou had told him, Chet was not very reassured. Sighing heavily, he tugged his waistcoat down over his growing paunch and did his best to put Beth Martin out of his mind. One of the company's brightest young executives, Leon Graham, a nephew of Clara Lou's, came into his office. Spreading documents on the desk, young Graham spoke confidently, outlining each problem and suggesting a solution. Chet listened attentively, and in every case agreed.

Leon Graham, he reflected, was one of the company's most valuable employees. Not yet thirty years of age, he was earnest and hard-working, the first to arrive at the office every morning and the last to leave every evening. Even though the mothers of many eligible young women had thrust their daughters at him, he was still a bachelor and lived a quiet, circumspect life in a small, neat house on Nob Hill, where he was attended by a staff of servants. From the little Chet had gleaned about him, he engaged in regular physical exercise, he ate and drank in moderation, and he avoided the gambling casinos and brothels that were San Francisco's legacy of the gold rush days. What he did with his spare time, and who his friends were, neither Chet nor Clara Lou knew, but certainly few young men seemed as upstanding.

A sudden idea came to Chet. Perhaps Leon could be persuaded to see something of Beth Martin socially and by acting as her escort, prevent less honorable men from endangering her.

When he went home for dinner that noon, Chet mentioned his thought to Clara Lou. "He'd be a perfect escort for Beth," she said happily, "and she'd be good for him, too. From what I've gathered, he spends far too many of his evenings home alone. I'll invite both of them to dinner, and I'll ask Leon to escort Beth to our house."

When Chet returned to his office after dinner, he gave his wife's invitation to Leon, while the Harris butler took Beth's to the Palace Hotel.

Both accepted, Beth realizing she could not put off any longer a visit to the Harrises. The following evening Leon stopped off at her hotel to take her to the Harris house in his carriage. By the time they arrived, they were chatting easily, like old friends.

Beth's gown of gauzelike silk was subtle and, at first glance, appeared quite modest; actually it revealed ev-

ery line of her lovely figure. She was animated and spar-
kling, and her blond hair glistened. Clara Lou had seen
few young women more attractive.

Certainly Leon Graham seemed fascinated by her.
Chet, taking no chances, made several pointed refer-
ences about Beth's husband, Rob, and discussed his current mission in the Sierra Nevada at some length.

Leon chatted about the state of grand opera in the
city, and Beth proved quite informed on the subject,
demonstrating that she had acquired a taste for San
Francisco culture in a short time. When Leon mentioned
a production of *Hamlet* the following evening in which
the great actor, Edwin Booth, would appear, Beth responded with enthusiasm.

The young man lost no time. "Perhaps," he said, "you
would do me the honor of coming with me to tomorrow
evening's performance? And join me for supper after-
ward?"

"I'd love it," Beth replied without hesitation. "Thanks
so much."

Chet and Clara Lou exchanged quick, satisfied
glances.

Wanting to make sure that Leon understood what was
expected of him, Chet called him into his office the following morning. "I hope you won't take offense at what
I have to say," the older man told him, "but your aunt
and I feel it's wise to clarify certain situations immediately. Beth Martin is an uncommonly pretty and vivacious girl."

"There's no question about that," Leon answered, grinning broadly.

"As the daughter of a major general, she's lived in all
parts of the United States—"

"I didn't know her father was a general," Leon interrupted in surprise.

"Indeed," Chet said. "He's commander of the Army of the West."

Impressed, Leon whistled softly under his breath.

"In spite of having had certain advantages—or perhaps because of them—she's more naive than she appears to be," Chet went on.

Leon looked blank.

Chet decided to pull no punches. "If I were your age," he said, "and a bachelor to boot, I might easily be misled by the way she looks and acts. But don't get any wrong ideas. She's very much in love with her husband, as he is with her, and she'd be outraged if you or anyone else were to make advances to her." No one, Chet told himself, could be plainer than that.

Leon's eyes widened. "I assure you, sir," he said earnestly, "I'm not for a single moment forgetting that Beth is a respectable married lady. I enjoy her company, and I flatter myself that she likes mine. But I'm very aware that there are limits to our acquaintance."

Chet was relieved. "Good," he said. "We understand each other, so there's an end to the matter."

As Leon made his way down the corridor to his own office, his lips froze in a half-smile. He had said what his employer and uncle by marriage had wanted to hear, which was something Leon made a point of doing. What Leon had told Chet about his intentions for Beth, however, was far from the truth. He couldn't remember a time when he had been as fascinated by a woman as he was by Beth Martin. He intended to explore every facet of her nature, and he told himself that there would be no holds barred.

* ❖ *

Toby Holt traveled by rail from Washington City to Minnesota, where he had left his stallion at Fort Snelling with an old army colleague. Staying only overnight at the fort, he set out early the next morning for the Dakota Territory.

It was late fall. Toby enjoyed himself immensely as he traveled on horseback to Dakota, maintaining a brisk pace. He was so eager to start in on his assignment that he often rode through the night, taking only short rests for himself and his horse.

As he rode, he pondered what was in store for him when he arrived in the Dakota Territory and began his work for the government. But he could make no concrete plans at the moment. He would have to wait for the right opportunities.

Also on Toby's mind was Clarissa, whom he missed terribly. He knew she would be all right with his mother and stepfather; there were few women as capable and self-reliant as Clarissa. But he missed her and wished she were with him.

Crossing the Red River, which delineated the border of Minnesota and the Dakota Territory, Toby headed for Fort Abercrombie, the small army post maintained jointly by the Corps of Engineers and the infantry, for peace-keeping purposes. The commandant of Fort Abercrombie had been notified by a War Department telegraph of Toby's arrival, and four engineer officers, who had worked on laying out the railroad lines across the territory, were on hand to greet him. Together, they would go out to inspect the lines they had charted, and the engineers had been told to make any alterations recommended by Toby Holt.

Toby ate dinner with the soldiers that evening at the

officers' mess, and for the first time since he had left the frontier, he dined on buffalo steak. One taste was enough to tell him that he had returned to the West.

Colonel C.C. Black, who had a thick, dark mustache and carried himself with an air of self-importance, was the senior officer of the group. He explained the situation to Toby. "Dakota is so confounded big," he said, "that we've surveyed for two lines, running east and west, rather than one. The northern route extends from Duluth pretty much due west, south of the Canadian border, and will hit in northern Montana. The other line extends west from St. Paul, Minnesota, and will enter the central part of Montana. This line will follow the route you and your partner already mapped out through the Washington Territory. The other line will run north of it, following a route the Army Corps of Engineers surveyed, and will merge with your line in the western part of the Washington territory."

"That makes sense," Toby said. "To have two lines located far apart means there will always be one of them running in the event of an emergency."

"You're thinking, Mr. Holt, of possible Indian troubles," one of the junior officers said.

Toby nodded grimly. "I am," he replied. "I don't know much about the latest developments with the Indians in the territory, but you're probably aware there's something afoot."

"So I am," Colonel Black told him. "But, I'm sorry to say, we're lacking details. We have only a small cavalry detachment here at the fort, and our infantry is in no position to range very far from the home base. All I can tell you is that something is indeed brewing."

"I aim to learn the details," Toby said, but did not reveal his assignment from General Grant to learn the ex-

tent and nature of the alliance among the Sioux,
Blackfoot, and Cheyenne, and to try to prevent them
from going to war.

The following morning, accompanied by Colonel
Black and three junior officers, Toby set out to inspect
the less northern line, which extended into the wilderness from the farmlands of Dakota. The weather was
cold, but there was no snow on the ground, and they
covered a considerable area in the next two days, riding
past numerous homesteads, each consisting of one
hundred and sixty acres, which the U.S. government
gave free to settlers who came to Dakota. Though the
fields had long since been cleared of crops, corn was the
staple product grown everywhere in this part of the territory.

The differences between life in the Dakota Territory
and that in Minnesota, which lay due east of it, were
significant. In Minnesota the Indians were few, and
there were not many dangers, but here in Dakota, farmers and their sons always had their rifles beside them,
and even the women made certain firearms were close at
hand. This was the "peaceful" portion of the vast territory, the part that supposedly had been tamed, but the
unwary nevertheless sometimes lost their lives and
scalps.

Most farms were near the Missouri River, which bisected the entire territory from north to south, and along the
banks of its tributaries. The land as far as one could see
in every direction was undeviatingly flat. One of the
most notable qualities of this portion of Dakota was the
complete absence of any trees. Most of America in its
primitive stages was covered with a thick forest, a sea of
trees that extended from the Atlantic Ocean to the
Pacific, but Dakota was different. Here there was unre-

lieved flat prairie, with rich, black soil and thick, waving grass that reached as high as a man's waist.

One of the consequences of this phenomenon was that log cabins, which were common elsewhere in the United States, were unknown in Dakota. Most pioneers built their homes of clay and of sod, though in the first months after they settled here, they copied the Indians and made their dwellings of animal skins.

Game flourished, attracted by the high, rich grass. As soon as Toby and his military associates started out on their journey, they saw large herds of buffalo, some grazing nearby, others visible in the distance. The farther they rode from civilization, the more herds they saw. As they rode farther and farther west, Toby saw deer and elk, antelope and moose, which, attracted by the nourishing dry grass, had wandered down from the Black Hills.

As the party traveled, Toby carefully inspected the site for the less northern of the proposed railroad lines. By the time they had reached the western boundary of the territory on the Montana border, he expressed his approval.

Thus, a little more than a week after leaving Fort Abercrombie, they had done what they had set out to do and were now heading back east. Then one day, shortly before noon, Toby became alert to danger. The sun was standing almost directly overhead in a cloudless sky as the group, with Colonel Black in the lead and Toby behind him, traveled back across the prairie, pausing from time to time to study maps drawn by the engineers. Suddenly Toby halted his horse. His eyes focused toward the left, and some intuitive sense told him that it was not an animal that had aroused his attention.

Peering into the distance, Toby at last saw what he

was looking for. Riding toward the small party was a group of at least twenty Indian warriors, all of them with feathers in their scalp locks, giving evidence of their bellicose intentions. Their faces and the upper portions of their bodies were smeared with the vermilion and white war paint of the Sioux.

Calling the attention of his companions to the approaching braves, Toby scrutinized the column swiftly. War parties seldom went out this time of year, but there was no doubting the hostile intentions of this group of Sioux, all of whom were armed with lances, bows, and arrows.

Reacting swiftly, Toby took charge, even though Colonel Black was the highest-ranking officer present. "They're Sioux," he said, "and they have war fever."

Colonel Black deferred to Toby. "What do you suggest?"

"If they follow the usual procedure of Sioux," Toby replied, watching the advancing braves, "they'll try to take us first with a headlong rush. If that doesn't work, they'll try forming a circle around us so we can't break out, and they'll take potshots at us. But we'll face that situation when we come to it. The best thing, Colonel, is for the four of you to form behind me in a point-shaped wedge."

"With you at the point?"

"Yes, sir."

"I don't know about that," Colonel Black said dubiously. "You'll be the target for every one of those warriors."

"That won't matter," Toby replied, speaking rapidly. "You and I and the other three have rifles, while they only have arrows and lances. It's going to take them time to get in range, and by then, I hope we'll have disposed of enough of them with our guns to scare them off."

The Sioux's horses were so close that the men could hear the thunder of their hoofs. The colonel gave a quiet order, and he and his men ranged behind Toby in a V-formation.

Again measuring the distance of the rapidly approaching braves, Toby checked his rifle, as well as the two six-shooters that he carried in his belt. Certain that his weapons were properly loaded, he laid the rifle in front of him across his saddle, and tugging his hat lower on his forehead, he squinted at the approaching Sioux, making no move until they came within rifle range.

The Sioux had expected the paleskins to break and run, to gallop away in an attempt to escape their charge. When they failed to be dislodged, the warriors admired them but nevertheless thought their behavior foolhardy.

The Indians rode in no formation. Each man pushed his horse as best he could, with the riders in the lead bunched together and a half-dozen or more men clustered behind them.

Toby caught a glimpse of a war bonnet with many feathers at the rear of the Sioux ranks, indicating the chieftain who was in charge of the assault. Ordinarily this individual would have been a prime target, but he was protected by most of his braves, so Toby ignored the chief for the present and instead concentrated on the warriors leading the charge.

Raising his rifle to his shoulder, he took swift aim, then squeezed the trigger. A brave threw his hands skyward and slid to the ground. He died before his body struck the ground and was trampled by the hoofs of the horses in the second wave.

The officers behind Toby were cool, experienced Inlian fighters, and four shots resulted in four more warriors tumbling to the ground. By that time Toby had reloaded his rifle and fired it a second time, disposing of still another foe.

By now the braves, their ranks reduced, thought better of their attack. They had suffered heavy casualties after sending only a few stray arrows ineffectively in the general direction of their enemy, and they knew they were being badly trounced. Once again, the superior weapons of the white man had proved too much for them, and the Sioux turned to flee.

As they turned, Toby recognized the chief in the war bonnet as Gray Wolf, one of the leaders of the Sioux in the battle with the Eleventh Cavalry in Montana. Almost without thinking, he seized the opportunity to begin carrying out the private mission given him by General Grant. He spurred his horse in pursuit of the war party, and after an instant's startled hesitation, the four officers followed him.

When Toby was within hailing distance, he drew both pistols. "Gray Wolf!" he called in the language of the Sioux. "Stop or you are a dead man! Take the word of Toby Holt, son of Whip Holt, for this."

The chief pulled his mount to a halt and stared in astonishment. The braves, confused, reined in behind him.

"If you had killed my comrades and me, you would have taken our scalps," Toby said, his pistols still aimed at the chief. "It is our right to remove your scalp and those of the braves whom you have led into battle. But I am willing to spare you on one condition."

"What is your condition?" Gray Wolf shouted hoarsely, as both he and his braves stared in wonder at the intrepid paleskin.

"Where is Thunder Cloud, the chief of all the Sioux?"

Toby demanded. "I wish to bring him a message from those chiefs who lead the United States. But I do not know where to find him in Dakota. It is said that he and his people have moved their village to a secret location. Take me to him and your life will be spared with honor."

Colonel Black, who knew the language of the Sioux well enough to make out what was being said, blinked at Toby in astonishment.

Toby, in an undertone, said, "It's true that I carry words for him from General Grant. If I can, I must persuade the Sioux to give up their plan to engage in a full-scale war against the United States. And if I can speak with Thunder Cloud, it will be unnecessary to speak to anyone else."

"You're taking a terrible risk, Holt," the colonel whispered.

"I think not," Toby replied. "They know me, just as they knew my father. Most of them know the many favors we have done for them over the years, and their sense of honor is so great that they would not dare to destroy their good names by killing me."

Colonel Black saw the sense in what Toby was saying.

"I accept the conditions of Holt," Gray Wolf called, and gave an order to his braves. Several of them promptly dismounted. Now that they were no longer fleeing, they took advantage of the opportunity to collect their dead, as was their custom.

Toby made brief farewells to Colonel Black and his men, then moved forward to take his place beside Gray Wolf. The Sioux braves fell in behind them.

As Toby rode off with the warriors, he unwittingly created another Toby Holt legend. The army officers would never tire of relating how he had killed two Sioux

in combat, had made demands of their leader at gun-
point, and then had ridden off with his attackers.

After riding for about an hour, Toby and the braves
came to a fast-flowing river, a tributary of the mighty
Missouri. They paused beside the bank to water their
horses and to eat shredded, dried buffalo meat, which
the Indians shared with their unwelcome guest.

The journey was resumed, and shortly before sunset
they encountered several Sioux sentries. Soon they came
upon a bustling village laid out on the prairie near a
bend in the river. Warriors sat placidly around the many
cooking fires. Carcasses of deer and smaller game—the
result of their day's hunting—hung from frames made of
poles. Squaws tended the fires, boiling water and cooking food for the evening meal, and small children were
shooed away and told to go play until supper was ready.
As nearly as Toby could judge, the village had two to
three thousand inhabitants, which meant that this was a
principal Sioux settlement and that it was undoubtedly
Thunder Cloud's own headquarters.

His guess was soon confirmed. Gray Wolf rode off,
leaving a few of his braves to stay with Toby, while the
others brought the horses of their dead comrades to the
corral. The bodies of the slain Indians would later be
given funeral rites.

Now Gray Wolf returned and led Toby and his horse
to the center of the community. Old men sitting on the
ground, half-drowsing in the warmth of the fires, stared
at the stranger, their faces expressionless. Their juniors,
however, were less polite. Warriors glared at Toby, as
did many squaws, and several small boys shook their
fists and hurled insults at him, only to be silenced by
their mothers.

Gray Wolf left Toby with several braves and entered

a tepee near the river's edge that was no larger and no more impressive than any other. A few moments later the entrance flap was thrown aside, and Thunder Cloud emerged, his full-feathered bonnet settled squarely on his head, his vermilion and white war paint streaking his face and torso.

Toby had seen the barrel-chested and brawny chief in the distance when they had engaged in battle in the Montana mountains. But this was the first time they had met face to face, and for a moment Toby was concerned that the hostile-looking Thunder Cloud was not going to acknowledge his peaceful intentions. Then the chief extended his right arm, the palm of his hand held upward, in formal greeting, and Toby did the same, relieved that the tense moment had passed.

Toby's horse was taken from him, to be looked after by some of the braves. He was allowed to keep his weapons with him, but he was always surrounded by three vigilant warriors, who watched every move he made. They followed him into the chief's dwelling, and they were right beside him as he and Thunder Cloud sat cross-legged on the ground, facing each other.

They were served a supper of broiled fish, stewed corn, and roasted elk heart, considered one of the greatest of delicacies by the Sioux. After the meal was finished and an appropriate period of silence was observed, Thunder Cloud nodded politely, indicating his guest could speak.

Toby began to talk. "The friendship of my family and the Indian nations goes back for many years," he said. "It began when my father notified the Sioux that they were going to be trapped by their false allies, the Crow, and the warriors of the Sioux not only escaped but defeated the Crow in battle."

"That is so," Thunder Cloud acknowledged. "I was young then, but I remember the occasion well."

"I have followed in the footsteps of my father," Toby went on. "It was not so long ago that I became brothers with the Nez Percé in the mountains of Washington, and I helped bring peace between them and the United States."

The Sioux leader nodded slowly. "It cannot be denied," he said, "that Toby Holt has been the friend of the Indians on many occasions."

"Now the time has come," Toby said, "for the Sioux to show they are friends to the family of Holt."

Thunder Cloud's expression did not change, but he sat more erect, as if bracing himself.

"I know," Toby said, "that the great Sioux nation has formed an alliance with the people of the Blackfoot and the people of the Cheyenne. The purpose is to drive white men from the Plains. Is this true?"

"It is true," the Sioux chieftain assured him solemnly.

"The reason for this alliance is not difficult to guess," Toby said. "The Sioux and their allies are angry because settlers from the United States are establishing their homes and farms and ranches in the hunting grounds of the Indian nations."

Thunder Cloud grunted assent as he folded his arms across his chest.

"The United States," Toby said, "has become a large and powerful nation. It has men by the hundreds of thousands. In factories men make rifles and pistols and cannon that shoot with great accuracy. If the Indian nations oppose the will of the United States, the United States will call her men to arms and will punish her foes."

Thunder Cloud remained impassive. "It is true that

many Indian warriors will die," he said, "but many white warriors will die, also."

"It is true that the battles would be fierce," Toby said. "Mothers and widows and orphans would weep for dead warriors on both sides. The tragedy is that they would have died in vain. The United States does not regard the Indian nations as her enemies. Her people seek only the friendship of the Indian tribes. My government has set aside vast tracts of land for the Indian tribes. No white men will be allowed to settle on those lands or to set foot on them without the express permission of the Indian nations. President Andrew Johnson, our present chief of chiefs, is committed to this policy, and so is General Ulysses S. Grant, his principal warrior. I have been authorized by them to make a solemn promise to the Sioux, to the Blackfoot, and to the Cheyenne. You do not want your young men to die in war; we do not want our young men to die in war. Sign treaties of peace with us, and I will guarantee you in my own name, and in the name of my father, that the United States will grant not one but many large reservations to each of your nations."

Thunder Cloud was unimpressed. "What will the people of the Indian nations do with this land?" he demanded. "Our lives depend on the meat that our hunters kill."

"The land you will be given will be your own," Toby said. "There your warriors will be free to hunt as they please and when they please."

A sour smile appeared briefly on the face of the Sioux chieftain. "In my lifetime," he said, "I have watched the Sioux move from the lands that are now known to you as Iowa and Kansas and Nebraska until they have finally settled here in what you call Dakota. Many white men

came to Iowa and Kansas and Nebraska, and they built
their houses. When I was a boy, herds of buffalo roamed
through the high grasses of those prairie lands. Now the
farmers grow corn and wheat there, and the buffalo
have disappeared. The deer that lived in those lands
have vanished, and so have the antelope. No Indian nation remains there because no Indian nation could survive. We are determined that the same tragedy will not
strike us here, for we have no other place to go."

"My government," Toby said, "has made many errors,
just as the Indian nations have made many errors. Because we were strangers to each other, we first suspected, and then hated, each other. But there is no reason
for such hatred. We can live together, side by side, in
trust and in friendship. We hold out the hand of friendship to you, and with it, we extend the promise that you
will have much land that will belong to you and your
children and grandchildren after you. As honorable men,
we cannot do more than this."

"Toby Holt," Thunder Cloud said slowly, "like his father, Whip Holt, has been the good friend of the Sioux
and of the Blackfoot and of the Cheyenne, just as he has
been an enemy to be feared in battle. I do not question
the word of Toby Holt. But I do not know your chief of
chiefs, Johnson, or his warrior, Grant. It may be that
they lie to Toby Holt and they hope that he will convince the Indian nations that he tells the truth. Then, after the Indians have broken apart their alliance and
have made peace treaties, they will discover that the
greed of the paleskins consumes them and they seek every foot of land for themselves. This trick has been
played on the Indian nations many times since the first
settlers came."

Toby did his best to counter the chief's argument.

"Let Thunder Cloud make a journey to Washington City
and take with him the principal chieftains of the Blackfoot and of the Cheyenne. Meet President Johnson and
General Grant. Hear what they say, and judge them for
yourselves."

Thunder Cloud shook his head. "If the leaders of the
Indian nations travel alone," he said, "far from their
homes, and are not surrounded by their warriors, who
can protect them? What is to stop the leaders of the
United States from chaining their wrists and ankles and
confining them in a prison?"

"I can assure you," Toby said, "that the President of
the United States and the chief of staff of our army are
honorable men."

"It may be you are right," Thunder Cloud said, "but it
also may be that you are mistaken. I wish to take no
chances, so I will stay here and will not go to these leaders. The gods who guide the destinies of the Indian nations show the greatest favors to those who are bold and
strong. So I shall continue to urge the people of the
Sioux to show those qualities in their dealings with the
white settlers."

His message was plain: He had no intention of trying
to reach an accommodation with the United States, and
Toby knew that his mission was on the verge of failure.
"Don't make up your mind in this matter too quickly. I
beg you," he said. "When the great thundersticks of my
people start to roar, they drown out the voices of reason,
the voices of mere men, even of leaders."

Thunder Cloud's nod was noncommittal as he rose to
his feet, indicating that the talk had come to an end.

The three junior warriors took Toby to a tepee of his
own to spend the night. That he had been allowed to
keep his weapons consoled him somewhat, though as he

lay in his blankets trying to fall asleep, he felt something was very much amiss. He went over his conversation with Thunder Cloud again. Something odd had happened in the course of that talk, something that struck him as strange, and he tried to recall it.

All at once Toby knew what was wrong. After the evening meal had been finished, it would have been customary for Thunder Cloud to light a pipe and offer it to his guest, expecting him to take alternate puffs. The fact that he had not observed this custom was significant, and Toby's jaw tightened as he guessed its meaning.

He rose swiftly to his feet and moved stealthily to the entrance of his tepee. Suddenly he stopped short. Only a few feet in front of the tepee were not three but ten burly warriors, all armed with long knives and stout clubs.

Toby knew instantly that Thunder Cloud had made him a prisoner and was ignoring the fact that Toby had come to him as an emissary of the United States.

Withdrawing inside his tent, Toby sat on his blankets, his legs folded beneath him and his arms crossed as he contemplated his situation. As a prisoner of the Sioux, he would be unable to talk to other Indian leaders of Dakota and explain why they should make peace with the United States. Thunder Cloud knew just what he was doing when he made Toby Holt his captive.

Still, the Sioux would have to handle his captivity with great discretion and, if possible, conceal it. He was a Holt, and he had defeated them fairly in a battle and had requested an interview with their chieftain. If the facts of his captivity became known, Thunder Cloud would lose face, not only with other tribes but also with many of his own people. He would be accused of betraying a trust, of acting dishonorably.

On the other hand, Toby had to exercise great care, too. He still had his rifle and pistols, so he could try to blast his way out of the village of the Sioux. But even if he escaped, warriors would be killed and wounded, and he could be accused of having abused the hospitality of the Indians. This was a grave offense and would be all that Thunder Cloud needed to blacken Toby Holt's name among the Indians in Dakota and, indeed, throughout the West. Also, at the very least, the sounds of firearms would waken the entire village. Therefore, Toby had to think of some more subtle method of making his way past the sentries. The task would not be easy.

One thing was plain, however: He had discovered that he'd been made a prisoner far earlier than the Sioux chieftain or his braves had intended him to learn of it. Thus, they would be guarding him far more loosely now than later, no doubt assuming he would be sleeping and would not yet have learned the truth.

Consequently, he had an opportunity to escape. Toby estimated the time as shortly after midnight. If the Sioux followed their usual custom, they would not change sentries until shortly before daybreak, so it would be wise to wait for a time. The longer the present guards were on duty, the more tired, bored, and lethargic they would become. His most difficult task would be to escape without using his firearms.

Toby decided the best thing he could do for the moment was to exercise patience. He emptied his mind; then, still sitting, he rested, even though he remained awake. His body gathered strength for the ordeal ahead.

Finally, when he estimated that dawn would break shortly, he knew the time had come to act. Walking out of his tent, he saw the ten guards sitting in front of the hut. Some were dozing, but others immediately rose to their feet and looked at Toby challengingly, their knives and clubs at their sides.

Toby calmly smiled. The guards looked perplexed but remained vigilant. Then Toby began to whistle softly.

The guards had no idea what this peculiar white man was doing, but he seemed harmless, and they made no move toward him.

Toby had noticed earlier that the Indians' horses, his own stallion among them, were corralled not far from where he was being kept prisoner. His whistle was a signal to his horse to come to him, and just as he intended, his stallion responded. The horse whinnied, paced back and forth a few times in the enclosure, then jumped over the rail and trotted over to his master.

Toby breathed a sigh of relief when the horse appeared. So far his luck was phenomenally good.

Grasping his rifle in one hand, Toby vaulted onto the back of his horse. There was no saddle, the Indians having removed it, but he could easily ride bareback. He kicked his heels into the side of his horse and galloped off, leaving the guards staring in bewilderment. They had no idea what to do about this totally unexpected turn of events, so they did not give chase. Instead, two braves ran off to find out from their chief what they should do.

This gave Toby all the time he needed to leave the Sioux village. He was aware, however, that he would encounter the Sioux sentries stationed outside the town, and he knew they might not let him get away so easily.

Indeed, he had not ridden more than a hundred yards when two armed braves stood in his way. They, too, did not know what to make of his unexpected appearance, but before they could do anything, Toby rode furiously at them, causing them to leap aside.

Now, beyond him stretched the limitless prairie, the high grass extending for miles ahead. It was still dark, and Toby could make out vague shapes only a few yards ahead.

He knew the village was protected by other sentries who concealed themselves in the tall grass. But he had no idea where they might be hiding. At best—or at worst—his horse would come upon them in the dark, and he might be forced to use his firearms after all.

But all he could do now was gallop forward.

Dawn came as light streaked the sky. Suddenly a Sioux sentinel, who had been completely hidden in the tall grass, leaped to his feet, a murderous tomahawk in one hand.

Toby reacted with instinctive speed. He grasped his rifle by the barrel and swung the stock with great force against the side of the sentry's head. The Indian dropped to the ground and lay still, and Toby hoped the brave was only unconscious, not dead.

Galloping on, he hoped there was not yet another ring of sentinels hidden in the grass farther from the village. His guards had undoubtedly notified Thunder Cloud by now, and it was likely a band of Sioux warriors would pursue him. He had sufficient respect for the speed of their horses to want enough of a head start to reach the wilderness and safety.

His stallion rushed forward, and Toby's luck was good, for he encountered no more sentries. Looking back over his shoulder, as the land became flooded with daylight, he saw that he was not being followed and had made good his escape. But his problems were far from ended; on the contrary, they were just beginning. He had been charged by General Grant with the responsibility of achieving a peaceful solution to the troubles that brewed between the United States and the Indian nations of the area. It was true that the principal chieftain of the Sioux, the largest and most powerful of these nations, had rejected the hand that Toby had offered him. But the young Westerner realized he had no choice. He had to keep trying to prevent an all-out war in the area, no matter how great the odds against him might be.

Tall, slim Andrew Brentwood, his boyish good looks something of a surprise in a colonel commanding an important military fort, checked the tunic of his blue uniform to make certain that his insignia were in place. Satisfied, he donned the jacket, buttoning it slowly as he stood at the bedchamber window in the commandant's house at Fort Shaw, and looked out at the majestic mountains that rose in the distance. He felt relaxed, at peace with the world.

The door opened, and his pert, auburn-haired wife, Susanna, entered. She had just finished attending to their nine-month-old baby, Sam, and had handed him over to Mrs. Ford, the wet nurse, for a morning feeding. Seeing Andy at the window, lost in thought, she crept up and put her arms around his waist. "Are you going to stand there all morning admiring the view, Colonel, or is it possible that I might interest you in some breakfast?"

"Breakfast it'll be," he told her, "since I'm assured of the pleasure of your company." He turned and kissed her, and then they stood together, both looking out the window. He sighed happily. "You know, Sue, I've really fallen in love with Montana now that peace has come to the territory."

"Now that you and the Eleventh Cavalry have made mighty good and sure that there's peace in Montana," she corrected. "If it weren't for you, the Sioux would still be raiding ranches, and the settlers would be prey to bands like that horrid Hastings gang."

"Peace is always relative in the West," Andy told her, buckling on his sword belt and taking his campaign hat from a peg as he followed his wife down to the breakfast table. "We haven't yet heard the last of the Sioux," he said. "I can't help wishing that we'd achieved an even more smashing victory than we did. I know Thunder Cloud, and as long as he can move and manipulate, he's not going to be satisfied to sit back and lick his wounds. He's sure to make another stab at us." He sat down at the table, and his wife served him a cup of coffee.

"You want the usual, I assume?" she asked.

He nodded vaguely, preoccupied.

Susanna went off to the kitchen to tell the cook that the colonel wanted fried eggs, bacon, and toast, as always, and when she returned, she took her seat opposite him.

"Strictly between us," Andy said, "Toby Holt has been given an urgent mission by the War Department. The Sioux have formed an alliance with other Indian nations. They want to make war against the United States, and Toby's been charged to persuade them not to fight."

"That's a tall order," Susanna said, shaking her head. "Do you think he can bring it off?"

He considered the question carefully. "I honestly don't know," he replied. "I'll say this, though. If anyone can bring off an impossible assignment like that, Toby can. I should be hearing from him fairly shortly because he wired me when he arrived in Dakota two weeks ago. I assume by now he's made at least preliminary contact with the Sioux."

Susanna, a veteran newspaperwoman before her marriage, discussed the book on which she was working, a series of interviews with pioneer settlers in the Western territories. She nibbled on a piece of toast and sipped a cup of steaming coffee as she outlined her latest chapter, while her husband, eating his bacon and eggs, listened with great interest.

They were still at the table when a knock sounded at the front door. Andy's orderly answered the summons and appeared at the dining room threshold moments later. "Sorry to interrupt, ma'am," he said. "Sir, that was the night duty sergeant at the door just now. The officer of the day received a message for you, and he thought it should be delivered to you right away."

"Thanks very much, Corporal," Andy said as he accepted a sheet of folded paper.

He scanned the document hastily, then read it more carefully a second time.

"Bad news?" Susanna asked. "You look grim."

"Speaking of Toby," he said, "this is a telegram he sent from Fort Rice in the Dakota Territory last night." He looked at the message again and scowled. "All he says is that he's had a meeting with Thunder Cloud, and he wants to confer with me as soon as possible. He's already left Fort Rice for a rendezvous point that we had prearranged in the Black Hills of Dakota not far from the Badlands. That means I'll have to get cracking."

"You don't know the results of his meeting with Thunder Cloud?"

Andy shook his head. "Toby doesn't say, so I assume he wasn't too encouraged. Ordinarily we don't put bad news into a telegram because it passes through so many hands. I have a hunch that I may have spoken a trifle too soon this morning when I said how much I love the West when it's peaceful."

"Oh, dear." Susanna bit her lower lip.

Her husband rose from the table, went to her, and patted her on the shoulder. "Don't fret, honey," he said. "Let's not borrow trouble until we have to. The army isn't maintaining my regiment in these parts in order to give the men a holiday. So I think it's fair to say that we may have some work to do."

Susanna realized that no matter how long she was married, she would never grow accustomed to the fact that her husband was in a dangerous profession.

"I'd appreciate it, Sue, if you'd pack a duffel for me with about ten days' worth of clothes and food, and I'll need a bedroll. I've got some papers to clean off my desk, and as soon as that's done, I'll want to get started."

She knew she was expected to maintain a calm façade, but she couldn't conceal her alarm. "Surely you're not going off into Dakota alone to meet Toby!"

He smiled reassuringly. "I may be a fool, but I'm not a complete fool. Don't worry, honey, I'll take a half-troop of cavalry with me as an escort."

Relieved, she raised her face to his for his kiss. "I'll include a packet of chocolate cookies for Toby. He's probably lived on army rations and dried meat for far too long, and since Clarissa isn't here to look after him, I elect myself to do the job."

"He'll be very grateful, honey, I'm sure," Andy replied. He refrained from saying that if Toby's news was as bad as he suspected it was, his good friend would be in no mood to enjoy a package of sweets. If Andy's estimate was correct, the entire future of the United States in the West, from the Great Plains to the Rocky Mountains, was at stake.

Ralph Hastings sat on the ground near the campfire in the Black Hills of Dakota, at the edge of the Badlands, his back propped against a stunted tree. His supper of buffalo stew sat untasted in a bowl on the ground beside him. Reeking of cheap gin, he muttered to himself unintelligibly; occasionally the words "Gentle Doe" could be heard.

Ma Hastings and the members of her gang thought Ralph was hallucinating, as he sometimes did when he drank too much liquor, so they paid no attention to him and concentrated instead on their food.

Ma had good reason to feel satisfied with herself and her gang. They had just returned to their hideout after raiding an isolated homestead the day before, and they had made an especially good haul, acquiring a large sum of cash, horses they could sell, and several weapons.

Ma Hastings ate heartily, as she always did when she was in a good mood, and not even the sodden condition of her son could dampen her feelings. The assault had been a stroke of good fortune, and her gang had earned enough to be satisfied for a time, at least until they had spent their shares on liquor and women. Ma intended to use the respite to good advantage by strengthening and solidifying her relations with the Indian nations, particularly the Sioux, with whom she had an informal alliance.

Tall Stone was cut from a bolt of cloth she understood and admired, and she was certain that they would do a great deal of business together in the months and years to come.

She had been fortunate, she told herself, that, thanks to the swift and decisive intervention of Toby Holt, she had been forced to leave the Montana Territory. That gave her a bond in common with the Sioux and had strengthened her relationship with them. In the long run, she reflected, she and her gang would make far more money for themselves being here in Dakota, where they could share in the booty resulting from the Sioux's war against the whites and where sooner or later she would have vengeance.

She had vowed when her son Clifford died not only to get his killer, Toby Holt, but also to see to it that her remaining son, Ralph, took the place of his brother. This last proved impossible. Ralph was much too far gone with drink, and in recent days, ever since they had visited the Sioux village, he seemed to be in a constant daze, muttering about a young woman he seemed to think was his wife. But he was the last of her kin left in the world, and even while acknowledging his weakness, she doted on him.

Gnawing contentedly on a buffalo chop, Ma Hastings heard the sound of approaching hoofbeats, and knowing she was expecting no visitor tonight, she reached for her rifle. Most members of the gang immediately followed her example but continued to eat. Though notorious when on a raid, the gang was rather undisciplined and lax when it came to defending their camp.

A ferocious-looking Sioux warrior, his head shaved on both sides of his scalp lock, his vermilion and white war paint visible in the light of the campfire, rode into the encampment. He was heavily muscled and carried himself with great dignity, which, by contrast, made the gang members appear all the more bedraggled and unkempt as they stood and pointed their rifles at him.

"Put down your firearms, you idiots," Ma commanded sharply. "Don't you know a friend when you see one?"

Turning to the new arrival, she smiled broadly and spoke in very good Sioux, a talent that never failed to impress her band members. "Welcome," she said, and lowered her head.

The warrior grinned at her, and before he dismounted, Black Horse raised his hand in salute. He had been somewhat reluctant to enter the pay of a woman, a paleskin at that, but he was pleased now that he had followed the advice given him by Tall Stone. Ma Hastings made him gifts of firearms and liquor, both forbidden to Indians under the terms of their early treaties with the United States, and she paid him promptly in hard cash for any information he brought to her.

On this occasion he felt certain she would pay him handsomely. But Black Horse was in no hurry to tell her what he knew. He had spent long hours crossing endless miles of the Dakota Territory, and having started at dawn, he was tired. So he accepted the steaming bowl of stew the woman offered him, and he looked long and hard at the half-consumed bottle of gin that rested on the ground beside Ralph Hastings. But he decided not to ask for any of the liquor.

Ma Hastings had lived for many years on the frontier, and she knew that the exercise of patience was the first rule in dealings with Indians. Certainly she was in no rush. She made no attempt to converse with Black Horse while he ate, but twice she ordered one of her men to refill his bowl.

He, too, observed certain rules. Not once did he glance in the woman's direction or indicate in any way that he had traveled a long distance to see her. Only after he belched loudly, indicating that he had finished his meal, did he raise his head and look at her.

Their eyes met briefly, and in that instant Ma knew

that the Sioux warrior had news of significance. She rose slowly to her feet and brushed off her dark, rumpled trousers. Then, acting as though she did not have a care in the world, she wandered off in the direction of one of the large, grotesque stones that dotted the Badlands.

A few moments later Black Horse joined her.

She leaned indolently against a strangely shaped stone, and the brave followed her example. Ma waited for him to break the silence.

Black Horse elected to speak in his own tongue, rather than to struggle with English. "Many moons ago," he said, "when Black Horse brought to the squaw-who-walks-like-a-man news that pleased her, she gave him a bag filled with silver. Does she remember that day?"

In dealing with Indians, there were conversational procedures that had to be observed, and Ma Hastings advised herself to show patience. "I remember well," she said.

"On that same day," he went on, "she told him that, if he ever gleaned any news about Toby Holt, the friend of Indian nations and son of Whip Holt, she would give him another bag, this one filled with gold."

She stiffened at the name of the man she hated most in all the world. "Do you have news of Toby Holt?" she demanded instantly.

Black Horse would not be diverted. "Do you remember the gold you promised me?"

She snatched off her hat, then took a heavy purse from her belt and emptied the contents into it. The purse contained her share of the loot from the previous day's robbery, and a shower of gold coins gleamed in the moonlight. "Of course I remember," she said curtly. "But I do not pay for merchandise I have not seen. If

you truly bring me important news of my enemy, all the
gold that now rests in this hat will be yours."

The brave's eyes gleamed avariciously as he moistened
his dry lips. "Six suns ago," he said, "the son of Whip
Holt and a party of soldiers from Fort Abercrombie
were attacked by a band of Sioux, many of whom were
killed. Gray Wolf, who led the raiders, has apologized to
the Sioux nation for his mistake and has said that if he
had known that Toby Holt was in the party, he would
not have attacked."

"No foolin'," Ma replied tartly.

"Yesterday," Black Horse continued, "a visitor to my
camp from the principal village of the Sioux brought
strange news. Toby Holt went to the village and tried to
persuade Thunder Cloud to give up his plan to make
war against the white men. Thunder Cloud refused."

Ma chuckled as she poured half of the coins in her hat
into the outstretched hands of the brave. "Good for
Thunder Cloud. Then what happened?"

The warrior, at the climax of his story, became self-
important. "Toby Holt," he said, "rode quickly to Fort
Rice. When I learned that news, I set out at once in
search for the woman-who-walks-like-a-man. The gods
of the Sioux smiled at me because this very day I saw a
scout of the Sioux, who told me that Toby Holt was seen
following the trail that leads into the Black Hills."

Ma Hastings could not contain her excitement. "You
mean he's here?" she demanded. "He's actually in this
very region right now?"

"I have already related all that I know," Black Horse
said, and sounded a trifle sulky, as though he suspected
she was trying to back out of her agreement with him.

Ma Hastings understood what was going through the
warrior's mind and promptly emptied the contents of her

hat into his waiting hands. "This is damn near too good to be true," she breathed. "The dirty swine who killed my son is nearby—right now—where my men and I can get at him. God, I ain't prayed in a long time, but I'm prayin' to ya now. Don't let my enemy hide from me. Let me find Toby Holt soon—real soon—so as he can be killed the same way he killed my own flesh and blood!"

IV

Gentle Doe worked in the fields with the other women of the village, harvesting the last of the carrots, beets, and other root crops before the ground froze solid. By the end of the day, she was tired, for the soil was rocky and hard and far less fertile than that found in other parts of Dakota. Vegetables and grains, particularly the corn on which the diet of the Sioux depended, had to be coaxed from it.

After work she ate her evening meal with the other unmarried women outside their lodge. Their meal was simple: fish that had been caught that day and a soup of boiled dried corn.

Gentle Doe squatted by herself near the fire and ate rapidly. She had almost completed her meal when she looked up and saw the large, bulky figure of Tall Stone approaching her. She had no idea why he wanted to see her but wished he would go away. The intensity of his stare and his unchanging, unfathomable expression made her nervous. The other women by the fire moved away.

There were customs to be observed, so Gentle Doe

treated the village chieftain with friendliness and grace, inviting him to sit and offering him the uneaten portion of her meal. Tall Stone matched her politeness. Declining her hospitality, he told her his business would wait; sitting, he folded his arms in silence as she finished eating.

Although he was not hurrying her, she nevertheless felt compelled to bolt what was left of her food. Then she smiled at him shyly.

"Gentle Doe looks as she always does," he said, "as though she is enjoying good health."

"I am well," she replied.

"In addition," he declared forcibly, "she is still the most handsome squaw in the village."

The compliment startled her, and not knowing what to reply, she remained silent.

"If the father of Gentle Doe were alive," Tall Stone said, "I would go to him, I would bargain with him, and I would strike a deal with him. I would learn from him the price he demanded for the hand of his daughter in marriage, and I would find out, also, what goods she would bring to me as my squaw."

She realized he was starting to propose to her, and panic swept over her. He was the last warrior in all the land of the Sioux she wanted to marry.

"Since the father of Gentle Doe has departed from this world and has joined his ancestors, I can force Gentle Doe to marry me, because I am her chief. But I would rather Gentle Doe came to me out of her own free will."

She had heard more than enough and hastened to stop him. "Gentle Doe will never come to Tall Stone to marry him."

Her reply stunned him, and he stared hard at her. "You prefer another warrior?"

"There is no other man in my life," Gentle Doe said. It did not occur to her that her candor might cause her trouble.

"Why do you reject me?" he demanded harshly. "It is my right to know."

She had hoped he would back off gracefully, but his stubborn insistence annoyed her, and she became more blunt than she otherwise would have been. "I would prefer the life of a permanently unmarried maiden," she said, "to the existence I would lead if I became the squaw of Tall Stone."

He clenched his fists, then leaned forward, and Gentle Doe thought he intended to strike her. She realized belatedly that she had gone too far. Her candor had transformed the village chieftain from a suitor into her mortal enemy.

He did not strike her, however. Instead, he rose and stalked off, his head high and his back rigid.

Gentle Doe shuddered as she told herself that at least she was rid of an unwelcome suitor.

Glowering at villagers he encountered, Tall Stone marched without hesitation to the lodge where the unmarried warriors resided. He knew that he could still force Gentle Doe to marry him, but this he did not want to do. He had another way to deal with this haughty, recalcitrant woman.

Entering the lodge, he found several of the warriors sitting in a circle, finishing their meal.

Tall Stone approached a young brave at random and pointed a thick forefinger at him. "You," he said accusingly, "have lain with Gentle Doe and have spent entire nights in her tepee."

The young man was shocked. "I don't know who has slandered me, but I have never lain with Gentle Doe." He rose hastily to his feet.

Drawing a tomahawk from his belt, Tall Stone hurled himself at the warrior and held the sharp-edged blade close to his throat. "Admit the truth!" he roared. "Lie to me again, and your blood will flow from your throat!"

The young Sioux looked into the eyes of a madman.

No single warrior present was the equal of Tall Stone, but the group together could have subdued him. All of them knew, however, what problems they would face if they became embroiled with the village chieftain. They would have been required to submit to interrogation from Sioux of the highest rank, and if they failed to satisfy their superiors, they would be liable to extreme, brutal punishment.

"Speak!" Tall Stone cried. "Admit the charge while you still have a voice!"

"I—I admit it," the young brave whispered. "I have lain with Gentle Doe."

Hurling the brave from him, Tall Stone caught another warrior by the ear, which he twisted viciously. "You will admit to the same guilt," he said, "or you will suffer the same fate that he would have met!"

It was better to admit an untruth than to be maimed or killed. "I admit it," the brave muttered. "I have also lain with Gentle Doe."

So great was the chieftain's anger that he was not yet satisfied. "Who else will make such an admission?" he demanded, glaring at each of the remaining braves in turn.

By now he had cowed them so thoroughly that two of the warriors spoke out simultaneously, both confessing to nonexistent affairs with Gentle Doe.

Tall Stone laughed maniacally and shouted, "Let the drums be sounded, and let all the people of the village be assembled!"

Soon the throbbing of a tom-tom summoned the braves and squaws of the village to a meeting on a slope where such infrequent sessions were held. Tall Stone paused briefly at his own tepee to don the feathered headgear that was the symbol of his rank.

Gentle Doe had no idea what was in store for her when she took her place with the other unmarried maidens.

Tall Stone launched into a long diatribe on the immorality of Gentle Doe. Not once as he spoke did he glance in her direction. Gentle Doe was so stunned that she stared at her accuser in openmouthed disbelief.

Tall Stone called on the four young warriors to repeat their misdemeanors in public. They complied, one by one, standing before the assembled throng and admitting that they had made love to the woman.

The bewildered, astonished Gentle Doe wanted to scream that she was innocent, but she was incapable of speech. As she looked around her at the disgusted expressions on the faces of those she had regarded as her friends, it dawned on her that her cause was hopeless. She had made an enemy out of Tall Stone by refusing his offer of marriage, and now he was getting even with her in the most vicious of all possible ways.

At last the village chieftain turned to Gentle Doe. Demented hatred was etched in every line of his face. "Let her who has erred pay the penalty," he said bitterly. "Let her be cleansed of her mistakes so she may once again be fit company for the people of the Sioux. Let the women of this village form a gauntlet, and let her run it!"

All at once Gentle Doe found her voice, but it was too
late. The women of the village, arming themselves with
clubs, lengths of rawhide, and tomahawks—which they
turned so the sharp edge would not cut their victim—
formed in two rows and faced each other, several feet
apart. Meanwhile, some of the women, brawny from
years of labor, seized the struggling, terrified Gentle Doe
and dragged her toward the double line.

Weeping and screaming, she protested her innocence.
The women paid no attention, however, and when she
tried to pull away, they lifted her off the ground and
carried her toward her fate.

As frightened as she was incensed by the injustice,
Gentle Doe could not think clearly. One of her last
memories was that of Tall Stone's face, his demon grin
maniacal as he watched her being carried to her unjust
punishment.

The women who were carrying her halted, placed her
on her feet, and shoved her forward so violently that she
stumbled and fell to one knee. Before she could regain
her feet, hard blows rained on her head, shoulders, and
back. The pain was excruciating, and she realized it was
useless to protest her innocence. The longer she remained within reach of the weapons, the more she
would suffer. She would escape only by running the
gauntlet.

Dragging herself step by tortured step, Gentle Doe
inched through the double line. The women, enjoying
their cruel sport, beat her unmercifully, and whenever
she managed to move somewhat more rapidly, one of
them reached out with a club and tripped her. Women
vied with each other to see who could strike the hardest
blows.

Her head aching and throbbing, her body aflame with

bruises, cuts, and welts, Gentle Doe struggled forward. The knowledge that she was innocent, that she was being made to suffer unfairly because she had injured a man's pride and vanity, gave Gentle Doe the strength to keep moving.

The actual running of the gauntlet took only a few minutes, but they seemed like an eternity to the battered, bruised young woman. The other women showed no mercy, and Gentle Doe could not blame them for their lack of compassion. She would have felt exactly the same way toward someone guilty of breaking the moral code of the Sioux.

Gentle Doe reached the end of the gauntlet by crawling the final yards on her hands and knees. Then, suddenly, the torture stopped.

Sobbing involuntarily, her whole body enveloped in pain so intense that it robbed her of the ability to think, Gentle Doe stretched out on the ground, her bleeding hands clawing at the rocky soil.

The villagers did not linger. The squaws, their work done, departed quickly for their own tepees. They were soon followed by the sober, silent warriors, including the four young braves whose false testimony had been responsible for the unjust punishment.

Soon only one person remained in the field with Gentle Doe. Tall Stone stood directly above her, looking down at the welts and cuts on her body, and he smiled, his eyes glittering with triumph. He knew what Gentle Doe was too far gone to realize, that he could not run the risk of allowing her to remain in the village. If she remained she would be a constant reminder of his treachery, and one or all of the braves he had intimidated into lying about her might be compelled to tell the truth. Thus, he had to get rid of her.

"Can you hear me, woman?" he demanded harshly, his voice like the sting of a whip. "Can you hear what I say to you?"

She was unable to speak but managed to nod.

"If you had married me," he said, "you would have stood first among the squaws of this village. Now, instead, you are an outcast. You have only yourself to blame. Now, get out! Leave this place and never return to it. I give you warning—if I see you here again, I will kill you on sight." He emphasized his words by kicking her in the ribs and then spitting at her.

So numbed by pain and terror that she scarcely felt his kick and was unaware of the spittle that ran down the side of her battered face, Gentle Doe summoned her final reserves of strength. She hauled herself to her feet, and staggering and stumbling, she fled from the village into the wilderness of the Dakota Badlands.

The half-troop of Eleventh Cavalry members forming a guard for Colonel Andrew Brentwood made their camp high on a slope among pines and spruce trees about five hundred feet away from the spot where a tent had been erected for the colonel's use. Their horses had been left at the bottom of the mountain slope, in the care of three of their men.

Now, following Toby Holt's arrival in the rugged Black Hills, a second tent was erected. A casual observer, stumbling on the clearing and seeing the two men dressed in frontiersmen's garb, would have assumed that the men were enjoying a hunting and fishing vacation.

Indeed, feeling invigorated to be at this mountain rendezvous, Andy and Toby took time out from their discussions to hunt and fish for themselves, leaving the men of the Eleventh to acquire their own game. Andy caught enough trout to enable them to eat their fill of fish at breakfast, and Toby brought down a fat buck, which gave them ample meat. The rest of the time they engaged in serious talk, sitting in the open, looking across the rugged, low-lying peaks of the Black Hills, mountains that had gotten their name because the trees and lesser foliage that covered them took on a black hue from a distance.

"The way I see it," Toby said, cleaning his rifle as he sat cross-legged on the ground, "we're headed for serious trouble, Andy."

Colonel Brentwood nodded slowly and pushed his beaver hat onto the back of his head. "I'm afraid you're right," he replied. "We're going to have our hands full."

"The Sioux are influenced by Thunder Cloud," Toby said, "and he's opposed one hundred percent to an amicable understanding with us. He's prepared to fight a full-scale war."

"Then he's a bigger damn fool than I realized," Andy replied harshly. "He can't possibly win."

Toby Holt shrugged. "Obviously Thunder Cloud doesn't agree. He feels that since the Sioux will be supported by the Blackfoot and the Cheyenne, the Indians are going to be blame near invincible, and between you and me, Andy, he may not be far off the mark."

"I've been assured," the colonel told him, "of the complete support of the War Department, and General Grant has a reputation for meaning what he says."

"I explained all that to Thunder Cloud," Toby said. "I told him that Washington will give us as many men and as much munitions as we need to enable white settlers to come here in safety. He didn't believe me, and I must admit I can't blame him. Dakota and Montana are enormous territories, comprising hundreds of thousands of square miles. It's difficult for me, much less for a savage, to envision troops being sent out here in sufficient numbers to guarantee the peace."

"I'm not underestimating the enormity of the job," Andy said. "It's sure going to be difficult."

"All I can do," Toby said, "is to visit as many Indian villages as I can. This is primarily the war of the Sioux, so if I manage to win the approval of even a few Sioux chiefs or their medicine men, the effect will snowball. Once some of the Sioux chiefs are on our side, leaders of the Blackfoot and the Cheyenne will start having second thoughts about allying with Thunder Cloud."

Andy nodded. "You really think you're going to get anywhere with these visits, Toby?"

"All I can tell you is that I'll be following the request of General Grant to the letter. I think it's possible for me to get results. If I didn't feel this way, I wouldn't be wasting my time."

Andy pondered the matter. "Neither the Sioux nor the Blackfoot are monolithic nations," he said slowly. "True, all the Sioux are related to each other, as all the Blackfoot are related, and that means that they usually act in concert. But they have no rigid laws that require them to stand together. If you can persuade some of them to show enough good sense to make a separate peace with us, I suppose it's always possible that the better part of the Sioux nation will repudiate the stand taken by Thunder Cloud."

Toby nodded. "At least I've got to act as though I believe it can be done."

"In the meantime, however, would you agree that I should also be ready in case things work out for the worst?" the colonel asked.

"Absolutely! To do anything else would not only be foolhardy but would also expose the settlers to unnecessary risks. We have to keep our powder dry and be prepared for the worst at any given moment."

"General Grant sent me a formal communication," Andy said, "in which he assured me that he'd take care of my wants, whatever they might be. He also assured me that I'll have the support of General Blake and the Army of the West."

Toby knew his stepfather would move mountains, if necessary, in order to keep his word.

"As soon as I return to Fort Shaw," Andy said, "I'll send a telegram to General Blake asking him to augment my force with as many troops as he can spare, preferably cavalry."

"Good," Toby said.

"Such a request, then, will have your support?"

"You can count on me all the way," Toby told him.

They planned to break camp early the following morning, with Andy Brentwood heading back to Fort Shaw, while Toby began to make his rounds of Sioux villages. The lieutenant in charge of Andy's escort was notified of their itinerary and was instructed to break camp at sunrise.

They were up early and had their last breakfast of fried trout beside their campfire. As the pair ate in the light of the predawn campfire, they heard rustling noises in the woods beyond their clearing but assumed that the soldiers had finished striking their own camp and had now come to dismantle and pack their tents. They were mistaken.

A shot sounded, and a rifle bullet whined overhead.

Toby and Andy reacted instantly. Toby dove behind a pine trunk, while Andy crawled several paces on his hands and knees to a large boulder. Both carried rifles, and both knew how to play the wilderness game of waiting for a foe to advertise his location. They did not have long to wait.

Fire erupted in the woods to their right and then to their left. They identified the location of the shots and instinctively divided the responsibilities, with Toby taking the foe on the left, while Andy engaged the one on the right.

Toby raised his rifle to his shoulder, made out a murky, indistinct form half-hidden in the foliage, and squeezed the trigger. A high-pitched scream of pain told him his bullet had found its mark.

At the same time, Andy Brentwood aimed his rifle and fired. His bullet struck home, and the body of a man tumbled forward onto the ground past the edge of the clearing.

The rifle fire alerted the men of the cavalry escort, and they raced toward the clearing, with the lieutenant who commanded the unit in the lead. He was the first to realize that a number of intruders were responsible, and he shouted loudly, "Spread out, men! Grab every stranger you see!"

He gave the orders too late for them to be effective, however. The enemy eluded capture and fled.

The man Toby had shot was still alive. As Toby approached, he was surprised to discover that his assailant was a white man wearing rough frontier clothes. Toby had assumed that he and Andy had been beset by Indians, for there were few white men who would have the stealth and ability to enter a large camp undetected.

Andy hastily joined him. "The man I killed was white, too," he said. "I don't understand this at all."

Toby dropped to one knee beside the fallen man and

saw there was nothing that could be done for him. He leaned close to him and spoke loudly and distinctly. "Who are you?" he demanded. "Why did you try to kill us? Who sent you?"

Perspiration streamed from the fallen man's face, and he tried hard to focus on the speaker. "You Toby Holt?" he asked hoarsely, his voice barely audible as he gasped for breath between each word.

"Yes," he said, "I'm Toby Holt."

The man reached for a knife in his belt, but his strength was ebbing so fast that the blade fell from his grasp, and he grimaced in pain. "Ma Hastings," he whispered, "promised to pay one thousand dollars in gold—a whole one thousand bucks!—to the man who killed Toby Holt. But I guess I ain't got no need for money, not where I'm going." Exhausted by his speech, he was attacked by a paroxysm of coughing, and Toby waited grimly for the man to stop.

"Who else came with you?" Toby demanded. "Who else got into our camp?"

The man struggled to speak. "Indian, name Black Horse. Led us in here. Escaped when he saw soldiers." This time the man's coughing attack was even more violent, and before he could recover from it, he died, his sightless eyes staring up at the early morning sky.

Toby rose to his feet, and a concerned Andy Brentwood led him off to the far side of the clearing while the soldiers dug a shallow grave for the two bodies. "Ma Hastings," he said, "is a vicious enemy. She must want your hide something fierce if she's offered a thousand dollars for it."

"She hates me because I put a bullet into her son's head back in Montana," Toby said. "But never fear,

Andy. I can look after myself, especially now that I've been warned."

"Maybe you can take care of yourself, and maybe you can't. But you heed my words, Toby. Take no needless risks from now on. With Ma Hastings gunning for you, you can't be too careful!"

Everyone in the audience at the fashionable San Francisco concert was aware of the handsome young couple sitting in the box at one side of the auditorium, the woman with a boa of ostrich feathers draped over her bare shoulders, her blond hair gleaming, and her escort impeccable in white tie and tailcoat. Some of those present had known Beth Martin during the years when her father had been commandant of the Presidio and had last seen her when she and her husband had honeymooned in the city. Others in the audience were acquainted with Leon Graham's uncle and aunt, Chet and Clara Lou Harris.

Watching Beth smiling up at her escort, her long lashes fluttering, her fingers reaching out to touch his arm as she chatted with him, they disapproved. She was a married woman, after all, and consequently had no right to be flirting so blatantly. But they said nothing, for she was the daughter of Major General Leland Blake. Some excused her conduct on the grounds that she was naive and unaware she was being provocative.

As it happened, that estimate was accurate. Beth, who had traveled to Europe and had acquired a modicum of sophistication, was still far from being a worldly woman. Right now all she knew was that for the first time in her life, she could afford to indulge her taste in clothes and had found a perfect escort who enjoyed her company but demanded nothing of her in return. She was enjoy-

ing herself immensely, making up for the dull years at
army posts.

Certainly she had no idea of her effect on Leon Graham. She knew him only as a hardworking investment
banker, in whom his uncle placed great trust, and as a
charming companion who entertained her royally. Had
she guessed that there was a darker side to his nature,
that he had become infatuated with her and was finding
it more and more difficult to refrain from making advances to her, she would have been horrified.

Even though he was perilously close to losing control
of himself, Leon managed to keep his emotions in check
for the time being. He reminded himself incessantly that
Beth was not only a married woman but that she was
also the daughter of one of the most prominent men in
the entire Pacific Coast area. Thus, he would have to
make his moves with the utmost care.

After the concert Leon took Beth's arm and guided
her through the crowd to his waiting carriage. He
handed her in, then spoke a few words to the coachman
before he joined her in the plush interior. "Instead of going on to a restaurant," he said, "I thought we might go
back to my house for something to eat. You've never
seen my home, and I'm rather proud of it. If you don't
object, that is."

She hesitated, then dismissed her fears. Leon's conduct had been impeccable. It would be insulting to refuse to accompany him to his house. Society had its
rules, to be sure, but they had to be tempered with common sense.

His house fitted the station he had achieved in life.
Located high on Nob Hill, with a view of San Francisco
Bay, it was a sturdy, three-story dwelling of pale brick,
staid and solid on the outside. But once they had en-

tered the place, Beth discovered that the interior was lovely.

The spacious living room had an Oriental decor, the bathroom—where she repaired her makeup—was glowing with polished marble, and the dining room, with its table and chairs of solid mahogany, its walls lined with mahogany paneling, was sumptuous and sedate.

The supper was perfect, as was the service. Leon's chef produced an excellent shrimp bisque, followed by a slice of cold beef and an asparagus salad, which were just right for an after-concert meal. The food was served with aplomb by a uniformed butler, and a second butler served chilled French champagne that was as delicious as it was head-turning.

Thanks to Leon's attentiveness, suave manners, and ability to engage in light, amusing conversation, Beth had never enjoyed an evening more.

After eating a dessert of fresh peaches in brandy, Beth was euphoric, at least partly because of the champagne. She eagerly agreed when Leon offered to show her through the rest of the house, and she had no inkling that he was suffering from barely effective attempts to restrain himself.

The solarium, where tropical plants bloomed, among them orchids and gardenia bushes, afforded a splendid view of the ships in the harbor and of the lower slopes of the hills leading down to the waterfront. The kitchen was a large, airy chamber and featured two hooded stoves, one of them wood-burning and the other fueled by coal. Beth was entranced.

Then Leon conducted her up the marble stairs, pointing out that the stairwell was illuminated by gas. It was one of the first private dwellings in San Francisco to have such lighting, and he intended, he said, to have it installed in the rest of the house soon.

Beth clung to Leon's arm as they mounted the stairs together, and she flirted with him even more brazenly, the champagne speaking on her behalf.

"This is my bedchamber," Leon said as he opened the door and waved his guest inside.

Beth was impressed. There was a dressing alcove with an easy chair and a pair of crossed pistols on the wall. The larger room, which also overlooked the harbor, featured a huge, four-poster bed and several other large pieces of furniture, including a divan and a coffee table.

Seated high on a perch in the far corner of the room was a mynah bird, an ugly creature with vivid metallic purple and green coloring. It had been idly pecking at some birdseed in a small container attached to its perch, but it looked up and brightened when the couple came into the chamber.

Everything seemed right for a seduction, and Leon planned his moves carefully. He would grasp Beth by the waist, turn her around to face him, and before she could protest, he would kiss her long, hard, and passionately. By the time he released her, she, too, would be aroused and would consent to his lovemaking. He had shown great forbearance; now, perhaps, his patience finally would be rewarded.

Suddenly the mynah bird spoke, its harsh words and raucous tone cutting through Beth's alcohol-induced fog. "Hello, wench! Hello, wench!" The bird's laugh was loud, shrill, and piercing.

Beth Martin reacted as though a bucket of ice water had been thrown over her head. The pleasant feeling, the sensation that all was right with the world, vanished abruptly.

"Hello, wench!" The bird laughed again, loudly, insistently.

Beth stiffened.

Leon was quick to note the effect of his mynah bird on his guest. "Be quiet, bird," he said. "The lady isn't amused."

The mynah bird knew it was being addressed and continued to cackle.

Beth rubbed her bare arms to rid them of a sudden attack of gooseflesh. She had no idea why she felt as she did. All she knew was that she had to control an urge to pick up her gown and flee not only from the room but also from the house.

"I'm sorry, Leon," she said, her tone cool, her manner suddenly remote, "but I'm afraid I have a sudden and dreadful headache. Perhaps you'll be good enough to take me home now."

So much for the seduction. He had no doubt that if he were to seize Beth now and try to kiss her, she would storm out of the house. "I'll order the carriage at once," he said, and withdrew.

She was left to follow at a more leisurely pace, and she paused to glance back at the mynah bird over her shoulder. It was ridiculous to be afraid of a bird.

Again the bird cackled.

Never had Beth heard such an evil, depraved sound, and she left the bedchamber in such haste that she almost stumbled and fell. When she was in the corridor again and the door was closed behind her, the bird's laughter was muffled, and she breathed more easily. Her heart pounded against her rib cage so hard that she found it difficult to breathe, and she wondered again why the harmless pet should have influenced her so adversely.

Leon Graham called for his carriage and driver, then helped Beth into the carriage. His suave smile concealed his disappointment. The bird had spoiled everything, but having come so close to success, Leon was determined to try again. And next time, mynah bird or no mynah bird, he vowed that he would allow nothing to stand in his way.

V

In Fort Vancouver, the school attended by the children of military personnel and civilians was located in the town that had sprung up about a mile and a half from the fort itself. The well-traveled road between town and fort led through pine woods and birch trees, and it was familiar to Cindy Holt and Hank Purcell, who made their way back and forth daily. Now, school having ended for the day, they were homeward bound to Major General Blake's house on the grounds of the fort.

Cindy was out of sorts. She hated having Hank tagging along after her, even though she had to admit that since they were going to the same house, it was only natural that he would walk with her. She could not help wishing, all the same, that he would leave her alone. Nothing infuriated her more than the teasing she received from some of her friends who saw her arriving with Hank every morning and leaving with him every afternoon.

"I'll carry your books for you, if you like," Hank offered.

Cindy shook her head. "No, thank you," she replied frostily.

"You haven't got any call to be unpleasant," he said. "I was just trying to be polite because you're supposed to be a lady. Carry your own books for all I care."

The teenage girl was miffed. "You're no gentleman!" she informed him.

"Well, if you ask me, miss high-and-mighty," he retorted, "you're no lady!"

The two young people fell into a hostile silence, Cindy walking with her head held high, Hank ambling beside her, swinging his schoolbooks by the strap that held them together. There was nothing out of the ordinary about their exchange. They bickered constantly except when in the presence of General and Mrs. Blake and Clarissa. Adults somehow became terribly annoyed over the incessant squabbles of people in their teens.

Leading away from the main road, there was a path through the woods that Cindy and Hank took as a shortcut to the fort. It was narrow, so they were forced to walk single file, Hank allowing Cindy to take the lead.

They heard the deep rumble of male voices ahead and then saw five young men sitting to one side of the path, passing a jug of whiskey around their circle. Hank recognized the group as new recruits who had been sworn into the army within the past ten days. All of them had short haircuts, and one carried a Colt six-shooter in his belt. It was a violation of army regulations for a service weapon to be carried when one was attired in civilian clothes.

Cindy had wandered almost into their midst when

they noticed her, and one of them called out something raucously unpleasant.

Before she could back away, the group surrounded her, grinning as they made comments about her face, her figure, and their intentions regarding her. Clearly they had no idea she was the stepdaughter of the general commanding the Army of the West, and had Cindy chosen to identify herself now, they would have been almost certain to conclude that she was fibbing in an attempt to extricate herself.

The men began to close in on her, and Cindy, terrified, realized she was in a serious predicament. Hank took a protective step closer to the girl.

The largest of the recruits, tall and broad-shouldered, grinned at the boy and brandished a heavy club. "Be on your way, sonny," he said, "and don't look back, or I'll have to knock your teeth out of your head to teach you manners!"

The threat was all Hank needed. Selecting the man who carried the pistol in his belt as his target, he spun the strap that held his schoolbooks, whirling it rapidly over his head, and then let fly with it.

The unorthodox weapon hit the man on the forehead and sent him staggering backward. Before he could recover, Hank leaped forward, pouncing like a mountain lion. When the boy backed off, he was holding the Colt six-shooter in his hand. He quickly checked the chamber to see that the gun was fully loaded.

"Take it easy, sonny," one of the men called. "That there gun is no toy!"

With a firearm firmly in his grasp, Hank Purcell's whole character seemed to change. His youthfulness vanished, and he was secure and self-confident, a man rather than a boy. He did not bother to reply in words but instead took quick, casual aim and fired the pistol twice.

One shot went through the crown of the hat worn by the man who had last spoken, knocking it to the ground, and the other shot splintered the club held by the biggest of the recruits.

The men stared at Hank in astonishment.

"There are four bullets left in this pistol," he said, "and there are five of you, which means only one of you is going to live, unless you do exactly as I tell you, when I tell you to do it. Beginning now. Reach for the treetops!"

The dazed recruits lifted their hands above their heads.

"Higher!" Hank commanded sharply.

The five men stretched their hands higher above their heads. The boy's tone of voice, as well as the two shots he had already fired, convinced them that he would make good his threat unless they obeyed.

"Cindy," he said, "I'll be much obliged if you'll bring my schoolbooks, and while you're about it, you had better bring that jug of whiskey, too. We'll want it for evidence."

Relieved now that the danger was ended, Cindy was uncertain whether to laugh or cry. She did neither, however, but obeyed Hank, picking up his books by the leather strap and fetching the jug of whiskey.

"Line up in single file, you no-good scum," Hank commanded, "and start marching back to Fort Vancouver. I'm only going to warn you once. If anyone steps out of line or tries any tricks, I'll split your heart with a bullet! Now, march!"

The strange procession started off on the path through

the woods, the five prisoners holding their hands high above their heads.

Cindy, bringing up the rear, began to see Hank in a new light. This was not the bumbling, inexperienced schoolboy she had known but a self-reliant man.

At last they came to the main northern entrance of Fort Vancouver, and the familiar challenge of the corporal of the guard rang out. "Advance and be recognized!"

The procession moved forward.

The corporal saw Cindy and Hank, whom he knew, and the five recruits with their hands high in the air. He summoned Sergeant McNamara, the senior noncommissioned officer in charge of the guard.

"What in the name of all that's holy is goin' on here, Miss Holt?" the bewildered McNamara demanded.

After Cindy explained the situation, McNamara turned to the recruits. "Is that what happened?" he demanded. "Is the story Miss Holt just told me accurate?"

Too late, the recruits realized that the girl they had threatened occupied a special place at the post. Two of them nodded wearily, unable to deny Cindy's charges.

Sergeant McNamara leaped into action. Members of the guard detail were summoned and promptly marched the recruits off to the prisoners' stockade. Then, barely able to keep a straight face, McNamara turned back to the young couple. "I'll relieve you of that six-shooter now, young fellow," he said, "and I reckon you can part with the jug of whiskey, miss. We'll need both of them as evidence."

Cindy was glad to be rid of the whiskey, but Hank seemed reluctant to part with the gun.

"I've heard tell you can do all kinds of magic with

firearms," McNamara said. "Maybe you'll give me a demonstration one of these days."

Hank was somewhat mollified. "Sure," he said. "Be glad to."

"You youngsters run along home now, so Mrs. Blake ain't going to be worried about you bein' late," the sergeant said. "I'll take care of notifyin' the general about the goin's-on."

Cindy and Hank started in silence across the parade ground, the most direct route to the commanding general's house. Suddenly the girl stopped and, reaching out, put her hand on the boy's arm.

"Thank you for stepping in when you did and saving me, Hank," she said. "I—I didn't treat you very nicely, but you sure didn't let that stop you. When I was in danger, you came to my rescue without hesitating, and I'm not going to forget it."

The boy flushed scarlet. "Shucks," he muttered, "I didn't do anything so special."

They exchanged no further words, but a new warmth surrounded them, and they walked close enough so that their shoulders almost brushed.

Clarissa and Eulalia had spent the day in a typical, hardworking fashion, doing housework and getting dinner ready, preparing for a short journey they planned to make together the next day to the Holt ranch in Oregon. Though Whip Holt's old Cherokee friend Stalking Horse was doing a splendid job overseeing the operation of the ranch, Eulalia wanted to pay a visit to review the account books and pick up a few things she needed.

They were sitting now in the comfortable parlor of the commandant's house. Eulalia had insisted that Clarissa, who was feeling some of the discomforts of pregnancy, get off her feet, especially since they had planned a big day for tomorrow. So Clarissa was sitting by the window, knitting a woolen blanket for her infant. She was lost in thought, and Eulalia, also knitting a sweater for the child, guessed that her daughter-in-law was missing her husband. Even the dog Mr. Blake, lying near Clarissa's feet, seemed to be aware of his mistress's feelings, and frequently he wagged his tail and raised his head, looking up at her solicitously.

The quiet mood was interrupted by the arrival of Cindy and Hank. Eulalia, from a parlor window, saw the young people coming down the walk to the house and said to her daughter-in-law, "Clarissa! Come here and tell me if you see what I see."

Clarissa joined her, saw the new closeness of Cindy and Hank, and giggled as she said, "I guess wonders will never cease. It looks as though they've buried the hatchet."

The teenagers came into the house but made no mention of what had happened to them on their homeward journey. They went directly to the kitchen for glasses of milk and a plate of the chocolate brownies that Clarissa had made that day.

They were still in the kitchen eating when Lee Blake came home and sought them out. The general hugged and kissed Cindy, then extended a hand to Hank. "I'm proud of you, boy," he said, "and I'm more determined than ever to recommend you for an opening at the military academy next year. You've also done me quite a favor. The army needs every recruit we can get these days, and I wasn't looking forward to discharging those five culprits from service. Now it doesn't look as though I'll need to. They've become the laughingstocks of the entire post because of the way you handled them, and they're so ashamed that I'll be able to keep them in line without punishing them much more, except to have them offer a public apology to you and especially to Cindy in front of the whole garrison. Do you two suppose you can tolerate such a ceremony?"

A furiously blushing Cindy agreed, as did a red-faced Hank.

"I didn't do a thing," the girl said. "I had no chance. Hank tamed them in a hurry, and the way he did it was astonishing!" She looked at him admiringly.

Hank muttered under his breath in embarrassment.

The wide-eyed Cindy looked at her stepfather. "Are first-year students at the military academy allowed to attend school dances?" she demanded.

Lee was startled by the question but nodded. "Of course," he said.

"And," she persisted, "is there any chance that you'll be going east to visit the War Department next year and taking Mama and me with you?"

He began to understand the drift of her conversation and nodded solemnly. "I'm sure it can be arranged, Cindy."

She turned to Hank and wagged a finger at him. "When you go to West Point, you'd better see to it that you invite me to your first school dance, Hank Purcell," she told him. "If you ask any other girl, I'll never talk to you again!"

Lee covered his mouth with his hand and averted his face so the two teenagers wouldn't notice his laughter. Eulalia, who had been standing with Clarissa in the doorway of the kitchen, sent Cindy and Hank off to do their homework.

After the teenagers had gone upstairs, Eulalia turned

to her husband. "Do you mind telling me what that was all about?"

Lee waved her and Clarissa into the kitchen, and while Eulalia put a pot of coffee on the stove to brew, the general described the incident that had taken place in the woods that afternoon.

"I'm not in the least surprised by Hank's expertise with a pistol," Clarissa said. "Next to Toby, that boy is one of the best shots there is."

"It's too bad he isn't a few years older," Lee Blake replied. "I have good use for him."

Eulalia thought she detected a hint of concern in her husband's voice. "What do you mean?" she asked.

"When the War Department gave me command of the Army of the West, I thought I'd be ending my army career on a quiet, tranquil note," he said. "But I couldn't have been more mistaken. It looks like there's going to be hell to pay in the West, all through Dakota, Montana, and Utah, and I need all the good men I can get. The Sioux, along with the Blackfoot and Cheyenne, appear to be on the warpath against us. This could turn out to be our biggest fight ever with the Indians. Not only is our immigration into the western territories threatened, but the new railroad we're building is also in jeopardy."

Eulalia's hand was steady as she poured the coffee. "How will this affect Toby?" she asked softly.

"He's involved with the whole process," Lee said, not wanting to worry Toby's mother and wife but at the same time feeling it was wrong to make light of the problems he faced. "That was the whole reason for his going to Washington City, to meet with General Grant to discuss ways of dealing with the Indians. He's in Dakota now, attempting to dissuade Indian leaders from their alliance. I just had a telegram from Andy Brentwood, who arrived back at Fort Shaw this morning after meeting with Toby in Dakota. Based on Toby's recommendation, Andy has put in a request for an additional five hundred men to be sent to Dakota as soon as possible."

Clarissa folded her hands in her lap and sat calmly at the kitchen table, even though her heart was pounding.

Lee spooned some sugar into the coffee Eulalia poured him, then stirred it vigorously, his mind lost in thought. "I'm afraid," he said, "I'll be obliged to forward Andy's request to the War Department. I just pray that they'll be able to give us the help we need."

"Oh, dear." Eulalia was upset. "Why refer to Washington, Lee?"

He smiled painfully. "The truth is," he said, "that I'm scraping the bottom of the manpower barrel already. The Army of the West simply isn't big enough to do all its jobs. I have troops in California and New Mexico and Nevada keeping an eye on the Apache. The Navaho in Arizona may kick up their heels at any time. The Nez Percé here in Washington have been pacified, at least for the time being, but it's anyone's guess for how long. The same is true of the Arapaho and the Cheyenne in Wyoming and in Colorado. Not to mention the problems that we face in the Dakotas, Montana, and Utah. Fires are smoldering all over the West, and there's no telling when and where a major blaze is likely to break out."

"President Johnson and General Grant have no right to expect the impossible from you, Lee," Eulalia said primly. "If they want you to take responsibility for maintaining peace in the West, then they've got to supply you with the manpower to do it!"

Lee Blake grinned wearily. "Based on pure logic, my

dear, you're absolutely right. But there are factors you fail to take into consideration."

"Such as?" she demanded.

"The most important thing to keep in mind," he said, "is that the United States is a nation of civilians. After a major war—especially a war as tragic as the Civil War— there's a national revulsion against military service. The army needs men, but we're not getting enough volunteers. So although General Grant promised to give us all the men we needed, he was, perhaps, being optimistic. There simply aren't the men available."

"Then how are you going to handle the problem?"

"As I said, I intend to scrape the bottom of the barrel. I'll reduce headquarters personnel—here, at the Presidio, everywhere—and in that way I can meet about half our current need. I'll have to do some juggling to get the other two hundred and fifty men, but I'll get them. I have too much respect for Andy Brentwood and Toby not to comply with their request."

In spite of his assurances, Eulalia was troubled. "I'm not sure I like any of this," she said.

"I can't say that I blame you," he replied, "but after we've been married for a time, you'll grow accustomed to this juggling act of mine. My subordinate commanders will scream and cry and beat their heads against the walls, but one way or another I'll manage to get the job done and to provide the manpower to the right commands at the right time."

"I've listened to you very carefully," Clarissa said, running her hand through her red hair. "You talk about the need for additional men to meet the threat of Indian uprisings in this territory or that territory, but you don't mention the exact situation of the men who are already in the field."

"You're thinking of Toby, naturally," Lee said.

Clarissa nodded slowly. "Of course, I am," she said. "Toby isn't even attached to an army unit. He's traveling alone, going from one Indian village to the next. He's in great danger every moment of every day and night."

"I'd be lying if I denied that," Lee said gently. "Toby is indeed in great danger, and he'll continue to be exposed until Colonel Brentwood's reinforcements arrive and the Indians are convinced to maintain peaceful relations with us."

"That's what I thought," Clarissa said, sighing.

Eulalia's sudden reply was quiet but emphatic. "This may sound foolish, Clarissa, dear," she said, taking her daughter-in-law's hand, "but if I were you, I wouldn't be too worried about Toby, no matter how great the danger he seems to be in. Toby can take care of himself."

The sun was shining in a cloudless blue sky, but the winter winds that blew across the endless prairies of the Dakota Territory were cold. Still, there had been very little snow, and Toby Holt traveled easily as he rode across the land. After he had met with Andy, he had returned to Fort Rice for a few days, to obtain from the fort's sutler dried beef and corn, flour and salt, and even bags of oats, in the event there were heavy snows and his horse was unable to graze. Toby had of course also acquired a new saddle for his horse, and in his saddlebags he even had room for small presents—silver combs and razors—to give to the Indians he would visit.

Now coming to a small, icy stream, Toby paused to drink, water his horse, and take stock of his situation. The first of the Sioux villages he intended to visit was a day's journey away. He felt confident that he would be able to see the chief, and he had no intention of allow-

ing the Indians to lay a trap for him the way Thunder
Cloud had. Relying on the Indian's sense of honor, he
would only stay in their camp if they pledged safe conduct. No, the big problem was what Toby should say to
the chief to persuade him to lay down the tomahawk.
What would his father say, for instance, in a similar situation? Neither Whip nor Toby had been trained as a
diplomat or peacemaker.

He sat beside the little river on the hard ground, the
bright sun warming him and his saddlebags protecting
him from the wind. As he pondered and sought a solution to his dilemma, Toby noted that something was
moving in the tall, dry grass some yards away.

The movement was infrequent, not like that of an animal busily burrowing in the ground or scampering to its
home. Toby waited for a moment, saw the movement
again, and got to his feet. Picking up his rifle, he walked
cautiously to the spot. Suddenly he halted and looked
down in the thick, dry grass at what he first assumed
was a young Indian boy. Not until he examined the figure more closely did he realize he was looking at a
young woman.

Her hair was matted and snarled, and dirt was caked
on her bare feet and hands. She was painfully thin, so
emaciated that her ribs showed beneath her tattered,
filthy deerskin dress.

She had been savagely beaten. There were welts,
bruises, and scabs on her arms and legs, her back, and
even on her head. At first Toby thought she was dead,
but then he became aware of her shallow breathing. He
dropped to one knee beside her, turned her over, and
tried without success to rouse her. Finally, he took a
small tin cup from his belt and, dipping it into the river,

filled it with water, then gently poured a few drops into the young woman's mouth.

She stirred without opening her eyes, drank several sips of water, then sighed quietly and lapsed into unconsciousness again. Toby lifted her in his arms and carried her to where his horse waited. After placing her on the ground beside his saddlebags, he wrapped her in a blanket.

A flight of wild ducks spurred him to action. He raised his rifle and brought down one of the birds with a single shot. After retrieving the bird, he unpacked a pot from his gear. He cleaned the duck, cut it into small pieces, and put it in the pot with some water. Then he started a fire with sticks he gathered and put the pot over the fire.

The Indian woman was half-starved and in her condition required soup. Toby took some vegetables, dried peas and corn, from his own supplies and added them to the pot.

While the soup was cooking, he decided to clean up the woman. If dirt contaminated any of her wounds, her recovery would be hampered. He took another pot from his gear, filled it with water, and put it over the fire to warm. Then he dipped a cloth in the water, and his touch surprisingly light, he began wiping the grime of the prairie from the woman's face, arms, and hands.

While he was attending to her, she opened her eyes, saw the face of a white man looming above her, and was filled with terror.

Toby reassured her. Recognizing from her fine, chiseled features that she was a Sioux, he addressed her in that tongue. "You have nothing to fear," he said. "I am your friend, and I am here to help you."

The woman heard his tone, saw the expression in his

eyes, and believed him. A hint of a tremulous smile appeared on her parched lips.

Toby was encouraged. She seemed to be stronger than she had appeared at first.

When the soup was ready, he poured some into a cup and, supporting the woman with one arm, fed her with his free hand. She ate the contents of the cup slowly.

At last she spoke timidly. "Is there more?"

"Much more," Toby told her. "Eat and drink your fill."

She ate two more containers of the soup before drifting off to sleep.

Toby knew that his mission had to take second place for a time. It was an inviolable law of the wilderness that the requirements of someone who was injured or sick came ahead of all else.

He realized that the Indian woman would need time to regain her strength before being able to travel again, so he decided to make camp at this spot for a few nights.

Believing no harm would come to the woman if he left her for a short time, he went hunting in earnest and soon picked up the tracks of a deer. Thanks to the speed and stamina of his stallion, he found and brought down a large buck and a doe. Returning to his camp with the catch, he skinned and cut up the carcasses, saving the sinews for rope or thread, and built up his fire in order to cook the meat. Wood was scarce on the prairie, and Toby was lucky to find several good-sized pieces that had come downriver and been cast upon the riverbank.

While the meat was roasting, he dressed the deerskins, spreading them out tightly and tying the corners to pegs he hammered in the ground. Then he scraped the skins clean, having reasoned that he would have good use for them in the future.

After sleeping for the better part of the afternoon, the young Indian woman awakened, and Toby again fed her several portions of the nourishing soup. He was surprised by the speed of her recovery. She sat up unaided, ate ravenously, and then said, "You are very kind."

Her praise embarrassed him, and he drew attention from himself by gesturing toward the fire. "Tonight you will have meat to eat."

She smiled, and it occurred to him that once she was really clean and gained weight, she would be pretty.

He introduced himself and was surprised by the look of awe that came across her face. "You know me?" he asked.

"Every Sioux," she said, "knows the name of Holt and tells stories of the prowess of the great hunters and warriors and guides who bear that name."

Somewhat flustered, Toby offered her the rest of the soup, which she eagerly accepted.

Gathering strength as she ate, she said, "I am Gentle Doe." Then she told him the story of how she had rejected the hand of Tall Stone in marriage and how the village chieftain had revenged himself.

"You needn't be afraid any longer," Toby assured her when she finished. "You are beyond the reach of your enemy now."

The young woman nodded, her eyes shining, and then, without another word, she curled up in the blanket Toby had given her and went to sleep again.

Recognizing the need to establish a more permanent camp, Toby spent the rest of the daylight hours scouring the area for buffalo chips—dried dung—that he could use for fuel to stoke his campfire. Then he took his other blanket from his saddlebag and prepared to settle down.

That night he and Gentle Doe ate venison, and at his

insistence his companion took his extra blanket while he made do sleeping wrapped in his coat and propped up against his saddle. The following morning he awoke early and made some biscuits in a pan on the fire.

While they were eating their breakfast, Toby caught a glimpse of a small herd of buffalo in the distance. He mounted his stallion, rode toward them, and brought down a large bull with a single shot. The carcass was so heavy that skinning and butchering it required considerable time, and he knew he would have to make several trips to the camp with the spoils.

A surprise awaited him on his return. Gentle Doe had found his pack of toilet articles, including a comb and soap, and had used warmed-up river water to bathe herself. She had washed her hair and somehow combed out the snarls, and she had cleaned her filthy dress, which was drying near the fire. She sat now, wrapped in a blanket.

By the time that Toby returned to camp for the fourth time, bringing the last of the buffalo meat with him, he discovered that Gentle Doe had been even busier. His largest kettle was on the fire, with buffalo bones, meat, and vegetables simmering in it, and she had heated venison for their noon meal. Not only had she revived physically, she seemed almost cheerful.

Curiosity overcame Gentle Doe, and childlike, she chose a direct method to satisfy it. "Why does Toby Holt travel alone in Dakota?" she asked. The blanket that Gentle Doe had wrapped around herself kept slipping as she ate, and she took her time tugging it back into place. Like most Indians, she was not embarrassed by nudity.

Toby hesitated, somewhat flustered by the glimpse of her bare shoulders. He decided he had nothing to lose by telling her the full story of his mission. He explained that he had been directed by the United States government to negotiate peace with the Indian nations. He stressed that he was empowered to offer them large reservations, where they would have their own hunting grounds and white settlers would be forbidden to enter.

He went on to say that although Thunder Cloud had rejected his terms, he intended to persist and offer them to the local chieftains of the individual Sioux villages.

Gentle Doe was surprised. "Has Toby Holt yet gone to these villages?"

He shook his head. "I was heading for one when I found you."

Gentle Doe was lost in thought for a time, her expression grave. Then she spoke slowly. "Gentle Doe knows the location of many villages of the Sioux in the Dakota Territory. She will travel with Toby Holt, and she will show him where these places are."

Toby was touched by her offer, but he was afraid traveling with someone else would slow down his mission. He started to protest, but she raised a hand to silence him and spoke with determination. "If Toby Holt had not come to her help," she said, "Gentle Doe would be dead now. He saved her life, and he asked nothing in return. He shot a duck, two deer, and a buffalo to provide her with food. Never before has Gentle Doe had such a good friend. No matter what may happen, even if she lives for one hundred winters, she cannot repay his kindness. But she must try and do that which she is capable of doing."

Toby demurred. "It would not be right for a woman to go from one end of Dakota to the other. The territory is large, and living conditions would be difficult."

She met his gaze and smiled. "I no longer have a

home of my own," she said. "If I go back to my village,
Tall Stone will kill me."

That settled the issue. Toby could not refuse protection to a helpless young woman who had nowhere else
to go.

The following morning, Gentle Doe, wrapped as before in the blanket, mended her buckskin dress. Toby,
meanwhile, smoked buffalo meat for their future use.
Suddenly a small party of Arapaho Indians rode across
the prairie, driving several mountain ponies ahead of
them. These animals had been captured in the Rocky
Mountains and had been trained by the warriors, who
were now intending to sell them to the Sioux or the
Cheyenne.

Toby struck a bargain with the warriors, giving them
a twenty-dollar gold piece in exchange for a lively mare.
When the Arapaho had gone, he presented the pony to
Gentle Doe.

His generosity overwhelmed her, and she was incapable of speaking.

"I don't want your thanks," he told her. "I bought the
pony for my own convenience. We'll be able to break
camp that much sooner—I'd say in the next day or two—
and we'll make far better time as we go through Dakota."

Gentle Doe nodded but made no reply, and Toby mis-
takenly thought that was the end of the matter. Had he
seen the expression in her eyes, he would have known
better.

Gentle Doe had never met a man like Toby Holt.
With the single-mindedness of the young and naive, she
was determined to stay with him, to make him her own.

That night, she insisted he sleep in his own blanket.
He took it reluctantly, wished her good night, and soon

lay asleep under the Dakota stars. Soon Gentle Doe slid
into Toby's blanket, her body pressing close against him,
her hands exploring him.

More asleep than awake, Toby wrapped her in his
arms, drawing her still closer, and dreamed he was home
on the Holt ranch, in bed with Clarissa, his wife.

Then he suddenly realized that the young woman he
was kissing and caressing was more slender and shorter
than Clarissa.

He opened his eyes and was stunned to find that he
was embracing Gentle Doe.

Releasing her instantly, he hoisted himself to one elbow as he stammered, "I—I'm sorry. I—I don't know how
we happened to be under this blanket together. I have a
wife. In Washington. I love her very much. She—she's
going to have our baby."

Gentle Doe put her hand on his mouth. "The squaw
of Toby Holt is not in Dakota," she said. "She is far
away. If she will soon bear him a child, she is not fit for
his lovemaking. Gentle Doe is here. She was weak, but
now she is strong again. She wants Toby Holt, just as
Toby Holt wants her. Let him take her, and let there be
an end to talk."

He felt desire, instantly countered by guilt. Hastily
pulling himself out of the blanket, he said, "I don't mean
to insult you, but I must be true to my wife."

She looked at him without understanding. "You do not
want Gentle Doe?"

He laughed ironically. "Indeed I do want you," he
said.

"Gentle Doe," she persisted, "also wants Toby Holt.
His squaw is far away, and Gentle Doe is here."

Toby knew that if he failed to keep his distance from
her now he would become embroiled in an affair from

which there would be no escape as long as he and Gentle Doe remained together. Explanations were useless. "Get some sleep," he said, speaking more harshly than he intended. "We're going to leave early in the morning." He left her the blanket and spent the rest of the night sitting up.

Gentle Doe completely recovered her health and strength, and her endurance soon matched Toby's. They rode from sunup until sundown day after day, and because of her knowledge of the locations of many Sioux villages, they were able to cover much ground.

When they camped for the night, they used one of the deerskins Toby had dried to make a small lean-to, though he elected to sleep in the open in order to guard their camp. With the other deerskin, Gentle Doe had fashioned herself a new dress, which made her look even more attractive.

No Indian town would have turned away Toby Holt, son of Whip Holt. Though he did not like to rest on his father's laurels, it certainly did no harm that the tall, wiry, sandy-haired Toby closely resembled Whip, who had befriended the Indians of Dakota and traded with them many years earlier. Indeed, there were many older warriors and chiefs who thought for a moment that they were seeing the ghost of the young Whip Holt. In addition, the presence of Gentle Doe with Toby proved to be beneficial. That he was traveling with a daughter of the Sioux gave him even greater acceptance, though in most villages it was taken for granted that they were sleeping together.

Toby spoke earnestly and at length with the village chiefs, medicine men, and principal warriors, stressing the futility of war and the advantages of a peace treaty with the United States. He did not ask for a commitment from the braves of any community, and on the few occasions when agreements were offered to him, he refused to accept them. His goal was to achieve unity within the Sioux nation itself. It would not be appropriate for individual towns to make peace with the United States and lay themselves open to charges of treason from their own people. It was far preferable, he insisted, for them to work from within and persuade their entire nation not to go to war. Then, and only then, would they give up the alliance with the Blackfoot and Cheyenne.

He was playing a delicate, dangerous game, with war or peace hanging in the balance, and he would not know the results of his efforts until Thunder Cloud summoned his people to take up arms against the United States. If at that time they refused, Thunder Cloud would have no choice but to break the alliance with Red Elk and Long Knife.

Gentle Doe, who accompanied Toby to his meetings, observed the Indians carefully, and felt certain that Toby was getting his message across to them. As she told him when they left a small Sioux village in the south of the Dakota Territory, "They are shy in the presence of a white man, particularly one who is a Holt. But they listened to what Toby told them, and in their hearts they agreed with him, rather than with their own tribal chiefs. You will learn that the words Gentle Doe speaks are true. When Thunder Cloud sounds the drums that summon his braves to war, those with whom Toby has held powwows will not heed that call."

"I hope you're right," Toby replied, "but I'm afraid we won't know for sure until the chips are down."

In the notebook he kept to record the results of each

session, he often made the notation: *Results of meeting
not known.* Still and all, he felt that he was not wasting
his time. He had at least some cause to be satisfied with
the progress he appeared to be making.

His personal life, however, was increasingly complex.
It was inconceivable to any of his hosts that a virile
young man and an attractive woman would travel and
not sleep together. As a matter of course, they were
given the same tepee when they were invited to stay
overnight.

For some days Gentle Doe appeared to accept Toby's
decision to have no intimate relations with her. Gradually, however, she became restless, and more than once
he caught her studying him surreptitiously. Still, he remained steadfastly faithful to Clarissa, and after he and
Gentle Doe retired for the night, usually after having
shared an evening meal with their hosts, he went to his
side of the tepee, rolled up in his blanket, and stayed
that way until morning. In both of them, though, tensions were building.

They were given a particularly cordial welcome in one
of the larger villages of the Sioux, located in the prairies
of south-central Dakota. The chief gave a banquet in
their honor, serving bear steak and heart of elk, and af-
terward Toby presented the chief with the buffalo skin
he had acquired when he first met Gentle Doe. Then all
of the adults joined in the meeting.

The people left little doubt where they stood on the
questions that Toby raised. Many warriors and almost
all of the squaws agreed with his arguments, that they
would be better off if they made peace with the United
States, accepted a tract of land as a reservation, and ignored the settlers who moved into the territory beyond
their own boundaries.

After the meeting Toby was in high spirits as he and Gentle Doe were led to a large tepee where they would spend the night. He saw a pallet of pine boughs covered with a wool blanket, which had been acquired in a trade with settlers. He had a premonition of trouble but shrugged it off. "You take the bed," he said. "I'll roll up in my own blanket on the other side."

Gentle Doe made no reply and lowered the entrance flap.

Toby did not look at his companion again, although he heard rustling sounds behind him. Then, as he was undoing his blanket, he felt Gentle Doe come up behind him. As he turned he saw that she had removed all of her clothing. Before he could say a word, she pressed close to him, reached up, and caught his head, then pulled it down and kissed him hungrily.

Before he quite realized what was happening, he responded to her embrace. Her lips parted for his kiss, her fingers wound themselves into the hair at his neck, and her warm, supple body pressed still closer. Toby felt himself becoming more and more aroused. Encouraged by his response, Gentle Doe redoubled her efforts.

Toby prided himself on his self-control, but he felt it waning under Gentle Doe's ardor. He knew he had to act at once before his passion got the better of him.

Exercising all of his willpower, he caught hold of Gentle Doe's bare shoulders and, holding her in place, disengaged himself. "No," he said softly. "We must not do this."

Gentle Doe did not advance, but neither did she retreat. "That which we would do," she said, "is natural."

"I reckon it is," he whispered.

"That which is natural cannot be wrong," she said, and laughed softly.

She was as bold as a hussy, and Toby wondered why he had thought that the name Gentle Doe suited her so well. It was impossible to make her understand his reluctance to make love to her, but he knew he had to try. "You know I am married," he said. "I love my wife, and when married people love each other, they must keep themselves only for their mates."

"I know you say you are married," she replied, speaking quietly but firmly, "but where is your squaw? It is the duty of the woman to stand beside her man, to cook his food, sew his clothes, and keep his house. It is her duty to go with him when he travels and to help him when he engages in work for his people. Toby is working hard for his government and his people, but his squaw is not at his side."

"You know she's at home," he replied, "because she's bearing our child."

Gentle Doe was adamant. "When the squaw of a chief is heavy with child, it is his right to take another squaw and to keep her beside him as long as she pleases him, until such time as his first squaw recovers and becomes a whole woman again. Toby Holt is a great warrior and a mighty hunter. It is his right to do as he pleases. If he wishes to take Gentle Doe as his squaw for a time and to make love to her, that is his right."

Toby clenched his fists. Never before had he faced such great temptation. Not the least of the young Indian woman's attractions lay in her innocence. "I must obey the laws of my people and of my God," he said.

She startled him by flinging her arms around his neck and clinging to him. "If Gentle Doe were a bad woman," she said, "she would find ways to make Toby love her. She would offer prayers to her gods, and she would prepare secret potions that she would place in his food. But she will do none of these things."

All at once she released her grip on him but continued to stand close to him, and she did not raise her voice as she continued to speak. "I know that you want me as much as I want you. I can see it in your eyes, I can tell it in all that you say and do, and in every way that you act. So I will wait. The day will come when you will give yourself to me as freely and willingly as I would give myself to you. When that day comes, we will be united!"

With that, Gentle Doe returned to her bed and slipped under the blanket. Within seconds she was sleeping soundly, her conscience, like that of a child, untroubled. But Toby lay awake for a long time, thinking of Clarissa. He had come to rely on his lovely, forthright wife in a way he had never depended on anyone, and he was lonely for her. They had been married too short a time to be separated this way; if he could spend just one day with her, Toby knew all would be right with his world again.

Ma Hastings chewed on the frayed, unlighted end of a cigar and looked out the window of the sod house at the corral beyond it. Propping her feet on the kitchen table, she shoved her broad-brimmed hat to the back of her head, then spat with accuracy at a bug that crawled across the bare floor about a dozen feet from her. The isolated property had been the home of a rancher, but he, his wife, and their two sons had been murdered by the Hastings gang, who had found the place convenient to use as a headquarters for several weeks. Now, afraid that the nearest neighbors—who lived forty miles away—might grow suspicious, Ma had determined that she and her band would have to take to the road again in the near future.

"I don't like it, Digger," she said to her swarthy, bearded lieutenant. "I don't like it worth a damn. All we hear from every last Sioux we meet is that Toby Holt—along with a good-lookin' Sioux gal—visited his village recently and made a heap of sense when he urged the Indians to keep the peace."

"I never even seen Holt until he beat the tar out of us when we set that ambush for him in the Black Hills," Digger replied. "All I can say is that he must be a mighty persuasive talker. Every Indian we see believes every last word that Holt has told him."

Ma Hastings spat again, even more vehemently. "Toby Holt is just like his pa," she said contemptuously. "He has more luck than sense. Ya boys bungled when ya set an ambush for him, but seein' as how he's a Holt, the story has got around that he did all kinds of heroic things. Just like when he killed my son. It was a sneak attack, but ya'd never know it when ya hear the stories."

Digger had been present on that occasion and recalled distinctly that Toby Holt had not been just lucky but had been an accurate marksman. It was useless to try to correct Ma Hastings, however. She was somewhat unbalanced on the subject of Toby Holt and would not listen to reason.

"Well, I tell ya straight out, Digger. If we don't put an end to Toby Holt once and for all, we'll have hell to pay. Now I ain't just talkin' about my own little bone o' contention with Holt." She spat vehemently still another time. "Nah, it goes even beyond that, now that he's goin' around talkin' the Indians into bein' peaceful. I tell ya, if the Indian nations of this here area don't go on the warpath soon and drive the settlers out, we're goin' to be in terrible trouble."

Her lieutenant scratched his beard and looked at her blankly. "How come?" he demanded.

Ma was exasperated. "If the Indians are peaceful and agree to move to reservations," she said, "people will migrate into the territory by the thousands. They won't just be comin' by wagon train, no sir. You've heard tell about the railroads that are goin' to be built out this way, and them trains is gonna be filled with settlers."

"It strikes me," Digger said patiently, "that the more settlers that move into an area, there's that many more folks for us to rob."

Ma looked at him in disgust and sighed. "Ya may be handy enough with a rifle," she said, "but ya sure was somewheres else when the Lord was handin' out brains! When a territory develops, it don't work out like ya say. Look at Oregon—and California—and Colorado. The more folks come into an area, the more need there is for services, and before ya know it, a whole city grows up. Pretty soon there's a whole slew of cities. That's when the righteous and the psalm singers take charge. They don't want no violence, but they're such cowards they can't put down the strong by themselves. They start shoutin' that the saloons and whorehouses are a bad influence and ought to be closed down. They cry and moan and carry on every time one of 'em gets robbed. So before ya know it, they go out and hire themselves a constabulary. Tough men who know how to shoot and ain't afraid of nobody. And if the constabulary ain't enough, the U.S. Army lends them a helpin' hand and sends in some cavalry units. Just exactly like they done in the Montana Territory not a year ago!"

"I begin to see what ya mean, Ma," Digger said.

" 'I begin to see what ya mean, Ma!' " she cried, mimicking him. "Gawd a'mighty, Digger! We been sent flyin' out of more territories and states in the West with our tails droopin' between our legs than we can count. We got one hell of a choice right now. Either we take a stand, or we admit we're beat and leave the Dakota Territory. We just plain retire. Maybe you're ready to get yourself a homestead and grub in the dirt for some rotten vegetables, but I don't call that kind of existence earnin' a livin'!"

"Yeah, Ma," the lieutenant said, "but I'm hanged if I can see what we can do about it."

"Sure as you're born, you'll be hanged less'n ya do begin to see the light, Digger," she told him. "Our hope lies in the Indians raisin' enough fuss, fume, and fury to drive the settlers out of the Dakota Territory for all time. And that," she added, her voice rising triumphantly, "puts us directly against Toby Holt, the man I hate more'n anybody else on earth. I aim to dance a real jig at his funeral!"

Digger looked at her dubiously, his expression mournful. "If I was you, Ma," he said, "I wouldn't try to tangle in too much of a hurry with that Holt feller again. The boys got stung pretty bad last time, so they're still kind of leery of him."

She gestured angrily. "I know better'n to count on ya yellow-livered prairie dogs for anythin'," she said. "That's why I sent that Sioux Black Horse packin'. He wasn't worth his weight in fleas when it came to doin' away with that Toby Holt. Anyway, I now got me a much better scheme in mind."

Digger made no attempt to conceal his great relief. "What's that?"

Ma's smile was a leer. "I tell ya, it pays to have friends ya can really trust. They come in right handy."

He looked at her blankly.

"Do ya remember a visit we paid to the chief of a Sioux village, name of Tall Stone?"

He thought hard for a moment, and then his face cleared. "Oh, yeah. I remember him now. Big feller, built like an ox."

"He's comin' to see me," Ma said, "and he's due to arrive here today. So ya better tell the boys to keep watch for him and his braves. They can keep their weapons, and they're to be treated nice and polite. Tall Stone don't know it yet, but he's goin' to do our dirty work for us and get rid of Toby Holt once and for all!"

"How are ya goin' to talk him into that?" the mystified lieutenant asked.

Ma's harsh laugh boomed through the kitchen. "From what I learned from that Black Horse before I fired him," she said, "Tall Stone was sweet on a young Indian girl, called Gentle Doe. She wouldn't marry him, so he made up a passel of charges about her and had her thrown out of the village. Damned if it ain't the very same Sioux girl who's now traipsin' around the Dakota Territory with Toby Holt."

Digger began to laugh, too.

"We'll not only be rid of young Holt once and for all," she said venomously, "but he won't be able to persuade the Indians to make their peace with the United States. You show Tall Stone in to me the minute he gets here, and keep everybody else away. I'll attend to the rest."

Several hours later the chieftain arrived, accompanied by a small party of warriors. He had not forgotten his pact with Ma Hastings to do away with Toby Holt, and now he had learned there was something brewing that required his presence right away. Tall Stone's braves were greeted at the supposedly deserted farmhouse with a warmth that surprised them, and the chief was conducted to the kitchen, where Ma Hastings went out of her way to be cordial. She even went so far as to offer him a drink, which was something that white settlers were careful never to do when dealing with Indians, whose capacity for alcohol was limited.

The village chieftain eagerly accepted, and Ma went to work on him. She explained in detail that it was their mutual enemy Toby Holt who was responsible for the reluctance of so many Sioux villages to join in the crusade being planned by Thunder Cloud. "This man is a menace," she said, "and he must die now. Then the ambitious plans of the leaders of the Indian nations can be fulfilled, and the land of your ancestors once again will belong to you."

She paused to let the words sink in, then resumed. "There's another reason why you should want to see Toby Holt dead right away."

Ma knew from the intensity of his wooden-faced stare that she had aroused his curiosity. "Gentle Doe," she continued calmly, "has become the woman of Toby Holt. She goes with him from one town of the Sioux to the next. They do not try to hide their relationship."

A cracking sound filled the kitchen, and Tall Stone stared down at the wooden mug he held in his hands. He had closed his fists so convulsively that the wood had shattered, and liquor dripped on his hands. He threw the remnants away and said in a voice of deadly calm, "Even though I have never seen him, Toby Holt is my enemy, as was his father before him. Tell Tall Stone what he must do."

"I will see to it," Ma said, "that a message is delivered

to Toby Holt. I will guarantee that after he receives this message, he will be present at a certain place on a certain day. Tall Stone will be notified of this in advance and can set an ambush for him. You will get rid of this man, who is your enemy and is the enemy of the Sioux, and your whole nation will rejoice."

"And what does Ma Hastings get from the death of this man?" Tall Stone demanded.

Her eyes and voice were equally cold as she replied, "The death of Toby Holt is all I want!"

VI

Leon Graham had decided to strike anew, and he planned the evening with infinite care. He had been seeing Beth Martin for a few months now, and this time he would not take the chance that she would run out on him.

Beth could have sworn Leon had invited her to dine at one of the hotels, but instead they drove directly to his house, where the dining room table was set for two. She didn't want to make a fuss over nothing; after all, she had been there for supper on another occasion, and Leon had been a perfect host then. Leon gave her a strong predinner drink of rum and fruit juice, which helped erase her inhibitions, and by the time they went to the dining room table, she felt quite at ease.

They were served an elaborate meal, and with each course Leon brought out a different bottle of wine. Once or twice Beth cautioned herself that she was drinking too much, but the wines were delicious, and her glass somehow was always filled.

After dinner they retired to the drawing room for

coffee and brandy, and Leon poured his companion a
generous portion of a rare and potent cognac. She
couldn't recall drinking it, but later she had the distinct
impression that he refilled her glass at least once, and
perhaps more often.

Then she dropped, suddenly, inexplicably, into a
deep, comalike sleep.

"Hello, wench! Hello, wench!"

The screaming of the mynah bird awakened Beth, and
as she came to her senses, she was confused and terrified.

She found herself on a large, four-poster bed, with no
covers over her. Her head rested on a pillow. Beside it
was another pillow that was indented where someone
else had lain.

Her hair had been piled high on her head when she
had dressed for the evening, but now it hung in loose
waves over her shoulders.

The mynah bird was still screeching. Beth's head
throbbed dully, insistently, and the horrified young
woman found she was clad—or almost unclad—in clothes
she had never before seen. On her feet were a pair of
high-heeled pumps, and she was struck by the incongru-
ity of wearing them in bed. Her legs were encased in
long, black stockings, which were held in place by frilly
garters around her thighs. Worst of all, she was wearing
a tiny garment of black lace that emphasized rather than
concealed her breasts and thighs. She could not figure
out how she had acquired this outlandish costume.

Swinging her legs to the floor, she struggled to a sitting position, and in the light cast by a pair of brass oil
lamps, she caught a glimpse of herself in the dressing-
room mirror opposite the bed. She was wearing more

cosmetics than she remembered applying, and the makeup, combined with her skimpy, sexually provocative attire, made her look like a trollop.

Her head ached so badly she could not think clearly. As she struggled to understand what had happened to her, the bedchamber door opened and closed.

Leon Graham carefully locked the door behind him, then dropped the key into a pocket of the handsome dressing gown he was wearing. "Hello, wench! Hello, wench!" he said, a sardonic smile on his face.

Beth looked frantically for something to cover her near-nudity but could find nothing. She tried to make the best of the sorry situation by smiling, but the effort was feeble.

"Here," he said. "I've brought you something that will make your head feel a bit better. I imagine you have a headache just about now." He handed her a large, chilled mug.

She took it, smelled brandy, and shuddered. "What's in it?" she asked, looking suspiciously at the dark brown liquid.

"Just drink it," he told her, and laughed.

The mynah bird echoed his laugh, sending a chill up Beth's spine.

She raised the mug to her lips and took two large swallows. For a moment she thought she would explode internally, but her insides soon settled down, and a warm glow spread up the back of her neck into her skull, easing her headache. She took another sip.

Leon had sunk into a chair across the bedroom from her and was watching her approvingly. "How on earth did I ever come to be in your bedroom?" she asked. "And how do I happen to be wearing this ridiculous costume?"

He continued to smile steadily at her. "One thing led to another," he replied.

She glanced at the two indented pillows resting at the head of the bed and steadied herself by gulping more of the potent drink. "Does that mean—what I think it means?" she asked faintly.

"You don't remember?" He pretended astonishment. "Why, you're the most passionate wench I've ever had!"

"Hello, wench! Hello, wench!" the mynah bird screeched.

The combination of shock and shame made Beth numb. She had been unfaithful to Rob and couldn't even recall it.

Leon was watching her closely, gauging her reactions. "The next time," he said, "we're going to have an even better time, because you'll be more sober. Suppose we start right now. I'd like to see you strut around in that outfit."

She blinked at him incredulously.

Leon reached behind the chair and amazed Beth by producing a long bullwhip. The leather thong sang as the whip uncoiled, and the end cracked only inches from her head.

Before Beth could move, Leon stood in front of her, gripping the handle of the whip. "Listen to me carefully," he said. "I've wined, dined, and entertained you for weeks, preparing for a night like this one. Now you are mine. You belong to me, and you exist only for my pleasure. Do as you're told, obey instantly when I give you an order, and you'll be rewarded. When I'm convinced that you're totally within my power, you'll be allowed out in public again. Until then, you'll stay right here. When I'm absent from the house, my servants will bring you food and drink. But that's all they'll bring you. Try to escape, and I'll beat you, just as I'll beat you anytime you fail to obey or please me."

Again the whip cracked, and the dumbfounded Beth felt weak in the knees.

"I've ordered you to parade for me. Then we'll have a tumble together. Either you do as I say, or you'll have your first beating here and now. Frankly, my dear, I wouldn't think the whip would be worth your acting the part of a prude. After all, we've already been to bed, you know."

Stalling for time, Beth drained the contents of the mug. The liquor weakened her courage, for she began to think that Leon Graham was right. He was insane, of course. But that was beside the point. What mattered at this moment was that he intended to whip her unless she did his bidding.

Placing the empty mug on the bedside table, Beth rose unsteadily to her feet. The heels of her shoes were so high she could hardly maintain her balance.

Taking a deep breath, she began to strut for Leon as he ogled her and caught glimpses of her from different angles in the bedroom mirrors. She felt cheap and ashamed.

Leon relished the exhibition. "Hello, wench," he murmured.

The mynah bird heard him and began to screech again, "Hello, wench!" Then the bird laughed, its piercing sound penetrating to Beth's very marrow. She could only pray that the nightmare would end soon.

Leon tired of the exhibition and, lifting Beth off her feet, carried her to the bed, where he removed the few pieces of clothing she wore. Then he began to paw her.

The humiliated, disgusted Beth made no protest, though his hands, his mouth, his body were repulsive to her. His foul breath made her gag, and the weight of his body suffocated her. But afraid of what the madman might do if she failed to react, she pretended that she, too, was aroused.

Leon's voice floated down from somewhere above her. "That's more like it!" he said. "You really are a lively wench! I'll let you in on a little secret. The extra pillow on the bed was arranged to make you believe that we'd made love before. We hadn't, really. I knew you'd be much easier to get that way, but this is actually the first time." His maniacal laugh filled the bedchamber, and the mynah bird joined in, shrieking loudly.

Beth was so sickened she could not even weep, and she continued to heave up and down in helpless abandon, her sweat mingling with that of the man who had so cruelly seduced her, just as his harsh laughter mingled with that of his mynah bird.

Three days later Beth Martin listlessly paced the length of Leon Graham's bedchamber, so discouraged that she did not even try the door, which she knew was locked. Finally, she sank into a chair, and feeling hopeless, she began to sob uncontrollably.

How she had gotten into this predicament she could not understand, but it seemed her life had steadily eroded since her mother's death. Rob, whom she loved, had somehow become a stranger to her, and she had been unable to control her outbursts at him. She had alienated her father's new wife, Eulalia, and she had probably come close to losing the affection of her father, too. Now she had sunk to the lowest point of her life, and she didn't know if she would ever be able to resume her marriage with Rob or if her family would ever accept her back.

But the most important thing this very minute was her own survival. And she could not survive another day as the prisoner of a madman.

The meal that Leon's butler had brought remained untouched on its tray, as did a potent drink of rum. The thought of drinking more liquor made her queasy, but she knew better than to throw it away. She would definitely need it to anesthetize herself when Leon again returned and made his weird sexual demands, holding his whip and ordering her to strut and parade, to subject herself to his lovemaking, and even to make violent love to him.

Her nightmare was endless. For three nights and three days she had been the man's prisoner in his bedroom, subject to his whims and his perverted fancies, and there was no escape in sight. Heaving herself to her feet, she began to pace again, averting her eyes each time she passed the full-length mirror that stood on one wall. Unfortunately, she knew every detail of her disgusting, gaudy appearance only too well: the heavily applied makeup; the black silk stockings held in place by frivolous garters; and worst of all, the single garment that enveloped her body, a dressing gown of transparent silk that clung to her as though it had just been soaked in water.

To think that she had regarded Leon Graham as honorable and respectable! All the time he had been hiding behind the façade of respectability, Graham had been planning his cruel and bizarre seduction. What was more, there was no doubt that Beth was not the first. She knew from the blasé reaction of his butler and the two hatchet-faced serving women that they were accustomed to their roles as jailers.

Suddenly the raucous sound of Leon's mynah bird,

laughing and cackling loudly, interrupted Beth's reverie. That bird, she thought, would drive her mad. "Shut up, damn you!" she shouted.

"Hello, wench! Hello, wench!" the bird called shrilly.

Clapping her hands over her ears, Beth began to pace again. It served her right, she told herself angrily, for speaking to the creature. Now she was in for another session of the bird's torture.

All at once she halted and stared up at the pair of crossed pistols that served as a wall decoration. She had barely noticed them before. Suddenly she was so excited her breath came in short gasps.

The pistols were too high to reach. She dragged a straight-backed chair to the wall, then lifted the long skirt of her diaphanous gown as she climbed on it. Her hands trembling, she took the pistols from the wall.

A swift examination proved that the weapons were old-fashioned, smooth-bore pistols, each capable of firing only a single shot. They were not loaded, but hanging near the pistols were a powder flask and a small leather bag that Beth quickly discovered contained dry powder and bullets. No doubt Leon Graham was ignorant about guns and thought the flask and leather bag merely added to the decor, but Beth, who had learned all about firearms from her father, could now turn the pistols into lethal weapons.

All at once she was no longer helpless. All the pain she had endured, all the anguish and misery, now were transformed into cold determination.

Stepping down onto the floor, Beth quickly moved the chair back to its place. Then, after quickly loading the two pistols, she cocked them, took them to the bed, and placed them beneath her pillow.

Frightened, trembling, she nevertheless knew what

had to be done and went about the task with an almost mechanical determination. First she pulled the bell rope to summon the butler, and when the man appeared, she did not try to hide her near-nudity. "I expect that Mr. Graham will be returning home soon," she said, "so be good enough to bring a bottle of champagne on ice with two glasses. We'll open it ourselves."

The butler bowed as he left the chamber and carefully locked the door behind him. He had to admit that Mr. Graham knew what he was doing. Most of the women he brought here protested their imprisonments for a time but eventually underwent a change and actually learned to enjoy their lot. This one had held out for seventy-two hours, which was longer than most, but now she was capitulating like all the others. After a night of intense lovemaking, she would be free to come and go as she pleased and would stay on voluntarily as his mistress. Most of them did.

In the bedchamber Beth went to the dressing table, and even though she already wore more than enough makeup, she applied kohl to her eyes and rouge to her lips and her cheeks. She glued a black velvet beauty patch to her chin and then fixed another one in the cleavage between her breasts. Why not? she thought recklessly. The more she could do to distract Graham, the sooner she would be completely free.

The butler returned with two glasses and a bottle of champagne in a bucket of ice. After he had withdrawn, Beth double-checked the pistols to make sure she could reach them swiftly beneath her pillow, and then, smiling slightly, she gulped her rum drink, which calmed her.

The mynah bird began to cackle again, but the sound seemed far-off to Beth.

She felt no guilt over what she planned to do. Her

freedom and the restoration of her dignity depended on her acting with firmness. She scarcely bothered to think of Leon Graham at all; if she had been pressed, she would have said simply that he deserved to die.

At last Leon arrived. He carefully locked the door behind him.

"I thought you'd never get here," Beth said. Her walk provocative, her expression sultry, she slowly crossed the room to him.

Leon was elated. His harsh, degrading treatment of the woman had been effective, and it was plain that she had undergone a complete change of heart. He particularly noted the beauty patches and rouge and realized that she had exerted herself to please him.

"I ordered some champagne that's been chilling," she said, "and I've hardly been able to wait until we make love. I don't know why it is, but I've been thinking about you—and the things you do to me—all day."

Giving him no chance to reply, she rubbed her body against him, raised her face to his, and pulled his head down for a passionate kiss. She continued to rub herself against him, and her hands roamed over his body. She succeeded in unbuttoning his waistcoat, shirt, and trousers. "Hurry, darling," she murmured. "I can hardly wait."

Leon laughed huskily. "We'll have to drink the champagne. We don't want it to get warm, do we?"

"Of course not," she replied as she continued to undress him.

By the time he opened the bottle of champagne and filled two glasses, she had succeeded in stripping him naked. He was already thoroughly aroused, but the champagne would ensure that he was entirely distracted from what she was going to do.

Leon made no protest as Beth gulped her own champagne, led him to the bed, and sat on his lap, caressing and kissing him.

This, Leon thought, was almost too good to be true. He had estimated when he had first met Beth Martin that she was capable of great passion but had never been awakened. Now, he was convinced, he had caused her metamorphosis. She was not like his other mistresses, whom he had tamed in the same way. None of them had been socially acceptable, and he had had to exercise great caution in his public appearances with them.

But Beth was a respectable married woman, the socially impeccable daughter of the commander of the Army of the West, and he could be proud to escort her anywhere in San Francisco, presenting her to any company. Yet, in private, as she was demonstrating at this very moment, she could transform herself into a complete harlot.

Leon returned kiss for kiss, caress for caress. Beth stretched voluptuously on the bed, writhing as one hand grasped the man, while the other slid beneath her pillow.

"Hello, wench!" the mynah bird shrieked.

Closing his eyes as he stretched beside Beth, Leon allowed her to do as she pleased with him. Then something hard and unyielding pressed into the left side of his chest. He opened his eyes onto the unwavering gaze of Beth Martin. She was as cold as the metal of the pistol she held.

"For God's sake—don't!" he whispered.

"Die, you filthy beast!" she said softly, and squeezed the trigger.

The shot boomed through the quiet house. Leon fell

back on the bed, dead. His blood turned the bedclothes crimson.

"Hello, wench! Hello, wench!" the mynah bird screamed.

Beth began to laugh hysterically. She would dispose of the bird she hated almost as much as she had despised its master. Still gripping a smoking pistol in one hand, she reached under the pillow for the other.

She rose, her own laughter wilder and louder as it mingled with the screams of the bird. She intended to blow off its head, but a pounding at the door distracted her. "Go away," she screamed. "I'm busy."

The pounding continued, making it difficult for her to think clearly. Suddenly she forgot what she had in mind as, giggling inanely, she stood staring down at the two pistols, one loaded, the other unloaded.

The mynah bird cackled with her.

In deep shock Beth stared at the creature, and she continued to giggle. Time lost all meaning for her, and she was surprised when she heard the bedroom door being smashed with a heavy ax.

Two members of the San Francisco constabulary burst into the chamber, both carrying drawn six-shooters. Behind them came the butler and the two serving maids, one of whom screamed when she saw the body of Leon Graham on the blood-drenched bed.

The mynah bird continued to cackle.

The astonished Beth found the pistols being snatched from her hands, and then one of the constables demanded, "What happened here?"

"I shot and killed Leon Graham," she replied in a daze.

One of the constables, she noted absently, scribbled in a notebook.

"Why did you kill him?" the other constable demanded.

"Because he was a loathsome creature," she replied promptly.

"He was your lover?"

Her laugh was as harsh as that of the mynah bird. "Really! What do you think?" she asked, and then, as the constables stepped toward her, she lost consciousness and fainted in their arms.

Not until the following day, when Beth woke in a cell of the Market Street prison and the jailer gave her the day's newspapers, did she realize what a sensation she had created. The wealthy Mrs. Robert Martin, wife of a prominent young railroad surveyor, daughter of the commander in chief of the U.S. Army of the West, had killed in cold blood the man she had freely admitted was her lover. Furthermore, the newspapers hinted, when she had been arrested in the bedchamber of her dead lover's house, she had been seminude, attired in a manner appropriate only to a prostitute.

The victim of the crime, Leon Graham, was a trusted employee of his uncle, the wealthy Chet Harris, one of San Francisco's leading citizens.

Only then did Beth begin to realize the seriousness of her plight. She knew she would be placed on trial for her life and that her reputation was destroyed. But she was not yet capable of feeling, and she did not care.

Toby Holt felt a sense of relief almost like that of coming home when he and Gentle Doe arrived at the banks of the broad Missouri River, which roughly bisected the Dakota Territory from north to south. They had been traveling for a few months and had visited one

Sioux community after another. Now it was spring, and
they were assured ample water, plentiful fish, and good
hunting as the wild animals came to the river for water.

They established their camp, pitching their animal
skin lean-to a short distance from the riverbank, and dig-
ging a pit for their campfire. By now their duties were
well defined, and Gentle Doe, like any good squaw, set
out in search of wood and buffalo chips with which to
make a fire. There were no trees in the area, but there
were driftwood and dead bushes, so more fuel than was
customarily found in Dakota was available. Perhaps,
Toby thought, they might even find young plant shoots
they could eat as a fresh vegetable.

It was his duty to fish and hunt, but he was in no rush,
knowing that fish were plentiful in the Missouri and that
game abounded in the region. His first task was to wash
the accumulated grime of several days' travel from his
body. The day was warm, and he stripped, leaving his
clothes and weapons at the top of the gentle slope of the
riverbank. He plunged into the Missouri, enjoying himself despite the coldness of the water. One of the joys of
wilderness travel, he reflected, was that of swimming
and cleansing oneself in a mighty river.

Refreshed and dripping as he emerged from the
water, Toby started up the bank to the place where he
had left his clothes and weapons, then paused in surprise. Standing some yards from him, grazing on the
new spring grass, was a large bull buffalo, at least one
ton in weight. Toby could not remember when he had
seen a large male buffalo separated from its herd, although he knew that occasionally a rogue was inclined
to wander off by himself.

As he climbed the bank, Toby grinned. The buffalo,
he thought, was saving him the trouble of hunting this

afternoon. To his further surprise, the buffalo neither bolted nor moved away but continued to nibble at the grass. This was extraordinary because the beasts were shy and never lingered in the presence of humans.

The buffalo lowered its head, its horns pointing almost straight at the man as it snorted and pawed the ground. Obviously it had no fear and, on the contrary, was demanding a direct confrontation.

Toby quickly retreated into the water, where he considered his dilemma. He caught a glimpse of the creature's tiny, bloodshot eyes, which looked glazed, and thought he knew the answer. Then he examined the grass as best he could from a distance, and the mystery was solved,

Every ranch owner in the West quickly learned to beware of a plant popularly known as "locoweed." It created violent belligerence in any animal unfortunate enough to sample it. The buffalo had become temporarily insane, and the huge creature, recognizing a foe, was eager to fight.

Twice more Toby tried to reach the pile of clothes and weapons, but both times the buffalo drove him back into the water. He was no match for the creature without his firearms, but the buffalo was a notoriously stupid animal, and perhaps he could capitalize on that. He called to Gentle Doe, cautioning her, however, not to reply, and to approach as quietly as she could.

She obeyed him, silently creeping toward the sound of his voice, then halted abruptly when she saw the huge buffalo grazing on locoweed.

"The critter is dangerous," he called to her from the river, "so make certain you stay upwind of him. Can you handle a gun?"

She was unfamiliar with firearms and looked miserable and confused as she shook her head.

"Never mind," Toby told her soothingly. "Just do as I tell you. Creep closer to my belongings yonder, take one of my pistols from its holster, and move back to where you're now standing."

She did so, taking great care not to arouse the buffalo's attention. Under ordinary circumstances it would have become aware of Gentle Doe's presence. But the powerful effect of the locoweed dulled its senses.

Toby breathed a trifle more easily when he saw his six-shooter in Gentle Doe's grasp. "Cock the gun," he called, and gave her precise instructions in how to perform that feat.

Gentle Doe obeyed silently.

"Now listen carefully," Toby said. "When I give you the signal, point the pistol at the buffalo and squeeze the trigger. The gun has a strong kick to it, so hang on. Otherwise, it'll jump right out of your hand. I know you've never before fired a pistol, so your aim may not be much good. Don't worry about it. It doesn't have to be good. Maybe the shot will scare the buffalo off. At the very least it will distract his attention long enough for me to reach my rifle. There are six bullets in the gun. Don't be afraid to use them."

Gentle Doe, although nervous, was determined. Looking far more afraid of the gun than of the beast, she pointed the six-shooter awkwardly at the buffalo, gripping the pistol with both hands.

"Now!" Toby called. He sprinted up the bank toward his clothes and the precious rifle that could mean the difference between life and death.

A pistol shot shattered the silence, and a gaggle of

geese rose into the air, honking loudly and flapping their wings. Confused by the explosive sound, the buffalo turned slowly toward it, blinking as it tried to focus on the noise.

Gentle Doe, her heart pumping wildly, saw that Toby still had several yards to go before he reached his rifle. Grimacing, she braced herself and fired the pistol again.

The second shot reverberated across the endless plains as Toby finally reached his rifle and bent and snatched it from the ground. The crazed buffalo managed to identify its new enemy as the dimly seen woman and started toward her. The terrified Gentle Doe fired the six-shooter wildly and missed the beast completely.

Toby knew that the buffalo would pick up speed as it charged. Consequently, he would have no time to reload, and that meant he would have to make good his first shot, or Gentle Doe would be trampled to death before he had a chance to fire a second time.

He heard the shot of the pistol again, then yet again, but he paid no attention to it. Gentle Doe was shooting wildly. The flashes and the sound of the pistol enraged the buffalo, and the ground shook beneath its hoofs as it pounded toward the woman.

Raising his rifle to his shoulder, Toby looked down the length of his barrel, sighted his target, and squeezed the trigger. The deep roar of the heavier weapon obliterated the sound of the pistol.

The huge buffalo stopped and stood still.

Toby assumed that the loud rifle shot had temporarily paralyzed the creature with fear but that the buffalo would recover momentarily and would resume its charge. He dropped his rifle and snatched his other six-shooter from its holster. Before he could fire the smaller weapon, however, he saw a spreading patch of crimson on the left side of the buffalo's shaggy coat, and the animal crumpled to the ground.

The awed voice of Gentle Doe broke the silence. "Toby," she whispered, "is the mightiest of hunters." She came up to him and put a trembling hand on his bare arm. "You have saved the life of Gentle Doe," she whispered.

Toby turned to her, intending to soothe her. "You also saved my life," he told her, smiling. "If it weren't for you, I'd still be standing down there in the river."

She looked up at him, her gaze direct and penetrating. Her hands slid up his bare chest, then clutched his back and pulled him close.

The emotional impact of the moment was so overwhelming that Toby was incapable of protesting, of stepping backward out of the woman's hold. Like Gentle Doe, all Toby knew was that they had looked death in the face and were still alive.

He was a healthy, robust male, who had been separated for far too long from the wife he loved. Gentle Doe was in love with him, and he stood nude as he embraced this girl who wanted him desperately.

Gentle Doe's teeth clamped on Toby's lower lip, she rubbed her body against his, pressed against him, and her nails clawed his bare back. Unable to control his own urges any longer, Toby crushed her to him.

Neither of them could later recall the details of how they had achieved their union. They had no idea whether Gentle Doe had removed her single garment or whether Toby had undressed her. They could not remember when he took the initiative and began making love to her as violently as she had initiated the exchange. All they knew was that the tensions that had built up between them had become unbearable. They found release in their explosive physical contact.

There was little conversation between them for the rest of the day. After they made love, they butchered the carcass of the buffalo and began the process of curing the hide. Then it was only natural for them to swim together in the Missouri River, and equally natural for them to resume their lovemaking when they emerged from the water.

That night Gentle Doe fell asleep cradled in Toby's arms, and the realization struck him that he was being unfaithful to Clarissa, the wife he loved, the wife who was bearing his child.

Vaguely Toby recalled hearing the story from his mother that, before marriage, his father had resumed relations with a young Indian woman with whom he had lived previously. The woman, apparently realizing that she stood in the way of Whip's real happiness, had vanished, and it had been assumed that she had done away with herself.

That was not likely to happen in this situation, nor would Toby want it to. But what was he to do? He was responsible for Clarissa and their baby. He was responsible, too, for Gentle Doe because he had lacked the strength to reject her. True, she had caught him at a moment when he had been defenseless, but that was no excuse. He had to face up to the realities of the situation. Still, how could he avoid hurting the people for whom he was responsible?

Gentle Doe sleepily pulled Toby's head down to hers so they could kiss, then nestled still closer to him. All Toby could think was that his dilemma appeared insolvable.

Chet and Clara Lou Harris were entertaining Wong
Ke and his wife in their white granite house on Nob
Hill, but the atmosphere in the Harris dining room was
not festive. Clara Lou was in mourning for her late
nephew, and Wong Mei Lo was in black, too, out of respect for her hostess. The conversation was labored because only one subject was on everyone's mind.

For a while, the men talked about business, but the
ladies felt so thoroughly excluded that they were actually relieved when Chet brought up the one topic all of
them had been avoiding.

"I understand from Sheriff Keeley," he said, "that Beth
is refusing all interviews. Every newspaper in San Francisco is eager to talk with her, of course, and correspondents have come from other papers all over the country.
The sheriff is willing to cooperate with them, but Beth
has flatly refused. She says she has nothing to say."

"I'm sure she doesn't," Clara Lou said bitterly.

Wong Ke and Mei Lo exchanged a quick glance, and
his wife's nod meant that she intended to intervene. "We
certainly understand how you feel, Clara Lou," she said.
"We know that you were fond of Leon and proud of
him. But we can't help feeling there's more to this case
than meets the eye."

"The facts speak all too loudly for themselves," Clara
Lou replied icily. "Beth Martin may be the daughter of
General Blake and may have masqueraded as a happily
married woman, but she's nothing but a trollop. Look at
the way she was dressed when the constables burst into
Leon's bedroom."

Chet was torn. "It's possible there may have been mit-
igating circumstances, dear," he said. "Ke and I have
discussed the whole, strange case several times, and it

seems to us that several pieces of the puzzle are missing."

Clara Lou shook her head adamantly. "I ask you—what was Beth doing in Leon's bedroom in the first place, and why was she half-naked? Answer those questions for me. The newspapers said that she flatly admitted having shot Leon. So I don't think there's any question of her guilt. I'll grant you that I have reason to feel more strongly than most, but I won't be satisfied until she's hanged."

Chet was shocked by the severity of his wife's views, but, loving Clara Lou, he did his best to understand how she felt. She was an independent, usually open-minded woman, but in this case someone dear to her—in fact, her only living relative, her sister having died years ago—had been taken from her, and she wanted to see the guilty party pay.

The opinion-makers of San Francisco—the industrialists and bankers, the newspaper editors and publishers, the shipping magnates and the manufacturers—were almost unanimous in echoing the opinions held by Clara Lou Harris. The men, meeting for lunch at their clubs, took it for granted that their peers felt as they did.

Their wives were even more adamant, and everywhere the reaction was the same: "I don't care what anyone says about her background, Beth Martin is nothing but a courtesan, and I feel sorry for her poor husband!"

Meanwhile, the object of all this attention was imprisoned in the Market Street jail, held without bail, as was the law in murder cases. She remained silent in her cell, refusing to communicate with the press and insisting that she required no legal representation. Sheriff Keeley chose not to press the matter.

Beth remained in a daze. She only picked at her food, and the deep rings beneath her eyes were testimony that she slept poorly. In addition, she was morose with her jailers, answering in monosyllables when they tried to make conversation with her.

"You have some visitors, Mrs. Martin," the sheriff said as he unlocked the door of her cell. "Come along to the visitors' room."

Beth stiffened. "I'm expecting no one," she said.

"All the same," he answered quietly, "your father and stepmother have come down from Fort Vancouver to see you."

She became panicky, clenching her fists and facing him defiantly. "I didn't ask them to come! I don't want to see them! They have no right to interfere!"

"You'll have to speak to General Blake yourself and tell him how you feel, Mrs. Martin." The sheriff was sympathetic but firm. "I was head of his military police detail when he was commandant of the Presidio, and I'm damned if I'm going to refuse him. So come along, please."

Beth tossed her blond hair defiantly, then stalked out into the corridor and followed the sheriff toward the visitors' room in the adjoining wing. She didn't feel as if she belonged to anyone. Her father and stepmother had become strangers to her, just as her husband had, and she wanted to be left alone.

Sheriff Keeley opened the door, and Beth stepped inside the room. The door closed softly behind her. Eulalia and Lee Blake, sitting on the far side of the chamber, rose.

Beth, facing them defiantly, noted that they looked tired and careworn. She noted, too, that her father was wearing civilian attire rather than his major general's uniform. He looked all the more unfamiliar to her, distant and strange.

No one spoke a word. They looked at her, and still standing, she looked about the pale blue walls of the stark room. Suddenly Eulalia broke the spell by swiftly crossing the room and taking Beth into her arms and kissing her. She was closely followed by her husband. Their affection was so unexpected that Beth was confused.

"We came," Lee said huskily, "as soon as I could get away from duty. Eulalia wanted to come ahead of me, but I preferred to have her wait and accompany me."

Eulalia put an arm around her stepdaughter's slender shoulders. There were tears in her eyes. "We just want you to know, Beth," she said, "that we stand behind you. No matter what the evidence is against you, we believe in you, and we know you've done nothing to be ashamed of."

"If you killed the man," Lee said, "you had good cause. If you were dressed as the press claims you were when the police burst in on you, we're sure there's an explanation for that, too."

Their belief in her, their solid, unquestioning support, so astonished her that she could not reply. She tried to speak, but the words wouldn't come, and all at once, unexpectedly, she burst into tears.

Eulalia cradled Beth in her arms and gestured to Lee, who produced a clean, neatly folded handkerchief, which he pressed into his daughter's hand.

Beth regained her composure and blew her nose vigorously. Then Eulalia led her to a chair as she would have led a small child and pressed her into it. "Your father and I," she said, "need no explanations. We'll have many opportunities to talk because we're staying in San

Francisco until this whole mess is resolved. If you want to confide in us, do, but it isn't necessary. We believe in you."

Beth threatened to break down again but managed to control herself.

Lee cleared his throat. "I wrote to your husband over a week ago and sent a military courier to find him."

"I'm sure he'll come to San Francisco as soon as he receives your father's letter," Eulalia said, then gently added, "His parents feel as we do and have confidence in you."

Beth clenched her fists and forced herself to look first at her stepmother, then at her father. "I owe both of you an apology," she said. "I hope you can find it in your hearts to forgive me. I hated you when you got married because I thought you were insulting Mother's memory. I realize now that I was mistaken, and I'm sorry for any heartache I caused you."

Eulalia reached out and stroked her arm and shoulder. "There's no need to explain, dear," she said. "We understand. As long as the air is cleared between us, that's all we ask."

Beth sniffed loudly. "I wonder," she said hesitantly, "if I could ask a favor of you?"

"Anything," Eulalia told her.

"Let me make it clear that I have no intention of hiding anything from either of you," Beth said. "I've made up my mind—since coming into this room—that I'm going to tell you the whole sordid story of what happened at Leon Graham's house. But I can't bring myself to talk about it yet. It's so disgusting that it makes me ill just to think about it. So, be patient with me, please."

"Of course we'll wait," Eulalia said.

"Satisfying our curiosity is the least of your problems,"

Lee added. "But I'm afraid you're going to have to speak frankly and fully to an attorney right away."

"An attorney?" Beth asked, and looked stricken.

"Apparently," Lee said somberly, "you don't grasp the seriousness of your situation. You face a trial on a charge of murder. If you're found guilty, you may be hanged. The court might show you leniency because you're a woman, but at the very least they'd sentence you to spend the rest of your life in prison."

"I know," Beth said, but it was obvious from her indifference that the enormity of the charge had not yet sunk in. She was still traumatized by the experience.

"I'm not unknown in San Francisco," Lee said, "and neither is your stepmother. We intend to use all our influence on your behalf. I'll engage the best attorney in San Francisco. We're fighting for your life, Beth."

His fierce loyalty, like that of Eulalia, almost swept Beth off her feet. She did not deserve such staunch, unquestioning support, she thought, and tears welled up in her eyes and streamed down her cheeks. She was not alone in a hostile, alien world, as she had assumed, and perhaps her future was not as bleak as she had imagined it.

VII

Rob Martin had been working seven days a week since coming to the Sierra Nevada to oversee the laying of the track for the Central Pacific Railroad, which eventually would join with the Union Pacific Railroad being constructed in the East. It was estimated that they would be joined somewhere in Utah, and then iron rails would span the North American continent. Rob, pleased with the progress of his crews, who were laying as much as a mile of track a day despite the difficult, mountainous terrain, believed the job would be finished ahead of schedule. The price for all this, however, was that he had been unable to get down to San Francisco to visit Beth as he had hoped. There was simply too much work to do.

Then the news arrived that meant his role in the building of the railway line would have to wait. He departed immediately for San Francisco, taking a special work train that traveled on the already completed tracks between Sacramento, California, and the construction site in the mountains.

Rob felt as though he'd been kicked in the stomach by a mule; it was hard for him to think clearly. The news in his father-in-law's letter had been so shocking that he was scarcely able to absorb it. It was almost impossible for him to believe that Beth, his restrained wife, who had been so unresponsive to his lovemaking of late, had not only had an affair but had also killed her lover in cold blood.

After the train arrived in Sacramento, Rob took the short steamboat ride down the Sacramento River into San Francisco. Throughout his trip, he tried desperately to organize his thoughts and his feelings. Regardless of what Beth had done, Rob knew that he had to help her. No matter how shaky his loyalty to his wife had become, he was prepared to do his duty by her. And thanks to the gold mine that he and Toby Holt had found, he had ample funds to meet the crisis.

Whether he remained married to Beth was another matter, one he was not yet prepared to face. He knew he had to be fair to her, that his marital loyalty was being put to the supreme test. All the same, he was jealous of the man for whom she had dressed in nothing but a pair of black stockings and what had been described in the newspaper he bought in Sacramento as a "filmy gown of transparent silk."

At the heart of his torment was a nagging question: Was it possible that Beth had been unfaithful to him for months before the separation that had taken him to the Sierra Nevada? He had no way of knowing. He knew only that she had been indifferent to him for many months. True, she had once admitted to him that the fault had been in her and not in him, that she was not in control of her emotions since her mother's death. But in spite of himself, Rob could not help wondering whether any feelings for him had been cooled because she was having affairs with other men.

When Rob arrived in San Francisco, he checked into a hotel, then went directly to the Market Street prison and identified himself to Sheriff Keeley.

"I'm awful glad you're here, young feller," the sheriff told him. "I've known your wife ever since she was a little tyke, when her father was commander at the Presidio, and I don't mind tellin' you, she's in a sorry state. She can use all the support and help she can get."

Rob was conducted to the visitors' room, and there he waited for his wife to be brought to him. Too nervous to sit, he paced the length of the chamber restlessly, thinking how odd it was that he and Beth should find themselves in this strange situation.

After a time the door opened to admit Beth to the chamber, then closed behind her. She stood uncomfortably, her hands at her sides, saying nothing.

Rob was momentarily stricken dumb, too. It had not occurred to him that she would be allowed to keep her own clothes, and he was surprised that she was wearing a dress that he had always liked. She wore makeup on her face, too, but the cosmetics could not conceal the lines etched in her forehead or the dark hollows beneath her eyes.

He knew he should go to her and kiss her, but his jealousy was so intense it rendered him motionless. She was in jail, he could not help thinking, because she had killed her lover.

"I'm sorry I couldn't have been here sooner," he said huskily. "I started as soon as I heard from your father."

"There's no need to apologize," Beth said in a small, strained voice. "I'm sorry you had to come on my account."

He searched his mind frantically for an answer. "It was the least I could do," he said, and immediately felt foolish.

She paused, uncertain, and the tension between them became greater as the silence became longer. "Won't you—sit down?" she asked formally, and in spite of herself, a slight, hollow laugh escaped from her lips.

Rob forced a smile as he sat on a plain, straight-backed chair and carefully brushed away an imagined speck of dust on his trousers. "I trust they're—treating you well here?" he asked.

"Oh, yes," she replied. "Sheriff Keeley is very nice. If there's any dish they are serving that I don't like, he sees to it that I get something else. Of course this isn't the Palace Hotel."

"If you like," Rob offered, "I'll have your meals sent into you from the Palace kitchens."

"Thank you, " Beth replied, "but I don't want you going to the expense and bother."

"Hang the expense, and it's really no bother," he said.

She shook her head, thinking it odd that they were conversing like two strangers. "I wish you wouldn't," she said. "I'm not all that interested in food."

His offer had been rebuffed, and he felt hurt. "Let me know if you change your mind," he said.

Beth wanted to scream, to claw down the wall they were erecting between them. But it was impossible for her to take the initiative, to put a hand on his arm and tell him how grateful she was that he had come to see her. She could guess how much that gesture had cost him, and what a blow the news had to be to his pride. But she couldn't explain how she had found herself in such a strange situation without telling him the whole, sordid story of her betrayal and captivity. It was too much to expect that any man, even a husband who had loved her, could believe that she could have been so naive, so trusting.

Rob took a deep breath, then tried to start a fresh conversation. "You're intending to put up a fight in court against the charges?" he asked.

She shrugged listlessly.

He became agitated. "You've got to fight," he said. "If you don't, you'll spend the rest of your life in prison."

"I'm not sure that would be the worst thing in the world," Beth replied.

"Thanks to our mine," he said, "we have no financial worries. I'm going to hire the best lawyer in San Francisco."

"Please don't bother," she said dully.

He was unable to conceal his irritation. "Damnation! It's no bother."

"I'm sorry, Rob," she said, penitent. "What I meant to say was that just a few days ago my father said that he was going to find a lawyer for me."

"I'll see your father immediately," he said. "I appreciate his offer, but I prefer to pay the attorney's fees myself."

Beth struggled to find the right words. "That's very kind of you," she told him, and hated herself because her reply was inadequate.

"It's the very least I can do," he told her. "Your name is Martin, and you *are* my wife."

"I am, more's the pity."

He looked at her sharply. "What is that supposed to mean?"

She looked at him sorrowfully and said, "I can never, as long as I live, find the words to apologize to you for dragging you into this and for trailing your good name in mud."

He waved aside her apology but was so stone-faced that she interpreted his generosity as indifference.

Beth knew that whether or not Rob believed her, the air would not be cleared unless she explained the lurid tragedy to him in full detail. But she could not force herself to speak of that day, even though she realized she was asking far too much of this man, who was her husband.

"What happened . . . that day," she began, "is . . . was . . . so complicated that I can't talk about it now. I'm sure, though, that all of the facts will come out in court."

Rob knew she was making a great effort, and his heart ached for her. At the same time, however, he was angry at her. She had told the San Francisco constables that she had shot Leon Graham. How she had happened to be in his house in such bizarre, intimate circumstances had never been explained, and, as before, he could draw only one conclusion.

Unable to tolerate the tensions any longer, he rose awkwardly. "I'll come to see you again, if I may, in the next day or two."

"By all means," she replied. "You're always welcome. I'll look forward to your visits."

Clenching her fists, she silently willed him to approach and kiss her. But Rob made no move in her direction. Bowing slightly, he reached for the bellpull that would notify the prison authorities that the interview had come to an end.

Not until Beth was making her way back to her cell, with Sheriff Keeley walking beside her, did she break

down. Then she covered her face with her hands and
wept silently.

The sheriff took her arm. "Keep your chin up, Beth,"
he told her. "You have a long, rough road ahead."

Rob, breathing the fresh air of freedom, walked rapidly up the hill to his hotel. He mulled over the meeting
he had just had with Beth, and the more he thought
about it, the more indifferent and cold she had seemed.
It was as though she didn't care whether he visited her
or not. He stopped suddenly and stared at his feet.
There was no reason for him to stay in San Francisco, if
that was how she felt. He had a tremendous job to do,
and rather than stay here and be an unwanted daily visitor to his wife—a nuisance to her, it seemed—he would
await the outcome of the trial in the mountains, where
work would take his mind off the tragedy. He determined to leave right away. After the trial would be time
enough to decide whether he could ever again live with
Beth as his wife. At this point he simply did not know
how he felt.

When Ernie von Thalman walked into a room, everyone took note. Though now in his early eighties, the
one-time Austrian baron still had a barrel chest, a mas-
sive head, and his years of marriage to the Pennsylvania
widow, Emily Harris, had added considerable girth to
his physique. His shock of white hair, combined with his
impeccable wardrobe, gave him a distinguished air, and
the horn-rimmed glasses perched on the bridge of his
nose added an intellectual touch. As his stepson, Chet
Harris, once remarked, "Your years as Oregon's delegate
to the U.S. Congress before the acquisition of statehood
really did things for you, Dad. You look so incredibly

like a federal judge that it's only natural President Lincoln appointed you to the bench."

Clara Lou Harris passed hot canapés to her in-laws and was gratified to note that Ernie, as always, ate everything that was offered to him. Meanwhile, Chet poured his mother a glass of sack and then handed his stepfather a stronger drink of whiskey.

"You two," he said, "are about the last people I expected to see turning up in San Francisco."

Emily smiled and nodded. "I'll admit we were planning on spending the whole spring at home in Portland," she said, "but we can't always do what we like."

"We have plenty of room here for guests," Clara Lou said. "We can offer you a whole suite to yourselves. So I hope you'll come here with us."

Emily and Ernie exchanged a quick glance, and the gray-haired lady shook her head. "Thanks, my dear," she said. "You're very gracious, but it just wouldn't be feasible. We've already engaged a hotel suite."

Chet could not conceal his disappointment. "A suite," he said, "won't offer you nearly as much comfort or as many conveniences as you'd have here."

Ernie sipped his drink and spoke decisively. "I'm sorry," he said, "but this is a strictly business visit."

"You're going to hear a trial here?" Chet asked.

Ernie nodded. "Yes," he said. "I've been assigned the case by the presiding judge for the Oregon-California Circuit."

"Are we allowed to know which case?" Chet asked curiously.

Ernie nodded. "I don't see why not. It'll be announced in the press in the next couple of days. I'm going to preside at the murder trial of Beth Martin."

The air was suddenly charged, and Clara Lou drew in

her breath. "I'm glad to hear it!" she said emphatically. "If there's one thing that Beth Martin deserves—"

"One moment! Don't say anything more!" Ernie commanded. "I find myself in a very odd position in this case. Remember that Emily and I came to Oregon on the first wagon train, so we've been good friends all these years of Lee and Cathy Blake, Whip and Eulalia Holt. And please don't forget that Bob Martin has been our family doctor."

"Not to mention the fact that Tonie Martin is one of our closest friends," Emily added.

"On top of everything else," Ernie said, "we've not only known Beth herself practically since she was born, but also the victim in this murder case was the nephew of my daughter-in-law. I tried hard to disqualify myself from the case, and I put in a formal request to the presiding judge of the circuit court to assign someone else to it. He refused, however. He insisted that I hear the case, and he made a point of saying that because I presided at other murder trials involving women, I was by far the best qualified judge in the district to hear it. So I've made several hard and fast rules, which must be obeyed." He sipped his drink and looked hard, first at Chet, then at Clara Lou.

Chet knew that expression of his stepfather's. When Ernie's mouth formed a hard, thin line and his eyes stared right through the person he was addressing, he could not be moved.

"I made my position clear to the Martins before we left Oregon," Ernie said, "and I intend to have a few words with Lee and Eulalia when we meet them in the next day or two. Under no circumstances will I discuss this case—or any aspect of it—with anyone. Beth Martin—past, present, and future—is a forbidden subject. So is Leon Graham, and so is anyone else involved to any degree, whatsoever, with this case. I will walk out of any group in which the subject is raised, and I not only won't talk about the trial, but I refuse to hear anything about it."

"We understand, Dad," Chet replied.

"Good," Ernie said firmly. "As I said, I didn't ask to be assigned this case, and I did my best to avoid it. But it's been given to me, and I'm going to do my damnedest to live up to my oath of office. I believe in letting justice be done, and so it shall, in the trial of Beth Martin!"

Repercussions of the murder of Leon Graham were felt keenly at Fort Vancouver in Washington. There, during the absence of Lee and Eulalia Blake in San Francisco, Cindy Holt and Hank Purcell continued to attend school daily, living under the watchful and protective gazes of Clarissa Holt, the Blake housekeeper, and the general's master sergeant.

One morning Cindy and Hank came down for breakfast at their customary hour. Clarissa, her baby due at any time, was sleeping in, and the housekeeper served them.

Hank began the serious business of eating his morning meal. It consisted of oatmeal, pancakes and sausages, bacon and eggs, and a salmon steak, all of which he consumed with great gusto. Cindy, however, merely nibbled at a slice of toast and barely touched her oatmeal.

"Hey," Hank said, "you ought to try some of this salmon that the sergeant caught last night. It's good."

"I'm sure it is," the girl replied listlessly, "but I'm not hungry."

Hank peered at her as he shoved the last big chunk of

salmon steak into his mouth. "What's the matter?" he demanded.

"Nothing," she replied vaguely.

"Ah, come on. Tell me what's wrong."

She hesitated, took a deep breath, and to his chagrin, her eyes filled with tears.

"It ain't—isn't *that* bad!" he protested.

"You have no idea how horrid it really is," she replied.

Aware that her distress was genuine, he softened his approach. "Can I help, whatever it is?" he asked.

"There's nothing you or anybody else can do," she told him. "What's done has been done—and that's that."

Hank's instinct told him to say nothing and to wait for Cindy to reveal the problem to him.

His hunch proved correct. She drew a deep, tremulous breath and then said, "It's that Billy Kramer and that whole bunch he runs around with. They surrounded me during recess at school yesterday, and Billy started off by asking me if I was going to be as big a whore as my stepsister."

"What?" Hank was astounded.

"That was just the beginning," Cindy said. "They said so many mean, awful things about Beth that I closed my ears to them."

He continued to stare at her openmouthed.

"I don't like talking to Clarissa about problems when her baby is due so soon, but I couldn't help myself last night," she said. "I went to her, and she wormed the whole story out of me."

"What did she say?" Hank asked.

"Well," Cindy said, "Clarissa told me she has every confidence in Beth, but I'm not sure she meant it. I think she was trying to convince herself. Anyway, she said to

let the insulting remarks of Billy Kramer and Karl
Gustafson and that whole crowd go in one ear and out
the other. But it's much easier to say than do."

Hank nodded, becoming tight-lipped. Leaning back in
his chair, he seemed to withdraw into a shell.

Moments later Clarissa, wrapped in a long dressing
gown, came downstairs for breakfast. Mr. Blake trotted
alongside her. Both Cindy and Hank were sensitive
enough to know that she had made the effort for their
sakes. Clarissa thought it only right that she say good-
bye to them before they went off to school.

"You ought to have some fresh salmon steak," Hank
told her. "It's terrific."

"Not for me, thank you," Clarissa said, smiling. "The
closer I come to having the baby, the less appetite I
have." She smiled up at Marie, the serving maid, who
brought her a pot of hot tea and a slice of dry toast.
"What were you two talking about when I came in? You
were both so serious."

"Nothing much. School, mostly," Cindy replied
vaguely.

Clarissa nodded. She suspected that the children were
discussing Beth Martin, as was almost everyone these
days, but she decided to keep the conversation going
along other lines. "I'm going to drop a line to Lee and
Eulalia later today. I'm sure they'll be relieved and
pleased to hear that you're both so serious about school."

Cindy sat at the table silently, obviously ill at ease.
Both she and Hank wore identical, strained expressions.
Then Hank excused himself and bolted from the table.
He did not return to the dining room but shouted to
Cindy that he was waiting for her in the front hall and
was ready to leave for school whenever she wished.

When she joined him, she noticed a bulge at his middle, beneath his sweater. But he made no mention of it, and her dread of further teasing by schoolmates preoccupied her so much that the bulge was soon forgotten.

Hank was reassuring. "You're going to feel a heap better today, and every day from now on," he told her solemnly. "Nobody in school is going to mention the name of Beth Martin to you again."

"How can you be so sure?" Cindy demanded.

Hank was evasive. "Just take my word for it," he said.

The house became silent once the teenagers had gone, and Clarissa sat alone in the dining room, sipping her tea. The baby kicked her, and Clarissa had to fight off a wave of loneliness. With the baby due to arrive at any time, she felt isolated and couldn't help wishing that Toby would appear at the door and tell her that he had ridden all the way from Dakota in order to be with her during her travail.

Clarissa was too sensible, however, to indulge in romantic daydreams. She had not heard from Toby since receiving a letter that Andy Brentwood had mailed for him from Fort Shaw after their meeting. The U.S. Postal Service did not operate in the wild hinterlands of the Dakota Territory in which Toby was traveling. Both of them had known that it would be weeks—perhaps months—after their baby was born before he learned about the state of the infant and its mother. This was one of the penalties they had to pay for Toby's acceptance of a patriotic duty.

She pictured him in her mind, rugged and handsome, and she smiled. How much she loved him, and she knew now that he loved her. The doubts, the tensions, the problems of the past were forgotten, and when he returned to her, she would hold him in her arms and not let him go for a long time. He was hers and hers alone.

Pouring herself another cup of tea and adding a little lemon and sugar to it, Clarissa reflected that her situation, no matter how sorry she might feel for herself, was far better than the terrible fix that Beth Martin was in.

She knew Beth well, having shared a house with her for months at Fort Shaw, and she felt desperately sorry for her. She was aware that there had been tensions between Beth and Rob and that Beth had indulged in some strange and temperamental behavior over the last two years. These things gave a certain validity to the charges being made in the press against her. All the same, Clarissa doubted that she was as dissolute as she had been pictured.

On the other hand, Clarissa had to admit it was inexplicable, at least according to the newspaper reports, that Beth had admitted shooting the man with whom she had been found in such a compromising situation. She had no explanation for that conduct.

She wished Toby would be coming home right away, for far more than her own selfish reasons. Rob Martin was her husband's lifelong, best friend, and if he'd ever needed anyone, she suspected that Rob badly needed a friend right now.

A violent cramp suddenly gripped Clarissa, almost doubling her over, and scattered her thoughts. Was her labor beginning? It was too soon to know for sure, though she had also experienced some irregular pains throughout the night. She remembered Dr. Martin's warning, however. As soon as she began to suffer pains at frequent intervals, she was to send a messenger across the river to his office to notify him, then she was to check into the post hospital at Fort Vancouver.

A cramp came again, this time even more severe, and as Clarissa cried out softly, Mr. Blake, sitting at her heels, barked.

"Go find Marie," Clarissa instructed the dog, too weak to call for the serving maid herself. "Go on, boy," she repeated, and gasped.

Mr. Blake dashed out of the kitchen, looking for the maid. She was not in the parlor or any of the upstairs rooms, and the dog understood she must be outside. All the doors were closed, however, and he scampered back and forth, trying to figure out what to do. Suddenly Clarissa cried out again, and at once Mr. Blake began howling. The back door opened, and the serving maid came in, her arms filled with clothes she was laundering. She dropped her bundle and followed Mr. Blake to the kitchen where Clarissa sat, breathing deeply. At once, the serving maid ran out of the house to find someone to go and get Dr. Martin.

Mr. Blake came up to Clarissa, and despite her weakened condition, she managed to pat him on the head and murmur, "Good boy, Mr. Blake."

Clarissa continued to take deep breaths, which eased the pain somewhat. *I've got to be big, brave, and strong,* she thought—*but oh! how I wish Toby were here with me!*

En route to school, Cindy Holt finally asked Hank Purcell about the strange bulge beneath his sweater.

"What you don't know isn't going to hurt you," he replied.

"Oh," she said, miffed.

He could never bring himself to admit that he was attracted to her and was going to do something to protect her. Such an admission would be mortifying. But he found a way around the dilemma of what to tell her in regard to his intentions. "General Blake always tells me that a lady has to be treated special-like," he said, "and so I've got something under here to let everyone know you're a lady."

Cindy was confused by Hank's words, but there were many occasions when he did not make sense. Anyway, his answer made her feel better, and she beamed at him. "Thank you very much," she said. "That's sweet of you to say, Hank."

His face reddened. His jaw jutted forward; he was more determined than ever to protect her.

He soon had his chance. As they drew nearer to the school, located in the center of a patch of woods outside the palisades of Fort Vancouver, he saw Billy Kramer and Karl Gustafson, two students Cindy had named as her tormentors, lingering in the wooded area. He suspected they were experimenting with chewing tobacco, for which they would get their ears boxed by the retired drill instructor who was one of the school teachers. But their reason for loitering did not interest him. He was glad to see them and immediately took advantage of the situation.

"You go ahead," he said to Cindy. "I'll see you in the classroom."

She looked at him, a question in her eyes.

"I have a mite of business to attend to," he said, and waved her ahead brusquely.

Her common sense told her not to protest or linger, and she went on to the school.

Hank sauntered toward the grove of trees and raised a hand in a half-salute to the two other boys. They eyed him suspiciously, for he was an outsider, a newcomer to the school. Also, he lived under the protection of General Blake, the highest-ranking officer at the post, and that automatically made them dislike him.

Hank smiled gently. "I hear tell," he said, "that you lads gave Cindy a rough time yesterday on the subject of her stepsister, Mrs. Martin."

Billy, who was bull-necked and brawny, almost a head taller than Hank, glowered at the smaller boy. "What the hell business is it of yours?" he demanded.

Hank continued to smile quietly and did not raise his voice. "I'm making it my business. Mrs. Martin is General Blake's daughter, and not only has he treated me pretty wonderful, but she was awful good to me, too, when I was down and out. So I don't take kindly to slurs and nasty remarks about her."

Karl Gustafson looked at Hank and sneered. "Who gives a hang whether you take kindly to something or not? If we choose to call a whore by her right name, what business is it of yours?"

Hank reached swiftly beneath his sweater, and suddenly a six-shooter appeared in his hand. He spun the cylinder expertly as he trained the pistol first on Billy and then on Karl. They backed away from him. It was rumored that he was an expert marksman, a far better shot than anyone in the infantry or cavalry at Fort Vancouver. Furthermore, they didn't like the gleam they saw in his eyes.

"This here," Hank said in a conversational tone, "is a precision weapon made in New England by Mr. Colt. It shoots six bullets, and I'd only need two of them to take care of you lousy, big-mouthed varmints forever."

Like all bullies, Billy Kramer was petrified by the

threat of superior force. "If you shoot us," he said,
"they'll arrest you and hang you!"

Hank laughed. "I never yet heard of anybody being
arrested for killing a rat," he said. "In some territories
they pay bounties for them. All I got to do is to tell
General Blake that I was protecting his daughter's honor
when you two called her a whore, and I guess he won't
be too strict about ordering the military police to throw
me in jail."

"You—you scare the liver out of me when you go point-
in' that gun at me," Karl cried. "Point it somewheres
else!"

"I'll do a heap more than scare the liver out of you,
Gustafson," Hank said, and his voice took on a frighten-
ing tone. "I aim to shoot your yellow liver right out of
your body unless I hear an apology for that name-calling
you did about Beth Martin."

"I'm sorry, I'm sorry!" Karl stammered. "Honest, I
am!"

The pistol pointed at Billy, who became panicky. "I
didn't say nothin'!" he cried.

Hank shook his head sorrowfully. "Instead of killing
you," he said, "I think I'll shoot off your lips and then
blast your tongue right out of your mouth. That way
you'll be a living example not to tell lies."

He was so in earnest that the color drained from the
bigger boy's face. "If I said anythin' bad about Mrs.
Martin," he said, "I take it back!"

"If I was you," Hank said severely, "I'd do a heap
more than take it back. I'd be careful never to say another word to a living soul about Mrs. Martin. And I'd
be very careful never to mention her name in front of
Cindy Holt again."

The other boys nodded, swallowing hard.

"Spread the word," Hank said. "Tell everyone that I've taken it on myself to protect the good name of Mrs. Martin, and I particularly don't want anybody upsetting Cindy Holt with name-calling and insinuations about her stepsister." Again he spun the pistol's chamber. The click was ominous.

Billy and Karl outdid each other in the vehemence of their protests that they would not make any more derogatory comments about Beth Martin, especially to her stepsister, Cindy.

They were interrupted by the ringing of a handbell. Students were being summoned to school, and any who failed to be in their seats within three minutes would be required to remain for an hour and a half of written exercises after the day's classes ended.

Hank's pistol disappeared quickly beneath his sweater. "You better step lively, boys," he said, "so you're not late for school. We want to grow up to be law-abiding, decent citizens, all of us, and being punctual is the first step." He smiled innocently as he followed the pair out of the patch of woods into the school building.

Hank knew he had not halted the gossip about Beth Martin, but at least Cindy would be subjected to no more vicious teasing, and that, more than anything else, was what mattered to him.

The day passed without incident, and that afternoon, when they got home, they were informed by the housekeeper that Mrs. Holt had been taken to the post hospital.

They raced as fast as their legs could carry them across the parade ground to the hospital. When they arrived, they were directed toward a sitting room, where they were instructed to wait.

Only a short distance down the hall, Clarissa Holt awakened in her small room. She dimly recalled having suffered such agonizing pains that Dr. Martin had given her a bitter drink of laudanum. After swallowing it, she had dozed. Now, opening her eyes, she saw the gray-haired doctor smiling down at her.

"Don't look so worried, Clarissa," the elderly physician said. "Everything is just fine!"

"How . . . how's my baby?"

"Seven and a half pounds," he answered heartily. "And in all of the years that I've practiced medicine, I've never seen a healthier little boy. He looks like a true Holt. In fact, if firearms weren't forbidden in this hospital, I daresay he'd have been born with a couple of six-shooters on his belt."

She laughed feebly. "When may I see him?"

"I'll have him brought to you as soon as you get your bearings. There's no rush about this," Dr. Martin added, "but when you decide on a name for the baby, let me know so I can complete the birth certificate."

"I can tell you right now," Clarissa said. "We're going to call him Tim."

Dr. Martin was surprised, having taken it for granted that a male child would be named Michael Holt, after Whip, his grandfather. "May I ask if the name has significance?" he inquired.

Clarissa smiled broadly. "Indeed it does, and Toby and I were agreed on it from the time we learned that I was going to have a baby. The first Tim Holt was the founder of the family in the New World. He came over from England in the seventeenth century, during the reign of Charles the Second, and he settled in Virginia. My father-in-law lost his parents when he was young, but he still remembered hearing about his forefather, to whom, apparently, all the male Holts bear a resemblance."

Dr. Martin chuckled. "In that case," he said, "I predict that your son is going to have a colorful life." He went out into the corridor and returned a few moments later, followed by a nurse carrying an infant wrapped in a blanket. The baby was handed to Clarissa.

Dr. Martin had long observed that all young mothers were radiant when they first gazed at their babies, and it was certainly true that Clarissa had never looked more beautiful than at this moment.

Holding the baby in one arm, Clarissa propped him on the pillow beside her and looked down at the tiny face. The pale blue eyes could have been those of her husband. "On behalf of Papa and me, welcome to the world, Tim," she whispered. "We're sorry—sorrier than you'll know for many years to come—that he isn't here to greet you himself, but he's very busy carrying out an assignment in the Dakota Territory for President Johnson and General Grant. I want you to have everything in the world that's good, and I'm going to help you in every way I can to grow up to be a man like Papa and Grandpa Holt."

Suddenly she was almost overcome by the feeling of loneliness for Toby, by a desire to have him near her. She knew she was asking for the impossible, but this time her practical, sensible nature did not assert itself, and she continued to want what she could not have. And Clarissa had a strong suspicion that she would feel this way until Toby came home to her and to the baby.

Ma Hastings appeared lost in thought as she rode at the head of her band across the Dakota prairie. Occa-

sionally she nodded and smiled to herself as though she
was well pleased. Suddenly she beckoned to Digger, and
her lieutenant spurred forward to the head of the
column and joined her.

"Ya know the Badlands pretty good, don't ya?" she
asked suddenly.

Digger, as always, was cautious. "I reckon so," he admitted.

"If I was to ask ya to meet me at a place called Five
Rocks, would ya know where to go?"

He laughed loudly. "I'd be stupid as all get-out if I
didn't, Ma," he said. "Everybody who's ever been to the
Badlands knows where Five Rocks is!"

He had answered her question, and she nodded,
pleased. "Digger," she said, "I worked out a perfect
plan. Ya can start diggin' a grave right now for that
there Toby Holt."

Digger knew that Ma had met with the Sioux chief
Tall Stone and had worked out some plan to do away
with Toby Holt, but he had not yet been informed of
the details. Even if he had been told, it was unlikely he
would have absorbed anything—Digger was known for
his shooting ability, not his brains.

"I've heard tell," Ma said, "that the best ideas are
simple ideas, and damned if it ain't true. This one is perfect. I'm gonna pay a Sioux brave to find Toby Holt and
give him a message. The brave will tell him there's goin'
to be an important powwow of Sioux chiefs to determine
if they're goin' to go to war with Thunder Cloud and the
Blackfoot and Cheyenne against the U.S.A. Holt is goin'
to tell himself that if he goes to the meetin', he'll be able
to talk the chiefs out of makin' war and will be able to
persuade 'em to sign peace treaties. Ya get it?"

Digger shook his head. "This is the first I've heard of any big meetin' with the chiefs," he said. "In fact, if anythin', I thought Toby Holt was gettin' them to change their minds about formin' an alliance."

Ma glared at him impatiently. "Sometimes," she said, "ya act as rattlebrained as my boy Ralph after he's polished off a couple of pints of gin! Of course there ain't no such meetin'! That's just the bait that'll send Holt racin' off to Five Rocks."

"If we set a trap for Toby Holt and kill him, Ma," Digger said soberly, "Colonel Brentwood and the whole blamed Eleventh Cavalry will track us and will shoot us down. They won't even bother to capture us and put us on trial."

Ma looked at him indignantly. "Ya think I'm so stupid I don't know that?" she demanded. "We'll be more'n a hundred miles from Five Rocks at the time. In fact, we'll go into some town and make ourselves known in the saloons and eatin' places, so we'll be able to blame well prove that we wasn't anywhere near the Badlands."

Digger was confused. "Then how—"

"Use your head!" Ma told him angrily. "Just remember we ain't the only ones in the world that ain't in love with Toby Holt. I already told ya, Tall Stone of the Sioux hates his livin' guts as much as I hate him, and he's gonna do our dirty work for us. I aim to let Tall Stone and any braves he wants to take with him represent us at Five Rocks. When Holt shows up there expectin' to attend a powwow of tribal leaders, it'll look for all the world like there's a meetin' goin' on. But Tall Stone and his braves will be lyin' in wait for him and will send him off to join his ancestors in one mighty hurry!"

Digger thought hard, reviewing the plan from every angle, and finally he chuckled. "I gotta hand it to ya, Ma," he said. "As near as I can see it, Toby Holt is as good as dead right this minute!"

VIII

Fort Pierre, a trading post located on the east bank of the Missouri River, was one of the principal American settlements in the Dakota Territory. It stood on an ancient site and originally had been the fortified capital of the Aricara Indians. Since the first settlers had begun to arrive in the territory in the early 1820s, it had become the trade center for traffic on the Missouri River. Settlers sent their wheat and corn to eastern markets via Fort Pierre, and the fur trade, although it had dwindled somewhat, was still an important industry.

Toby Holt had no reason to tarry in Fort Pierre, as his business in Dakota was with the Indians, not with the settlers. His desire to leave the town was influenced by his discomfort over his relationship with Gentle Doe. Having made love with her one day, he could not turn his back to her the next, and he was self-conscious about staying in Fort Pierre with the Indian woman who was so obviously his mistress.

Toby wanted to avoid flaunting his relationship with Gentle Doe. He felt guilty for the intimacy that had oc-

189

curred between them, and he prayed that this would never come between him and Clarissa. Still, for now, there was the situation to deal with. He was responsible for Gentle Doe, and until they went their separate ways, they were a pair, bonded as close as if they were man and wife.

Toby and Gentle Doe stayed in Fort Pierre just long enough to pick up needed supplies, to eat a noon meal at the Aricara Tavern, and to pick up the latest news there from Missouri River boatmen. From them he learned that with summer approaching, Thunder Cloud, Red Elk, and Big Knife had begun traveling to the various towns of the Sioux, the Blackfoot, and the Cheyenne, trying to rally their warriors. To be sure, some of the braves had the war fever, but most of the other braves of the three tribes were remaining strangely quiet. In fact, no uprisings had been reported, and no settlers had been attacked.

Toby concluded that his efforts to keep the peace had been effective and that the message he was trying to hammer home in his talks with the Indians was having the desired effect.

After dinner, he and Gentle Doe stopped at the U.S. Post Office in Fort Pierre, where he sent a telegram to General Grant and another to Colonel Andy Brentwood, telling them what he had learned. But he could not bring himself to write Clarissa, even to ask about their baby, who, he realized, had been born by now. His mind was too jumbled, too filled with thoughts of his relationship with Gentle Doe, and he could not find the words that he wanted to say to Clarissa.

Thus, Toby and Gentle Doe left Fort Pierre and headed back into the wilderness. They had gone only a short distance toward the north, however, when Toby became aware of a lone Sioux warrior, who rode behind them, his pace unvarying as he neither fell behind nor came forward.

"I'm afraid we're being followed," he said. "We'd better stop and find out what this is all about." He halted and turned his horse to the rear, one hand resting lightly on the butt of a six-shooter.

The brave, continuing to advance, raised his left hand over his head, palm outward, in the Indian gesture of friendship. Toby returned the salute, but his right hand remained on the butt of his pistol.

"You are Holt of the mountains, son of Holt of the mountains," the warrior said, speaking in the language of the Sioux.

Toby inclined his head but made no comment.

Gentle Doe, meanwhile, was watching the brave carefully. Her large eyes narrowed as she observed his facial expressions and listened to his tone.

"I have heard much of the travels of Holt," the brave said, and having been briefed by Ma Hastings, as well as having been promised a generous reward of liquor and gold from her, he spoke self-confidently and glibly. "I approve of the visits that Holt has made to the towns of my people, and it is my great hope that he will succeed in persuading them to exchange the wampum of peace with his government."

Toby nodded quietly.

"I want to help bring peace for all time to Dakota," the warrior declared earnestly. "So I have sought Holt of the mountains in order to give him news that will help him to make peace with the Sioux."

"What is the news that my friend brings to me?" Toby inquired politely.

"In the time of the half-moon," the warrior said, "leaders of the Sioux will gather to discuss the matter of war or peace. If Holt of the mountains were to go to that meeting, he could influence the chiefs, and they might vote in favor of peace, rather than war."

The words seemed almost too good to be true. Rather than continuing to traipse from one Sioux camp to the next, Toby would be able to reason with a number of chiefs all at one time.

"One rides through the Black Hills and comes to the Badlands," the warrior said. "There at a place called Five Rocks, the leaders of my people will gather."

"I know the place," Toby replied, thinking it odd that a rendezvous should be held in such a remote spot, "and I will be there in the time of a half-moon."

The brave's expression did not change, but he could not help thinking how easy it had been to earn the rich reward that Ma Hastings had promised him.

Gentle Doe, however, was not satisfied. "Why have you ridden far from your home and sought Holt of the mountains in order to tell him of this meeting?" she demanded.

Her unexpectedly aggressive question was almost too much for the young brave, and he came close to stumbling. But he managed to recover his aplomb sufficiently to reply in a manner that was convincing. "I seek the same goal that Holt of the mountains seeks," he said. "I have seen too much of war; I have seen my wife and children suffering because of war; and I want there to be peace between white and red. For this reason I have come to Toby Holt with news that I know will be of great value to him and will help me and my people, as well." Unwilling to run the risk of further questioning, he raised his left hand in a farewell salute, then turned and rode off quickly.

Toby sat in his saddle, watching the warrior's departure. "It may be that what he says is true," Toby said. "We have much to gain and little to lose by going to the meeting at Five Rocks."

"There is no village of the Sioux that is near to this place where we now pause," Gentle Doe said thoughtfully. "It is strange that a warrior of my people would ride a great distance to tell Toby Holt of the powwow of leaders in the Badlands. The Sioux will ride for vast distances through the wilderness when they know there will be a herd of buffalo waiting for them at the end of their journey. But never have I heard of a warrior of my people who has traveled a great distance when he has nothing to gain immediately."

Respecting her opinion, he removed his broad-brimmed hat and ran his fingers through his sandy-colored hair. "I hear the words that Gentle Doe speaks," he said, "and I shall heed them. We shall go to the rendezvous, but we shall keep our eyes and our ears open."

On the Dakota prairie, Ralph Hastings sat alone at one side of the campfire. His plate of venison and baked beans was untouched beside him, as was his mug of coffee. The liquor was beginning to wear off, so he turned his back on the others, reached beneath his shirt, lifted a bottle of gin to his lips, and drank greedily. A dulling of his senses was what he craved. He supposed that sooner or later the liquor would kill him, but he didn't care all that much.

Ralph occasionally admitted to himself that he was tired of the existence that he led and was ashamed of being the son of the leader of the most notorious gang of robbers in all of the Dakota and Montana territories. He took no pride in the band and respected neither his mother nor her associates. He hated them as he hated himself for his weakness.

It was much preferable to drift into the near oblivion that gin caused, to daydream idly, and to be in such a state that he could no longer differentiate between dreams and reality.

He never tired of his favorite dream, that he was a successful rancher respected by his neighbors and by himself. He imagined himself owning a vast spread that included a ranch house, barns and other outbuildings, a corral stocked with fine horses, and a herd of ever-increasing numbers of cattle.

Best of all, in his dream, he was married to a wife he loved and who loved him, Gentle Doe, the Indian girl to whom he had lost his heart when he had seen her during his mother's visit to Tall Stone. In his dreams he himself was a man of integrity, recognized for his virtues by all who knew him, and Gentle Doe, his wife, loved him because of his high standards and refusal to compromise with evil.

Again taking a swallow from his bottle of gin, Ralph was vaguely conscious of his mother's voice.

"I tell ya, Digger, the whole scheme worked perfectly," Ma said, chuckling. "It couldn't 'a' been better."

"Ya really think Toby Holt fell for the warrior's line?" Digger asked.

"That's what I'm tryin' to tell ya!" Ma was emphatic. "Our warrior watched with his own eyes from a safe distance, and Holt and the Indian girl who's travelin' with him were headin' due north from Pierre, but they turned west toward the Black Hills and the Badlands. He took the bait, hook, line, and sinker."

Ralph forced himself to concentrate. Gentle Doe, he knew, was traveling with Toby Holt, and he was interested in anything that concerned her, particularly anything that his mother might be planning. The very sound of her laugh was evil.

Listening attentively, straining so hard against the effects of the alcohol he had consumed that beads of sweat trickled down his face from his forehead, Ralph was able to piece together the scheme. His mother, he learned, had hired a Sioux brave to waylay Toby Holt and Gentle Doe and to convince them that leaders of his tribe were intending to hold a meeting in the Badlands at a place called Five Rocks. Then Ma had notified Tall Stone, the chief who had reasons of his own to hate Holt and the woman Ralph worshiped from afar. The couple was riding into an ambush, and Tall Stone and his followers would see to it that Toby and Gentle Doe lost their lives.

The scheme was so much worse than any other plot his mother had concocted that Ralph was horrified. He was both terrified and infuriated that Ma was planning an ambush in which Gentle Doe would be a victim.

He was in no condition to think clearly, much less to act. Before he could do anything else, he had to get sober. Picking up his mug of black coffee, he gulped half the contents, paused, gasped for breath, and shoveled venison stew and beans into his mouth. He had no appetite, no desire for food, but at the same time he realized that it was essential that he eat. Forcing himself to finish his meal, he then reached out to the coffee pot, which was still bubbling over the coals, and poured himself another hot mug. One way or another, he thought grimly, he had to get sober.

Ralph was not conscious of the passage of time. When he finally felt sober, other members of the band had rolled up in their blankets and gone to sleep. He alone was still awake. It was far easier for him to think coherently now, and he made his plans rapidly.

He knew that his mother's plan was already well advanced. Toby Holt and Gentle Doe were riding toward an ambush in the Badlands, and Tall Stone, along with his braves, would be lying in wait for them. The only way to prevent this violence would be to reach Holt and the woman and tell them about the scheme. That meant he would be forced to ride as he had never before ridden and display stamina greater than any he had ever exhibited previously.

Putting his plan into action without hesitation, Ralph helped himself to supplies from the band's store, taking bacon and beans, flour and parched corn, as well as dried venison and buffalo meat. He already had ample ammunition for his rifle and for his six-shooter, inasmuch as he had not fired either weapon in months. His horse was well rested, and he knew there was enough grass for the gelding to graze his way to the Badlands and back.

Ralph saddled his mount quietly, so as not to awaken the gang. Then he paid a last visit to the store of supplies that Ma kept. There he had hidden a spare bottle of gin, and on sudden impulse he took it, unable to resist the temptation. Thus, shortly before midnight he started off for the Badlands, which lay to the west.

By daybreak Ralph was aware of the enormity of the task he had set for himself. He simply was not in physical condition for a grueling ride across the prairies. Yet he knew he had to persist and somehow reach his goal. If he failed, Gentle Doe—the one person on earth he loved, or at least thought he loved—would die.

Conscious of raging thirst, Ralph stopped at a small stream and drank large quantities of the cool, clear water. His spirits improved, and he rode on, surprised when the sun rose and the prairie was bathed in daylight.

As Ralph gazed out over the sea of grass that stretched all the way to the horizon, he began to suffer doubts. It would be extraordinary if he could somehow save Gentle Doe from death, but he was determined to succeed.

In spite of his resolve, the fear of failure continued to niggle at him as he rode west. After a time he wanted a drink. Gradually the craving grew until it was almost irresistible, and he faced his first crisis. He halted by another small river and decided to make camp for a time. He removed his saddle and allowed his horse to graze, then he drank water and forced himself to eat some dried buffalo meat and cold beans. He had no appetite but hoped that by putting some nourishment into his stomach, he would rid himself of his craving for liquor.

His efforts failed. Uncertain whether he was asleep or awake, Ralph reached into his saddlebags for the bottle of gin. His hand trembling, he removed the stopper, and as the familiar odor of the potent, cheap gin assailed him, his nerves felt soothed. He raised the bottle to his lips, then paused. Suddenly, scarcely aware of what he was doing, Ralph flung the bottle from him and sat watching the contents trickle into the rich soil of Dakota.

This, he reflected, was the only way he could put

temptation behind him. With the bottle empty, he could no longer obtain a drink anywhere in the vast wilderness of Dakota. No matter how intense his craving, he would be unable to satisfy it.

Ralph drifted off to sleep and fell into a deep slumber for several hours. When he awakened, the sun was high overhead, and once again he was assailed by a terrible craving for liquor. Seizing the empty bottle from the ground, he lifted it to his lips, but only the faint odor of gin remained.

"Serves you right, you stupid bastard," Ralph muttered, and threw the bottle out onto the prairie. Never in his life had he regretted anything so much as the impulsive emptying of the gin bottle. His withdrawal was painful, and no relief was available. He had no choice but to go on.

He continued to ride westward, and every body-jouncing step of his horse was agonizing. He told himself repeatedly that his suffering was worthwhile, provided that he reached Gentle Doe and Toby Holt in time. But at the same time he would have given his soul for a drink. But no drink was available, and he would be able to obtain none until he returned eastward and went to a saloon in Fort Pierre en route to Ma's bivouac area.

The thought of food and coffee nauseated Ralph, but he forced himself to eat and drink at regular intervals, knowing that otherwise he would lack the strength to complete his mission. Often he hallucinated and imagined himself strong and upright, married to Gentle Doe, who loved and respected him. Then the reality of the hard ride, and the lack of liquor, overtook his dream, and he was nearly crushed by it.

Still, Ralph somehow found the strength and courage

to ride on through the rugged Black Hills into the Badlands of Dakota. The knowledge that he had never done anything in his life of which to be proud spurred him and was a major factor in enabling him to go on, past the point of sheer physical exhaustion and mental collapse.

Pausing at a small, friendly Sioux village located in the heights of the Black Hills, he learned that Gentle Doe and Toby Holt had passed that way two days earlier. They seemed to be in no hurry, he was informed, so there was a possibility of overtaking them.

He pushed on, driving himself to the limits of his endurance. As he neared the Badlands, he came at last upon their camp. They were eating their evening meal beside their fire when Ralph hailed them, dismounted, and started toward them. Before he could reach them, however, he stumbled and fell unconscious to the ground.

Gentle Doe did not recognize the young man, who had become gaunt from his travail. His suffering was etched in the lines of his thin face. They knew only that he was in trouble, and they reacted accordingly.

Toby attended to the stranger's horse, noting that although its master was in a deplorable state, the animal appeared to have been well-tended. Meanwhile, Gentle Doe prepared some broth. Then, cradling the unconscious Ralph in her arms, she coaxed him awake and fed him from a gourd.

Taking the nourishment gratefully, Ralph looked up into the lovely face of the Indian woman. He thought that he was hallucinating again. His fondest dreams were being realized, and he was in a delirium of happiness. The strong broth fed his body, and Gentle Doe's care nourished his soul.

That night Toby and Gentle Doe relinquished the use of their small, deerskin shelter to Ralph. They slept in the open, and in the morning, for breakfast, they had fish, which Toby had just caught, and ducks' eggs that he gathered from the edge of a nearby pond.

Recovering swiftly, Ralph realized that for the first time in more years than he could recall, he was completely sober. His long ride across the wilderness of Dakota had tempered him, as steel was tempered by fire, and he had recovered his sanity.

Ralph took a long, hard look at himself and was disgusted by what he saw. The time had come, he knew, to rehabilitate himself, to compensate for the mistakes he had made, and above all, to make up for lost time.

Eating ravenously, he told them the story of the plot against them. Gentle Doe reacted only once, when Ralph mentioned Tall Stone. Her memories of the vicious cruelty of the Sioux chief were still fresh in her mind, and she rubbed her bare arms as she listened.

Toby, however, revealed no emotion. When Ralph was finished speaking, Toby confined himself to a single question. "Gentle Doe and I are strangers to you," he said. "Why did you seek us out at such great cost to yourself in order to warn us of the plot to kill us?"

Ralph knew they would think him mad if he confessed his love for Gentle Doe. So he looked her full in the face as he replied slowly, "For years, I was ashamed of my mother's criminal ways. But I was too weak to leave her. I took refuge in liquor, and I sopped it up the way dry ground soaks up rain. In time I became useless, good for nothing, a bum. I needed something like what I've just done to win back my self-respect."

Toby clapped him on the shoulder. "What you've done is a courageous and wonderful thing. We owe you our lives, and I don't know of any way we could ever repay you."

"I want no repayment," Ralph said gruffly.

"Now that we know of this plot," Gentle Doe said, "what shall we do about it?"

"I'm not sure," Toby replied thoughtfully. "Tall Stone will suspect that we've learned of the ambush when we don't appear at Five Rocks. So perhaps we can surprise him there and treat him to a dose of his own medicine. Otherwise, there will probably be another plot hatched against us, and the next time we might be far less fortunate."

"I agree," Ralph said. "Tall Stone must be stopped and prevented from notifying my mother her scheme has failed. Otherwise, I know her well enough to realize that she is certain to try again to have you killed."

"Instead of traveling on to Five Rocks," Toby said, "we'll sit on the problem right here for a day or two until the solution comes to us."

Later that morning Toby shot a bighorn sheep high in the Black Hills. Ralph pitched in, butchering the carcass for Gentle Doe, making a fire for her, and then hunting along the banks of a small river for wild onions and other vegetables that she could use in preparing their evening meal.

Late in the day a cold breeze swept southward from Canada, and despite the fact it was summer, the weather suddenly turned chilly. The campfire felt good, but Ralph, not completely recovered as yet from the ill effects of his journey, could not stop shivering.

Toby was concerned and lent Ralph his fringed jacket

of buffalo leather, a distinctive garment that was identical to one that his father had worn for many years.
Ralph was reluctant to use it but finally was persuaded
and was grateful for its warmth. He ate heartily but
silently, his eyes following every move that Gentle Doe
made.

Toby was conscious of Ralph's reflective, somber
mood, and thought he was feeling guilty because he had
betrayed his mother. Whatever he was feeling, Toby
knew better than to probe.

For his own part, Ralph was only vaguely aware of
the inner turmoil he was suffering. He knew he had con-
quered his craving for drink, but that was not enough.
Now, he reasoned, he had to do something strong and
positive that would not only command the attention of
Gentle Doe but would also win her respect. He knew
she would never love him, and he recognized the
hopelessness of his dream. All the same, he wanted
Gentle Doe to look up to him.

An idea came to him out of nowhere, striking him
with such force that he became even more silent. He did
not pause to consider its good points and its shortcom-
ings. All he knew was that it appealed to him, and he
decided to put it into effect. He would have to await an
opportune moment, however, so he curbed his impa-
tience.

Gentle Doe, like Toby, was sensitive to the prolonged
silences, and she finally announced that she was going to
sleep. She insisted that Ralph again take the shelter, and
she wrapped herself in the blankets she and Toby
shared. Toby joined her, and both of them were soon
asleep under the stars.

With great reluctance Ralph Hastings went under the

shelter, but it was almost as chilly there as it was in the open, so he did not remove the jacket he had borrowed from Toby.

People who had suffered together through Indian attacks, floods, and rockslides, icy winter cold, and blistering summer heat, formed bonds that lasted a lifetime. As Lee and Eulalia Blake knew, they had no better friends than Ernie and Emily von Thalman, and the U.S. Circuit Court judge and his wife felt the same about them. They had endured endless hardships and sorrows together, burying two of Emily's sons in the wilderness of the Great Plains, watching their youngsters grow to adulthood, and struggling to achieve places for themselves in the world.

Of all those who had crossed America in the first wagon train to Oregon, certainly these four had won renown and status. They knew each other so well that there was no need for them to put on airs. They were fast friends, and they relaxed in one another's company.

Now, enjoying their first reunion in many weeks, they gathered in the hotel suite engaged by the Blakes in San Francisco. Eulalia had ordered cold appetizers of shrimp, abalone, and the delicious crab that was unique to the San Francisco area. Lee opened a bottle of wine, and after pouring drinks, he raised his glass.

"To our oldest friends," he said. "Long may our friendship flourish."

"Amen to that," Ernie von Thalman replied, and all four sipped their wine.

"I hope you don't mind," Eulalia said, "but rather than go down to the dining room for dinner, we've ordered it served here. That will save a great many complications."

There was no need for her to explain what she meant by "complications." Neither the parents of the notorious Beth Martin nor the judge who would officiate at her forthcoming trial wanted to be annoyed by representatives of the press. By remaining in the hotel room, the party would not be subjected to the stares and whispers of other dinner guests, and they would be spared the comments of citizens who could not resist offering their opinions of Beth's guilt or innocence.

"I think it's very wise," Emily said. "We know we've been friends for many years, but most people don't know it, or at least don't stop to think about it, and they're likely to jump to the wrong conclusion when they find out that Beth's parents and the judge appointed to her case are dining together."

Ernie sighed gently. "I assume you know," he said, "that I tried like the very devil to be relieved of the case, but the presiding judge wouldn't hear of it."

Lee nodded. "I guessed as much. Let me just say that I understand your predicament, Ernie, as does Eulalia, and you have our complete trust and faith."

"Thank you." Ernie von Thalman inclined his head. "It goes without saying that I've never had a case I've anticipated with less relish. I'd give my soul if I didn't have to preside at it."

Lee Blake cleared his throat. "In my lifetime in the army," he said, "I've had many assignments that I've found unsavory. But I've never once avoided doing my duty, no matter how much I've hated it, and knowing you, Ernie, I don't expect any less from you."

"As long as we're being frank," Eulalia said, "I'd like to make a little speech, too. I promise you it's the very last you'll hear from either of us on the subject. Both of

us love Beth very much. Lee sired her. I've known her
since she was a tiny baby, and her mother was my
closest friend. In spite of what we've read in the press,
we cannot find it in our hearts to believe that Beth is a
trollop who murdered her lover in cold blood. That
doesn't fit the picture of the Beth we know and love. We
could be proved to be wrong, however, and if we are,
we will be the first to insist that justice be done. We've
engaged the best attorney we can find for her, and we're
entrusting her defense to him. With so many rumors and
so much controversy surrounding the case, we don't
know what to think, but we're happy and relieved beyond measure by one thing." She paused for breath.

Her husband intervened quickly. "Our minds are at
rest," he said, "because we know you'll be on the bench,
Ernie. For better or for worse, we know that our daughter will have a fair trial, and that's all we can ask. Under
no circumstances will we try to intervene in this case in
the name of our old friendship."

"Thank you," Emily said. "I might have known that
you'd clear the air of any doubts that might cast
shadows on our friendship."

"The older I grow, the more I believe in ancient prov-
erbs," Ernie said quietly. "If you'll allow me to quote
from the Latin, 'Fiat justitia, ruat caelum.'"

"I'm afraid I've forgotten what little Latin I learned in
school," Eulalia said.

"I'll translate for you," Ernie said. "'Let justice be
done, though the heavens should fall.' That's my motto,
and I believe in it with all my heart."

Lee Blake raised his glass. The others followed his example, and they drank a toast in solemn silence.

❊   ❊   ❊

Three hundred miles away from the Palace Hotel, in the vast desert of the Arizona Territory, a small, canvas-covered wagon was making its way along the trail toward the state of California. Seated on the front of the wagon, holding the reins of the team of horses, was Millicent Randall, a young woman from Baltimore who was touring the West with her cousin, Jim. A one-eyed veteran of the recent Civil War and a retired regular army officer in the Corps of Engineers, Jim had agreed to accompany Millicent on this Western tour after she learned that her fiancé, Major Isham Jentry, had been murdered en route to the Montana Territory. Millicent felt a long trip such as this would offer some consolation for her loss.

Intrepid as they were bold, the cousins were thoroughly enjoying the towns and forts they had visited so far: Fort Shaw in Montana, where they had met Colonel Andy Brentwood and Rob Martin the previous year; Fort Vancouver in Washington, where of course they met General and Mrs. Blake; then south to Denver and Santa Fe. Just recently they had left Fort Lowell in Arizona and were heading west to Los Angeles, then San Francisco, where they would enjoy civilized comforts for a spell before deciding what they would do next.

Jim, leaning comfortably against the back of the wagon seat and holding his rifle in his arms, looked over and watched Millicent for a time. He was filled with admiration for his cousin. In Baltimore, where she had no family but her cousin, she had been a highly promising student of music at the conservatory; here in the West, she seemed equally talented, whether it was driving a wagon or making a camp for the night.

"I have a feeling," Jim said quietly, enjoying the swaying and jostling of the wagon, "that we're not going to

want to stay that long in a big city like San Francisco. If
I know us, we've both come to enjoy the wide open
spaces too much."

"I think you're right, Jim," Millicent replied, grinning.
Like her cousin, Millicent had dark brown hair and
brown eyes. She was of average height, and there were
those who called her plain. But when she smiled, as she
was doing now, or when her eyes lit up with excitement,
she was transformed into a beauty. "Still," she went on,
"I'm looking forward to seeing San Francisco at long
last. I just hope we weren't foolish setting out on our
own like this."

Jim nodded thoughtfully. They both knew that a
good-sized wagon train, escorted by army troops, would
surely have formed up at Fort Lowell before too long, if
they had wanted to wait—there were already a couple of
families waiting at the fort to go to California.

"Don't you worry, Millie," Jim now said. "The commander at Fort Lowell thought we'd be fine driving a
wagon by ourselves. I'm a crack shot with a rifle, and, of
course, it wasn't so long ago that lone wagons were making the same trip we are. They didn't even have the lux-
ury of military posts or settlements along the trail."

Millicent knew Jim was right and felt no apprehension. She and her cousin could certainly take care of
themselves if any emergency arose.

At noontime they stopped to rest and water their
horses. They had, of course, brought water bags, which
hung from the sides of their wagon, in the event they
encountered no water holes along the trail.

Jim went out a short ways to hunt. Even with only
one good eye, he was a fine shot, and he brought back a
pair of rabbits. Millicent pitched right in, skinning the
animals and cooking the meat, then prepared biscuits.

They set out again late in the afternoon. They had only gone a few miles, however, when they saw way ahead of them on the flat terrain a number of mounted Indians halted along the wagon trail. The Indians—who would be the dreaded Apache—were still more than a mile away, and it was impossible to tell what their intentions were. But there was something very ominous about the presence of so many braves waiting on the trail. Though the Apache had signed peace treaties with the United States, there were still some warlike braves who went out and attacked settlers and wagon trains.

"What do you suppose they're up to?" Millicent asked, trying hard to control her growing fear.

"I'm afraid it may mean trouble, Millie," Jim replied steadily. "They're probably waiting for us to get closer, and then they're going to strike. In any case, I'm not taking any chances." With this, Jim quickly checked his rifle and raised it to his shoulder, ready to fire once they were within range.

"But, Jim," Millicent cried, "there are at least a dozen of them. What good can your rifle do against so many?"

"What choice do we have, Millie? If we turn the wagon around, they're certain to give chase."

Millicent stared at the distant braves for a moment, then suddenly said, "I've got an idea. Here, hold the reins." Before Jim could protest, she had thrust the reins at him, then reached back into the wagon and pulled out her leather-covered flute case. Quickly assembling the instrument, she moistened her lips and put the flute to her mouth. Then she began to play.

The sound of the flute lifted out across the vast desert. The Indians sitting their mounts along the trail heard the music, and they were taken aback. They had planned to attack this lone wagon coming toward them, but now it seemed as if some spell were being cast, as if the white people driving the wagon were working some kind of magic.

Millicent played with all her heart as Jim slowly drove their wagon along the trail and right into the midst of the Indians. Jim, his rifle on the seat beside him, tried hard to keep calm as he looked at the faces of the braves lined up along the trail. Their expressions showed no hostility or anger. The Indians kept their horses still as they watched the wagon pass, their eyes following the woman who was playing the flute.

Millicent continued to play until they had driven past the line of Indians and had gone several hundred feet farther down the trail. The braves continued to sit their mounts a little longer, until finally one of their number called out a command, kicked the sides of his horse, and galloped off. The others immediately followed suit, riding off into the hills from whence they had come.

Millicent put down her flute. Beads of sweat stood out on her forehead, and she wiped them away with her hand.

"You were just terrific, Millie," Jim said, his voice filled with admiration. "I don't mind telling you, I thought we were in for some real trouble, but that flute of yours saved the day."

Millicent smiled wanly. "They say music soothes the savage breast, Jim. I guess we just proved it. Now if you don't mind, I'll ask you to continue to drive the wagon for a bit. I think my hands are going to be shaking from here to California."

Jim reached over and took one of Millicent's hands in his for a moment. "I'll be happy to drive, Millie. You just lean back and relax. We'll be in California before you know it." With this, he flicked the reins, and the team of horses moved out at a faster pace.

There were no other problems for the cousins as they drove through the mountains of California to the bustling trading center of Los Angeles. Made up mostly of hundreds of adobe buildings, Los Angeles didn't offer very much to see, and after spending the night in a little inn, they continued their journey along the Pacific Coast, admiring the breathtaking views of the ocean from the heights.

At last they arrived in San Francisco, a city in every way as cosmopolitan and bustling as Baltimore. They left their vehicle with a wagon maker, whose warehouses were located on the outskirts of the city, and next they checked into a small, comfortable hotel on California Street. Then they learned some news that shocked them.

Jim and Millicent had cleaned up in their rooms before coming down to the hotel lobby to meet for dinner. When Millicent came downstairs, Jim was already waiting for her, his expression grim.

"Millie, read this," he said, handing her a newspaper.

Millicent read the headline on the front page, and her face turned pale. The headline read: BETH MARTIN TRIAL SET A WEEK FROM TUESDAY. The rest of the story told of Beth Martin's refusal to make any statements to the press, then repeated in lurid detail all the facts that had led up to the trial.

Millicent had not met Beth at Fort Shaw in Montana, but she had come to know Rob Martin fairly well and was grateful to him for the concern and warmth he had shown when she first learned of the death of her fiancé. Lowering the newspaper, she said to Jim, "We've got to do something for Rob. He's going to need a lot of support during this difficult time."

"What do you have in mind?" Jim asked.

"I'm not sure," she replied slowly, "but let's try to locate him or General Blake and see what we can do. He was so good to me when I was troubled, the least we can do is offer our help in return."

IX

Gentle Doe stirred uneasily in her sleep, and Toby, instantly awake, sat up and simultaneously reached for the rifle at his side. Gentle Doe opened her eyes and was mildly surprised at seeing Ralph Hastings moving about. He had no idea he was being observed.

Preoccupied, his face showing determination rarely reflected there, Ralph rolled up his blanket and put it in his saddlebag. Then he went off a short distance for his horse and proceeded to saddle the mount.

"Where is he going at this hour of the night?" Gentle Doe whispered as she sat up.

Toby silenced her with a gesture and continued to study Hastings. It seemed to him that Ralph had reached a climactic point in his life. Toby had been aware that the man was undergoing a struggle of some sort. It appeared that now he had reached a decision that he was putting into action.

It would be wrong, Toby concluded, to come between a man and his conscience. So he signaled to Gentle Doe to lie down again and then did the same himself as he continued to watch Hastings through half-closed eyes.

Ralph attached his saddlebag to his mount, then buckled on his belt. Almost as an afterthought, he removed his pistols from their holsters one by one, examined them, and dropped them back into place again. He appeared satisfied, and mounting his horse, he looked back over his shoulder at the couple he thought were sleeping.

The resigned stoop of his shoulders, outlined against the night sky, was so unusual that it haunted Toby for many days thereafter. Hastings's attitude exhibited pride and, at the same time, deep hurt.

Spurring forward, the rider went off in the direction of the Badlands and soon disappeared into the night.

Gentle Doe hoisted herself to a sitting position again and shook her head in wonder. "He was only half-alive when he came to us," she said, "and now, before he has had a chance to recover his strength fully, he is gone again. What business could take him into the Badlands at this hour of night?"

Toby shrugged. "All I can tell you," he said, "is that we had no right to stop him."

This was a concept that Gentle Doe could readily grasp. "When one goes to meet one's destiny," she replied solemnly, "it does not matter whether the sun shines or the moon glows, whether it is morning or night. It is said by the medicine men of our nation, who know of these things, that the gods who guide the destinies of the living do not measure time as we know time."

"That is so," Toby replied, nodding in agreement and looking off into the darkness. The son of Ma Hastings could not have led an easy life, and Toby felt sorry for him. Whatever the mission was that drove him, the young Westerner could not help but wish him well.

Ralph Hastings felt anything but sorry for himself. On the contrary, he was gripped by an exhilaration unlike anything he had ever before experienced. He knew now what had to be done. He was going to compensate for all the opportunities he had missed, for all the years he had lost.

Gentle Doe was even lovelier than he had imagined, but she was beyond his reach; he had done nothing to earn the respect of such a woman. He intended to earn it now, however. She was certain to learn what he had done, and regardless of the outcome of his adventure, whether he lived or died, she would be forced to admit that Ralph Hastings was truly a man. That was all he asked in life.

His plan was simple. According to the scheme his mother had concocted for the murder of Toby Holt, Tall Stone and his braves were already waiting at the Badlands rendezvous to open fire on Toby when he approached. He would not be keeping that appointment, however. Ralph Hastings would be riding there in his stead, and rather than being shot down in a surprise move, he intended to fire first.

Thus, if he was successful, Tall Stone would pay for his perfidy with his own life. Not only would Toby Holt's life be spared and his mother's plot thwarted, but Gentle Doe would look up to him.

Ralph rode steadily through the long hours of the night, and not once did he crave a drink. His newfound determination gave him a buoyancy he had never before possessed, a strength to see a project through to the finish. His regrets over what might have been, over his many mistakes and the weaknesses he had shown throughout his life, were all behind him now.

Ralph paused once to let his horse drink from a brook. As for himself, his euphoria shielded him from ordinary human desires such as hunger, thirst, and the need for sleep.

He smiled to himself when he rode into the region of the Badlands where already bizarrely shaped stones seemed even more exaggerated and twisted by the night. There had been a time when the Badlands had frightened Ralph because the area corresponded all too closely with his nightmares. Tonight, however, he was free of fear. He was confident and looked forward only to the successful termination of his venture.

Pausing from time to time to get his bearings, Ralph increased his pace as he drew nearer his destination. How he would enjoy putting a bullet between the eyes of Tall Stone! He had hated the long hours of practice shooting with pistol and rifle when he had been younger, but now, at last, that unrewarding labor was about to pay him handsome dividends.

Ralph slowed his mount to a walk when he saw the five giant slabs of stone that comprised the rendezvous looming ahead in the predawn darkness. A Sioux warrior, he knew, was concealed behind each of those large stones, and hidden behind the rock in the center of the formation was Tall Stone.

Smiling to himself, feeling truly fulfilled for the only time in his life, Ralph Hastings slowly reached for the two pistols at his sides.

His unseen foes had been aware of his proximity, however, and thinking that he was Toby Holt riding into the ambush, they had watched his every move. Now, when they saw him about to draw his pistols, they struck first.

An arrow pierced the night, making a slight singing sound as it was released from the bow. It punctured Ralph's cheek. At that same instant, another of Tall Stone's braves threw a tomahawk at the white man. The primitive weapon found its target, making a deep gash in its victim's forehead.

Ralph Hastings pitched forward and rolled from the saddle to stare with sightless eyes at the black sky above the Badlands. The attack had been so swift that he never knew he had failed.

Tall Stone, though he showed no emotion, was pleased that the ambush had been so easy. He looked scornfully at the body of Ralph Hastings and failed to recognize him because of the hideously disfiguring wounds. In the black night he saw only the shape of his enemy.

"Where is the woman who travels with him," he asked, staring at the braves. They did not know but spread out looking for her. After half an hour they reported that the white man had been alone; there were tracks of only one horse. Tall Stone shrugged contemptuously. Gentle Doe, he was sure, would not last long by herself, without the protection of the white man who was now lying maimed at his feet. "The warrior who fired the arrow," he said, "may have the scalp of the white man. Wrap his body in his blanket and tie it to the saddle of his horse. We will return to the woman bandit with it to claim the reward she has promised us."

Glenn Chapman was regarded as the brightest, shrewdest, and most aggressive of the younger generation of attorneys in San Francisco. Certainly he was the most ambitious, so he promptly accepted the challenge of defending Beth Martin when her father offered him the opportunity. The enormous interest the case had aroused guaranteed a notoriety that would rebound in publicity for him. If, by some miracle, he managed to get the young Martin woman off free, it would be a legal feather in his cap.

Tremendous amounts of work had to be done before he could try to establish Beth Martin's innocence, however, and no one realized more acutely than Chapman the need for her to take him into her confidence.

Clean-shaven and well-groomed, wearing an olive-colored suit of tweed, he arrived at the Market Street prison late in the afternoon. The sheriff had him escorted to the visitors' room where, after a brief wait, the door opened and Beth Martin was admitted.

Clad in a plain dress, her manner withdrawn, her face wan, and her body painfully thin, Beth bore no resemblance to the young woman about whom legends were being created. She had lost all interest in her appearance and did not care what dress she wore or if her face was made up. Perhaps it had been the recent, icy meeting with Rob that was responsible, but whatever the case, Beth had withdrawn entirely into herself. She did not want to talk to anybody, not even her parents. She did not care what happened to her.

The attorney rose. "I'm Glenn Chapman, Mrs. Martin," he said. "Your father hired me as your attorney."

"That was very sweet of him," Beth replied, sinking listlessly into a straight-backed wooden chair across the table from him. "But I don't need representation."

"You're mistaken," he said quietly but forcefully. "Under our system of jurisprudence, you're required to be represented by a lawyer at your trial. We have a far better chance of winning your freedom than you apparently think."

Beth looked at him and shook her head in disbelief.

"As I understand it," the attorney said, "you've issued no statement since you were arrested following the murder. You've said nothing in public or in private—not even to your father and stepmother—regarding the circumstances that resulted in Leon Graham's death."

"I see nothing to be gained by rehashing the whole matter," Beth said, looking down at her tightly folded hands in her lap. "The facts speak for themselves. All I want is to get the trial over with and done. I've seen enough of what the newspapers printed to realize what a sensation they're creating. Frankly, Mr. Chapman, I'm not interested in providing a circus."

Glenn Chapman replied in the incisive tones he usually reserved for judges and juries. "Your trial, Mrs. Martin, will be conducted in the Circuit Court of the United States, not in the press. The less you're willing to speak, the more conjecture you'll be creating for the newspapers. When they have no facts to write, they rely on rumor, innuendo, and guesswork, and the circus you're trying to avoid will be all the more gaudy."

Beth shrugged wearily. "That's out of my hands, Mr. Chapman," she said. "I can't control what the newspapers write."

He saw nothing to be gained by arguing that point with her. "You may be right, and you may be wrong. But there are certain to have been extenuating circumstances. Why were you in Graham's house? Why were you dressed and made up, if you'll forgive me for putting it this way, like a trollop? What were the facts of your affair with him, if you indeed had an affair? You've got to provide me with information, Mrs. Martin. If I go into court without facts, your case is hopeless. At best you'll be sent to prison for the rest of your life!"

Beth laughed harshly. "And what's the *worst* that can happen to me, Mr. Chapman?" she demanded.

"You'll be hanged," he replied bluntly.

Her face did not change, and there was no expression in her voice as she replied, "You can believe this or not, Mr. Chapman, but I honestly don't care."

Never had he seen an accused person so lethargic. He wanted to shake her. "God helps those who help themselves, Mrs. Martin," he said.

Beth shrugged. "God gave me up long ago."

Chapman made a supreme effort to cut through her paralysis. "Listen to me, Mrs. Martin!" he said. "I don't know what happened in Graham's house or why you were there in the first place. I can't possibly know unless you tell me. I want your story, all of it—the whole truth. Believe me, at this point in your life, you have no cause for shame or for self-recrimination. I assure you, I'm not trying to dig the truth out of you for prurient reasons. I'm trying to save your life."

Beth sighed and gazed at the wall behind his shoulder.

Chapman was frustrated. He couldn't be sure that she had heard a word he had said to her.

A gong sounded somewhere in the distance, and Beth dragged herself to her feet. "I must be going back to my cell now, Mr. Chapman," she said. "They're about to serve supper—such as it is." She rose and made her way to the door, then paused with one hand on the knob. "I know you mean well, Mr. Chapman," she said politely, "and thank you for coming." The door opened, and a sheriff's deputy appeared, to conduct her back to her cell.

Glenn Chapman watched her as she disappeared down

the corridor. This case was going to be even more difficult than he had imagined.

Tall Stone led his party across the prairie to the place
where he had arranged to meet Ma Hastings and her
band. The meeting site was remote and was located on a
minor tributary of the Missouri River that had no name.
The one advantage of holding a reunion there with Ma
Hastings was that no one—neither settlers nor Indians—
had any community within many miles of it.

The Hastings gang had made themselves at home in
the wilderness. Animal-hide shelters had been erected.
The smell of fish and venison cooking told the approaching Indians that game was plentiful, and Tall
Stone and his companions were looking forward to
claiming their reward and enjoying a few days' rest.

Ma Hastings had been dismayed when her son Ralph
had disappeared from the camp, but she decided that he
had probably ridden off to Fort Pierre for liquor. He
would show up, she was sure, or be found in a drunken
stupor by one of her gang. Ralph was pushed far from
her thoughts as she emerged from her shelter, her eyes
glittering, and searched the expression of the Sioux
leader.

Tall Stone, to whet the appetite of the loud old
squaw, had his braves keep the horse bearing the corpse
beside them so that it was out of sight. Now he faced
Ma Hastings impassively, as she looked first at him, then
for a sign of the body. Enjoying the suspense he had
created, he raised his left arm in greeting, forcing the
white people to reciprocate, despite their eagerness to
find out what had taken place.

Digger, Ma Hastings's lieutenant, finally remembered
himself and asked the Sioux to join the gang for a meal.

Tall Stone accepted, and before any business was conducted, the group sat in a circle around the fire eating chunks of smoking meat, which they hacked off the deer carcass with their knives.

Not until everyone had eaten his fill was it appropriate for Ma Hastings to make inquiries regarding the success or failure of the Indians' mission. She herself had eaten nothing, having all she could do to control her excitement.

"As you can tell from the food we have eaten," she said, "the hunting has been good in these parts. I hope that the warriors of the mighty Sioux have enjoyed equally good hunting in the Badlands of Dakota."

Tall Stone remained silent, increasing the suspense. Then, his face expressionless, he nodded gravely. "The warriors of the Sioux," he said, "enjoyed their hunting. They found the quarry they sought, and they destroyed him."

The woman's wrinkled, leathery face softened, and she was unable to control the tremulous sigh that welled up within her.

"It may be," he said, "that you wish to see our prize for yourself."

"I would like that," Ma replied, her voice husky and barely audible.

Tall Stone rose and led the party to the place, located downwind, where he and his companions had left their mounts. The stench of death was strong as he stepped to the bulky blanket and cut away the thongs. He lifted the blanket-covered corpse from the horse and put it on the ground. Beside him, disturbed, Ma Hastings studied the horse and blanket, which looked peculiarly familiar.

Tall Stone pulled away the blanket, revealing the

bloody, mutilated face and slack body of the scalped
Ralph Hastings.

Ma Hastings stood as though she had been carved out
of stone. Rigid and still, her face ashen and her fists
clenched, she stared down at the body of her dead son.

Suddenly a wild, uncontrolled scream was torn from
her. In it were the rage of thwarted vengeance, the ag-
ony of a mother who had lost two sons, and the madness
of ineffable despair. The scream rolled across the
endless, flat prairie of Dakota.

The members of her band looked at each other in con-
sternation. Ever since they had known Ma, she had been
in command of herself, just as she had commanded
them. Never had she displayed any emotion other than
anger. Now, however, it was evident that she had lost
her reason.

As she continued to scream, the Indians watched her
uneasily, not understanding the reasons for her overwhelming grief. They knew madness when they encountered it, however, and there was no question in their
minds that Ma Hastings's wits had deserted her.

Digger, who stood next to Tall Stone, muttered to the
Sioux in his own tongue, "You killed Ma's son, not Toby
Holt!"

Tall Stone was surprised, but he refused to worry
about it. One white man was like another. His only regret was that he had not done away with the man who
had stolen the affection of Gentle Doe.

The members of the band were hard-bitten frontiersmen and gunslingers who had killed and robbed and
broken laws of every sort for years. But Ma's screams
were so penetrating and shrill that they sent shivers up
and down their spines.

She could no longer lead them, that was sure, and

though they felt vaguely sorry for her, every member of the gang thought first and foremost of himself. They wasted no pity on Ralph, whom they regarded as useless, beneath contempt.

Two of the younger members exchanged glances, understood each other, and stole away, quietly folding and packing their tent, stuffing their belongings into their duffel bags, and then saddling and mounting their horses.

No one halted them, no one raised a voice objecting to their departure. Instead, they caused a quiet stampede. Others in the band soon followed their example, looting the gang's storehouse and also taking extra horses. Soon the Hastings gang was scattered, its members riding off in all directions.

The Sioux, unnerved by Ma's unremitting screams, decided the time had come to absent themselves also. They moved off quietly at a signal from Tall Stone, mounting their horses and leaving in a body. They increased their pace to a gallop in order to shut out the soul-wrenching sound of the woman's screams. But they continued to hear her voice in their imaginations for many hours.

When only Digger remained, Ma Hastings suddenly stopped screaming. She shuddered, reached for her rifle, and approaching the corpse of her mutilated son, sat on the ground beside it. Her eyes were those of a madwoman.

She began to mutter, and Digger had to strain to hear her.

"Ralph is my son," she said. "He's a good boy, and nobody ain't goin' to hurt him. If anybody tries, I'll drill 'em full o' holes!"

"Listen to me, Ma," Digger said.

The woman paid no attention. He knew that it was

impossible to reason with her, that she was beyond appeal. So he divided the remaining food, packing part of it in his own saddlebag and leaving the rest, along with a jug of water, on the ground beside Ma.

Then, gathering his own belongings, he, too, rode off. Looking back over his shoulder, he caught a final glimpse of Ma Hastings, once the most feared and hated woman in the West. She was sitting cross-legged, her rifle under her arm, doing sentinel duty over the body of her dead son. He knew it was only a matter of time before she, too, would join him in death and their remains would be finished by the coyotes that came down from the Black Hills.

Not only were all the San Francisco newspapers represented at the trial of Beth Martin, but there were also correspondents for major journals from around the entire United States. There were so many reporters that the bailiffs had to set up two extra tables in the front of the courtroom to accommodate them.

Susanna Brentwood, the wife of Colonel Andrew Brentwood, and a former newswoman who had worked on the *Denver Tribune* and *Virginia City Times*, put aside the book she was writing about life in the West and came down from Montana to attend the trial. Andy's duties as commander at Fort Shaw prevented him from also traveling to San Francisco, and little Sam Brentwood, now more than a year old, was in the care of his nurse. Susanna disliked leaving her family even for a short period of time, but she felt if ever there was a reason to make a comeback as a newspaper reporter, this was it. No less a prestigious journal than the *New York Herald* had hired her to write the story, and Susanna believed that she had a responsibility to state the facts accurately, regardless of the fact that the woman on trial was her husband's cousin.

Interest in the case was so great that huge crowds filed into the courtroom the moment the doors were opened, and within moments they had taken every seat.

Chet and Clara Lou Harris, dressed somberly, sat quietly in the reserved seat section, with Wong Ke and his wife next to them. The two couples, under considerable tension, did not converse.

On the opposite side of the room, a couple entered. They were the cousins from Baltimore, Jim and Millicent Randall, who had come to the trial because they wanted to offer whatever comfort they could to Rob. The cousins had been surprised to learn from General Blake, however, that Rob had returned to his work on the railway; he apparently had no intention of witnessing his wife's trial. Neither General nor Mrs. Blake expressed any disapproval of what Millicent found to be his decidedly odd behavior, however, so she kept her thoughts to herself.

Lee and Eulalia Blake created a stir when they came into the courtroom, the press immediately noting that the general was wearing full uniform, complete with all his many medals. Eulalia, the widow of Whip Holt, now married to the distinguished general, was dressed in refined good taste. Her hand on his arm, she avoided the stares of the curious and quietly took her seat with her husband.

Attorney Glenn Chapman turned in his chair at the defense table in order to have a few words with the Blakes. "I visited Beth again yesterday at the prison," he told them in a low tone. "It was my seventh visit to her in as many days, and I'm sorry to say that I seem to have been wasting my time."

Eulalia drew her breath in sharply. "She didn't tell you, then, how she happened to be in Leon Graham's house?"

The lawyer shook his head glumly. "I appealed to her in every way I knew," he said, "but I might as well have been talking to a stone wall. She didn't respond."

"I'm afraid we know what you mean, Glenn," Lee Blake said heavily. "We saw Beth the night before last, and we talked ourselves hoarse begging her to tell the court the whole truth of the matter. But we got nowhere."

"I'm afraid," the lawyer replied, "that this is going to be an exceptionally difficult case for the defense. All of the evidence points strongly toward Beth's guilt, as does her insistence on waiving her right to have a trial by jury. Unless she reveals at least enough of the truth to convince the court that she had valid reasons for killing the man, I'm afraid that Judge von Thalman will have no choice but to find her guilty."

He broke off as the door to an anteroom opened and Beth came into the courtroom flanked by two United States marshals. She appeared composed and, thanks to makeup, looked less haggard than she had of late. She showed surprise when she saw Susanna, but then her face became inscrutable again as she noted her father and stepmother. Inclining her head to her lawyer, she slipped into her chair beside him.

Although she did not show it, Beth was bitterly disappointed. She had scanned the reserved seat section swiftly and had seen no sign of her husband. She could only assume that Rob, who had not returned to the jail to visit her, was notifying her by his absence that their marriage was at an end.

What she did not know was that Rob had indeed gone

back to work in the Sierra Nevada to await the outcome of the trial but at the last moment had decided he should be with Beth. Because there was no work train for several days, he had been forced to travel by horseback to San Francisco from the railroad construction camp in the mountains. He slipped into the courtroom minutes before the trial began, and Beth did not notice him. He was still wearing his work clothes: heavy boots, corduroy pants, and wool shirt.

Looking around as he caught his breath, he was pleased to find Millicent Randall sitting beside him.

"Jim and I came here to wish you and your wife well," she whispered, pleased to see that he had arrived after all. "Is there anything we can do for you?"

Rob ran a hand through his hair. "I'm very grateful, but there's nothing I can think of."

Millicent patted his arm in encouragement. She would not press herself upon him, but she would make it very clear that she and Jim were available if Rob needed them.

Rob was pleased by Millicent's gesture, but he was too confused to analyze his feelings. He wouldn't be able to think clearly until the trial was behind Beth.

The chief prosecuting attorney, Amos Gallagher, gray-haired and lean, came into the courtroom, followed by two assistants laden with documents and law books. He went to the table adjacent to that occupied by the defense and promptly came over to shake hands with Beth's attorney.

Glenn Chapman shook hands with him and then presented him to Beth.

"How do you do?" she murmured inanely, thinking that the whole experience was like a bad dream. It was difficult to imagine that this amiable gentleman was

present for the purpose of sending her to the gibbet to
be hanged, if he could marshal enough evidence to persuade the court of her undeniable guilt.

The rapping of a bailiff's gavel cut through the buzz
of conversation in the courtroom. "United States Circuit
Court, Judge Ernst von Thalman presiding, is now in
session," he said. "Please rise."

Everyone in the courtroom rose as the judge, clad in
flowing black robes, appeared from his chambers and
mounted the bench. He took his seat and rapped his
gavel once. The principals and spectators resumed their
seats.

"The United States of America versus Beth Martin,"
the bailiff intoned.

A chill chased up and down Beth's spine.

Judge von Thalman peered over the rim of his glasses
at Beth and asked, "Will the defendant please rise?"

As she stood it occurred to her that this stern-faced
man bore little resemblance to the "Uncle Ernie" she
had known all her life.

"Mrs. Martin," he said, "I want to be certain that you
understand your rights. You are, you know, entitled to a
trial by jury. I've been informed by your counsel that
you have elected to surrender that right and entrust
your future instead to this court. Is that correct?"

"Yes, Your Honor," she replied in a voice so soft that
members of the press had to strain in order to hear her.

"Very well," he replied. "So be it. Mr. Prosecutor, you
may open the case."

Amos Gallagher made a brief, cogent opening statement, in which he said that he intended to prove conclu-
sively that the defendant was guilty of murder, as
charged. He then began to call a parade of witnesses.

Taking the witness stand, one after another, were

Leon Graham's cook, butler, and chambermaids, and the two constables who had been summoned after he had been shot. Their testimony was damaging to Beth, for out of loyalty to their late employer, who had paid them well, they distorted the facts. They described in detail her scanty, provocative attire, the heavy makeup she had worn, and her drunken condition. By the time their testimony was completed, there was no doubt in the minds of the majority of people in the courtroom that Beth was a wanton who had murdered Graham in cold blood.

Clara Lou Harris looked indignant whenever her gaze settled on Beth, and even her husband appeared angry.

The defense attorney had no weapons to fight back with, so he chose not to subject any of the four witnesses to cross-examination. He did the best he could under the circumstances, however, when he said to the court, "I note that among the servants of the deceased is one Chang Wu, who was the houseman. May I ask if there's any particular reason he has not been called to the stand?"

The prosecutor replied easily, "Chang Wu has a limited command of English, so I decided that in order to expedite matters, his testimony was unnecessary."

Glenn Chapman took a chance. "May I ask the court that he be called to the stand, if you please?"

"Certainly," Judge von Thalman replied, and declared a recess until the houseman could be fetched. In less than an hour the trial resumed.

It was obvious that Chang Wu knew no more than a smattering of English, and the judge looked around the courtroom. "I wonder," he said, "if this court might impose on a distinguished citizen, Mr. Wong Ke, to act as an interpreter for the witness?"

Wong Ke was surprised but promptly rose to his feet. "I shall be glad to do anything I can, Your Honor," he replied, and came forward.

The witness relaxed when the interpreter explained his mission to him.

"If it's satisfactory to the prosecution," Attorney Chapman said, "I suggest that the witness be allowed to describe the events in his own way."

"By all means," Gallagher said.

Wong Ke, addressing the witness in Cantonese, asked him to describe what he had seen.

The witness spoke slowly, somberly, and his opening statement, which Wong Ke translated in a soft, unemotional voice, created a sensation. "Leon Graham," he said, "was a very bad man."

This was the first hint that the deceased was anything but a pillar of San Francisco society and an honorable citizen. There was a buzz of excitement, and Judge von Thalman had to rap for order.

The houseman's testimony became even more sensational. He indicated that Beth Martin was not the first woman Leon had entertained in his bedroom. She had been a prisoner there, he said, and she was the last in a succession of young women who had been subjected to similar treatment.

The excitement in the courtroom became so great that the judge ordered another recess.

Glenn Chapman turned to Beth, his voice urgent. "Is the testimony of the houseman true?" he demanded. "Was Graham actually holding you as a prisoner in his bedroom?"

Beth had sat stonily through the testimony. "I've already lived this nightmare," she said grimly. "I don't intend to go through it again."

Chapman was exasperated. It occurred to him that his client simply did not grasp the consequences of her reticence. In the few days he had known her, he had realized that the young woman was still in shock. Also, she had had a privileged upbringing on army posts as the daughter of a commanding officer, and probably at a deep emotional level, she did not really believe that she could be hung or incarcerated. Furthermore, he was sure she felt deserted by her husband. Although she had said nothing to Chapman, he had noticed the pained look in her eyes when she learned that Rob had returned to the mountains. All these circumstances conspired to render her mute. Even so, he leaned closer and whispered urgently, "My God, Mrs. Martin, if you tell me what happened, I can save your life! But I can do nothing for you if you remain silent! I beg you, help me!"

Beth compressed her lips, folded her hands, and stared straight ahead.

The defense attorney sighed in frustration.

When the court reconvened, Chapman recalled the Graham cook, butler, and chambermaids to the stand and grilled them. All admitted, with some reluctance, that Beth Martin, indeed, had not been the only woman to be entertained in Leon Graham's bedroom. There had been a succession of young women over a long period of time.

As to whether these women had been there voluntarily or had been prisoners was something that none of the household staff were willing to say for sure. If the young women had been prisoners, they assumed that had been a part of a game of make-believe. As one chambermaid said, persisting in a distortion of the facts, "They must have liked the game, whatever it was. If they didn't like it, there was nothing to stop them from leaving."

Court was adjourned for the day, the prisoner was taken back to her cell in the Market Street jail, and Attorney Chapman headed for the Palace Hotel to eat dinner with General and Mrs. Blake. They had invited Rob to join them, but he was too weary from his journey and went to his hotel.

In the elegant, gaslit surroundings, the trio sat at their table and drank glasses of predinner sack, discussing the case.

"What do you think?" Lee Blake asked anxiously.

The lawyer shrugged. "The testimony of Chang Wu," he said, "opened a window. It's the first break we've had in this case, the first indication that Graham may not have been the paragon of virtue that he's been made out to be. But I can't persuade Beth to shed any more light on the matter. She's as closemouthed as she was the first time I saw her."

Eulalia sighed. "I think I know what Beth is feeling," she said. "She's so ashamed of what happened that she can't bring herself to talk about it."

Lee was angry. "But she's being so shortsighted, damn it!" he exclaimed.

"We see it as shortsighted," his wife replied, "but she can't see clearly. I'm sure she's more worried about her marriage than about her guilt or innocence."

They were interrupted when a waiter approached and handed Glenn Chapman a folded note. He opened it and read it, then passed it to the Blakes. It was written in a bold, feminine hand: *May I speak with you on a matter of importance, relative to your current case? Kale Salton.*

"Who is Kale Salton?" Lee demanded.

Chapman nodded his head slightly toward the far side of the dining room, where the note had come from.

The Blakes saw a young woman sitting at a table by herself. She was watching them, and when she saw them looking at her, she smiled and inclined her head. She had violet eyes and long blue-black hair gathered in a bun at the nape of her neck. She wore a brilliant red salve on her lips, a rim of kohl around her eyes, and a velvet beauty patch on one cheekbone. Her clothes were seductive and emphasized her voluptuous figure. Her neckline was so low that Lee was shocked. "If you ask me," he said, "she's a prostitute."

"I don't think there's any question about it, General," Chapman replied. "She's a member of that very special breed of expensive prostitute who's been prominent here ever since gold rush days." Like Lee, Glenn Chapman seemed to be dismissing the young woman.

Eulalia protested. "Her vocation and morals are irrelevant," she said. "If she has something to contribute that will win Beth's freedom, we've got to listen to her."

Lee looked at her and nodded slowly. "Eulalia is absolutely right," he said.

Chapman rose. He started across the room to the young woman's table, but seeing him coming, she jumped to her feet first and met him. She was a tall, statuesque woman, and her walk was deliberate and sensual, much to his embarrassment.

Kale Salton smiled as she extended a warm, firm hand, and a dimple showed in one cheek. "This meeting isn't accidental," she said.

She allowed the explanation of her remark to wait until she joined his table and met General and Mrs. Blake. She was struck in particular by the cordiality of Eulalia.

The older woman went out of her way to be friendly and did not condescend to her, which Kale appreciated.

Lee Blake ordered a glass of wine for their guest, and after it was served, Kale Salton looked at each of the trio in turn. "I'm pleased that you're making this easy for me," she said. "Believe me, you won't regret it. I've been following the case of your daughter with interest because, but for the grace of God, I might have been in her shoes at this very moment."

Eulalia broke the tense silence that followed. "What do you mean?" she asked.

The younger woman was forthright. "I was Leon Graham's mistress for a time," she said, "and I suspect my experience was very similar to your daughter's. Leon followed—ah—certain patterns. If you wish, I'll tell the whole sordid story in court."

Glenn Chapman looked hard at her. "Why are you making this offer?" he demanded bluntly.

She grinned at him. "I knew you'd ask that," she said, "and I can answer you very briefly. Hate is as powerful as love. I hated Leon with all my soul, and I hate him still. It will give me a great sense of satisfaction to contribute what I can to putting his memory in its proper perspective. I've been infuriated these past weeks by the press's attempt to make him appear like a saint. He was no saint, believe me!"

The defense called Kale Salton as a surprise witness, and there was a hum of excited comment in the courtroom as the provocatively attired young woman made her way to the witness stand and was sworn in. It was apparent from Defense Attorney Chapman's attitude that he considered her important to his case, and certainly it was obvious to everyone present that the young woman herself was enjoying the drama.

Beth, who had been told nothing about Kale, showed no interest in her.

"Be good enough to tell the court your name, age, and occupation," the defense attorney said.

She smiled sweetly and addressed herself exclusively to Judge von Thalman. "I am Kale Salton," she said, "and I've reached the age of consent, so the number of years I've spent on earth doesn't particularly matter. As for my vocation, I'm a professional prostitute."

Her candor caused a stir in the courtroom. The members of the press, sensing a juicy break in the case, scribbled furiously as they listened attentively. Susanna, for the first time in her career as a newspaper reporter, was torn between her concern for the welfare of her subject and the sensationalism of the article she was writing.

"Perhaps you'll be good enough, also," Attorney Chapman said, "to explain your own involvement with Leon Graham."

Before she could reply, Prosecutor Gallagher was on his feet. Chapman, however, gave him no opportunity to interrupt. "If my colleague Mr. Gallagher will show a little patience," he said, "I think the importance of this witness to the case will be well established."

Gallagher sat down again.

"The better part of a year ago," Kale Salton said, "I was introduced to Leon Graham by a mutual friend. I'm not being vague, Your Honor, quite the contrary. I make it my business to keep the names of my clients strictly confidential, and, therefore, I prefer not to mention the name of my friend in public. If you wish to hear it, however, I'll be glad to tell it to you in private."

"That won't be necessary," Judge von Thalman told her dryly. "I'll take your word for it. Go on."

"Leon knew that my services were available to him for a fee," she said. "In fact, he had been the client of two other girls of my acquaintance and was known in the business as being a generous customer, provided one went along with his rather odd wishes."

"'Odd'?" Judge von Thalman asked, raising an eyebrow.

"I'll come to that, sir," Kale replied. "In any event, after introducing us to each other, my friend left Leon and me alone. It didn't take him long to make me an offer. Specifically, he offered to pay me one thousand dollars, half of it in advance, if I would pretend to be his captive in his house for three days and nights."

The judge interrupted again. "What do you mean by captive, Miss Salton?"

"Supposedly," she replied, "I would be his prisoner. My clothes would be taken away, and I'd be given some flimsy undergarments to wear, but nothing else. Anytime that he was not present, I was to remain in his bedchamber suite with the doors locked. My food and drink, and the return of my clothes, were to depend on my ability to please him in bed."

Again her bluntness caused a stir in the courtroom. Even Beth was paying close attention now.

"The pay was generous," Kale said, "so I accepted the offer."

"One moment," Judge von Thalman said. "You didn't consider the suggestions made to you rather bizarre?"

Kale shrugged. "In my business," she said, "you meet all kinds, and some of them have strange quirks. My motto has always been that if it doesn't do any harm and if they pay enough, I see nothing wrong with going along. Anyway, that's how I felt toward Leon Graham."

Glenn Chapman interjected his comments into her recital for the first time. "Were you surprised by the unusual offer made to you by the late Leon Graham?" he asked blandly.

"Not at all," the witness replied. "As a matter of fact, I'd been warned by the two girls who had previous experiences with him, and they told me exactly what to expect. He always followed the same pattern."

"So you accepted the offer," the defense attorney said.

Kale nodded. "Yes, sir, I'm sorry to say."

"Sorry?"

"You bet! He double-crossed me. Instead of holding me as his captive for three days, he made me his prisoner for a total of five days, and for the last forty-eight hours, I really was his prisoner. I had no clothes, no means of escape. He had a nasty whip, and I had to obey him in all things, at all times, or he threatened to use it."

The defense attorney bowed to the witness. "Thank you, Miss Salton. I relinquish the witness to the prosecutor if he has any questions to ask."

Amos Gallagher was on his feet instantly and fired one question after another at the young woman with the rapidity of a Gatling gun. He was trying to shake her credibility, but his efforts failed. She held her ground and answered him without hesitation, and it was clear that she was telling the truth.

At the conclusion of the cross-examination, Judge von Thalman adjourned the case until the following day.

Beth was white-faced, her lips compressed, and without looking again in the direction of the witness, she went quickly to the anteroom where the United States marshal waited to escort her back to the Market Street jail.

In the courtroom Rob Martin sat still for several long moments. He still didn't know what to think or what to do, and like the previous day, after court had been adjourned, he just wanted to go back to his hotel room and see no one.

He slowly stood, and someone said to him softly, "I'm so sorry you're compelled to go through this frightful ordeal."

Rob was pleased to see it was Millicent Randall who spoke. "I didn't know you were here today. I didn't see you."

"I was sitting in the back of the room," she said. "I had to come alone. My cousin Jim had a meeting to go to. In fact, I have to meet him in a few minutes. But I know he'd want me to give you his best regards, too."

"I thank you—both of you—for your kindness," Rob said. He could not help looking directly in her dark brown eyes and noticing the concern and sympathy there. Indeed there was something indefinably lovely about this young woman, whom he had met in Montana in what seemed like another lifetime. Then it had been she who was in distress, bereaved as she was over the death of her fiancé, but now she looked self-possessed, attractively attired in a white summer dress and a straw hat decorated with little flowers.

"I feel even sorrier for your wife," Millicent said. "It must be a nightmare for her."

"I—I reckon it is," Rob replied. "I can't say that I know what's going through her mind these days. She's like a stranger to me."

Millicent put a hand on his arm. "For your own sake,

as well as for hers," she said, "don't judge her too harshly, Rob. She must be suffering horribly."

Before he could reply, she hurried away.

Meanwhile, Kale Salton retired to an anteroom with the defense attorney in order to escape the press, who were clamoring for interviews with her. There, General and Mrs. Blake soon joined them.

"Thank you for your testimony," Lee said.

"But your testimony," Eulalia added, "was just the beginning. I watched Beth the whole time you were talking. It was impossible to tell what she felt. Her face was like a mask."

"Well, I'm ready now for the next step, Mrs. Blake," Kale said. "We'll do what we can to pound some sense into her."

A carriage awaited the two women outside the courthouse. They rode off in it together, accompanied neither by Lee Blake nor Chapman. At Eulalia's insistence, the task had to be done by the two women.

Eulalia and Kale rode together to the Market Street prison, and there they were admitted to the visitors' room. Beth, who had just been returned from the courthouse, was ushered into the chamber.

"I thought it important," Eulalia said, "that you two meet. Beth, your father and I are with you. I just beg you to remember that only you can save yourself by telling the court your full story." She turned to Kale, giving Beth no opportunity to reply. "I'll be in the sheriff's office, whenever you're ready to leave," she said. Turning on her heel, she quickly left the room. There was a brief, awkward silence as the two young women took each other's measure.

"I'm indebted to you," Beth said. "Your testimony must have given my standing with the court a boost."

Kale grinned at her. "I'll bet that what I said sounded familiar."

Beth did not reply.

"As a matter of fact," Kale went on, "I'm sure you were the only person in the entire courtroom who wasn't surprised by what I had to say. In fact, you could have probably told my story almost word for word."

Beth stirred uncomfortably. "What makes you say that?"

Kale showed her irritation. "Lady," she said, "let's level with each other. That's the only way I operate. I volunteered to testify in your case because I hated Leon Graham. I'm on your side, and once both of us know it, we're going to get along one hell of a lot better."

Beth stared down at the cement floor. "I'm sorry," she murmured.

"The hell with that, too," Kale said. "Look, Beth, I understand your position. You feel that Graham made a jackass out of you and took advantage of your innocence when you should have shown a little bit of savoir faire. You're scared of your reputation—or what's left of it— and you're frightened silly that your marriage is going to go up in smoke. Now listen to me, and I'll tell you the way it was."

Beth nodded uncertainly.

"Leon was a smooth, experienced operator who understood women and knew what makes them tick. I'll bet my soul that he made a play for you, a very subtle, refined play, and then seduced you when your guard was down."

Beth smiled ruefully. "That's about the size of it," she said. "He fed me enough liquor to knock me out."

Kale nodded sympathetically. "That sounds like the dirty rotter," she said. "And once he got your clothes off you, he had you exactly where he wanted you. That's when he forced you to play his game that he paid me to play with him—and paid a number of others, as well. You were a real prisoner, and—my God!—how he must have loved it."

"That's true," Beth said, blinking back the hot tears that came to her eyes. "How he delighted in humiliating me."

"Ha! I had ample experience in that department myself, thank you. I swear, he enjoyed making a woman crawl, denigrating her and abusing her, even more than he liked actually taking her to bed. He was the most obnoxious worm I've ever met."

"Surely you—of all people," Beth said passionately, "can understand why it's impossible for me to admit in open court what I went through. I'm so ashamed that just the memory makes me cringe. How can I ever hope to hold my head high again if I admit the truth of what happened to me in that horrid man's bedchamber?"

"The way I see it," Kale said harshly, "you have a choice between being honest and admitting a lot of painful things and winning your freedom, or hugging your shame to yourself and going to prison for life—or perhaps being sentenced to be hanged. I don't see any real choice. It'll be obvious enough to everybody that you had no alternative but to give in to Graham. When you're half-naked and being subjected to beatings, you're not in any position to demand your own terms. Certainly your parents will understand, and although I haven't yet met your husband, if he's half a man, he'll understand, too."

"You're probably right," Beth answered, sighing, "but I—I just can't bring myself to come out with the whole story. It requires greater courage than I possess."

Kale did not pursue the point. "There were so many things about Leon Graham that I couldn't stand," she said. "For one thing, there was that horrid sanctimonious front. Here he was a major member of his uncle's investment company and supposedly one of the leading citizens of San Francisco. Actually he was a warped degenerate!"

"There's no question about that," Beth replied.

"You probably were too miserable, and if you don't mind my saying so, too inexperienced to notice," Kale said, "but his lacks as a lover were outstanding."

Beth shrugged. "I felt as though I were under the influence of laudanum the entire time he held me captive," she admitted.

"Well, you can take my word for it," Kale told her flatly, "he was a rotten lover. He was so damned selfish, seeking only his own pleasure and not giving a damn about his partner. It was typical of him."

"Now that you mention it," Beth said, "I see what you mean." In spite of herself, she was beginning to relax.

"Worst of all," Kale said with a sudden, abrupt show of feeling, "was that damned mynah bird of his. I gladly would have wrung its neck. 'Hello, wench! Hello, wench!'" she added, doing a creditable imitation of the bird.

Beth was startled for a moment, but suddenly she began to laugh. "Oh, I know what you mean! I hated that bird as much as I hated Leon Graham himself. I could have pulled out its feathers, one by one! 'Hello, wench! Hello, wench!'" She, too, imitated the mynah bird.

Both women laughed spontaneously. They looked at each other, and their cries and gasps were so loud that a guard opened the door and peered at them.

Beth searched in vain for a handkerchief, then wiped

the tears of laughter from her eyes with the back of her hand. "Whatever became of that bird, do you suppose?"

"I don't know," Kale said, "and I honestly don't care. But if I ever see it again, I'll strangle it on sight."

"Not if I see it first," Beth told her, and again they both whooped with laughter. The last barriers that separated the general's daughter and the prostitute had been washed away by mirth.

Kale extended a hand. "Thank you," she said, "for doing away with Leon Graham. You did what I lacked the courage to do, what a number of us also lacked. We're in your debt."

Beth grasped her hand, and as she shook it, a measure of self-respect began to return to her. The discussion of the mynah bird had been the key to unlocking the gates behind which her emotions had been penned. All at once she felt freed of the fears that had paralyzed her, and she no longer cared what people thought. She had done all she could to preserve her life and her sanity, and she had succeeded. Certainly she felt no remorse at having killed Leon Graham. Faced with the same circumstances, she would perform the same deed again, with no reluctance.

"You've opened my eyes," she said, "to what I should have realized all along. I'm not the only one Leon abused and humiliated and subjected to his horrid fancies."

"I'd hate to estimate how many of us there are in this world," Kale replied gently, and picked up her handbag. "Mrs. Blake is waiting for me. We'll talk again."

They shook hands, and Kale smiled as Beth rang for a guard and was escorted back to her cell. Then the young woman went on to the sheriff's office and joined Eulalia Blake, who was waiting for her.

They did not speak until they reached their carriage. Eulalia looked at the younger woman, a question in her eyes.

"I'll be very much surprised," Kale said, "if Beth doesn't testify and tell her whole story."

X

Defense Attorney Glenn Chapman created a sensation in the courtroom when he called Beth Martin to the witness stand to testify in her own defense. Wearing a dress of black with white collar and white trim, her face devoid of makeup, Beth mounted the witness stand and was sworn in.

An expectant hush settled over the spectators as her attorney said, "I think it might be best, Mrs. Martin, if you tell the court your story in your own words."

Beth looked out at the courtroom, and her eyes met Rob's. She had not seen him the previous day or the day before that, and she was taken aback that he was there.

She knew now that Ernst von Thalman would not be alone in judging her; her husband also intended to weigh her testimony and make up his mind whether or not to stay married to her. Certainly it was significant that since his return to San Francisco, he had not called on her at the jail, nor sent her any messages.

Putting Rob and everyone else out of her mind, she began her recital slowly and carefully, explaining that she had met Leon Graham at the home of his relatives, who were family friends, and that he had acted as her escort.

Attorney Chapman interrupted her recital. "Did you develop an intimate, personal relationship with him?" he wanted to know.

Beth flushed indignantly. "I did not! If he had even hinted at an advance, either verbal or physical, I would have stopped seeing him instantly. He understood that I was a married woman who had an affection for her husband, and I did nothing to encourage him to think otherwise." She refrained from glancing in Rob's direction, but she couldn't help being conscious of his presence as she spoke.

Eulalia Blake exchanged a glance with Kale Salton, who was seated beside her. The younger woman, distinguished by her conspicuous attire and makeup, was smiling in satisfaction.

Kale, Eulalia thought, had succeeded where everyone else had failed.

Beth went on with her recital. She had had a dinner date with Leon, she said, and he had escorted her to his house for supper. As this was the second time she had been there, with nothing inappropriate having taken place, she thought nothing of it. She still was uncertain whether he had plied her with liquor or whether her drink had been drugged. But in any event, she explained, she had awakened from a stupor to find herself unclad, in his bedroom.

Her voice faltered as she related that Graham had told her that he had already enjoyed her favors. Then he had produced a whip and threatened to beat her unless she gave herself to him again. "My head was still spinning, I was confused, and I was incapable of thinking coherently," she said. "So I gave in to his demands and allowed him to do what he pleased."

There was such a loud buzz of comment in the courtroom that Judge von Thalman had to pound his gavel for order. "The witness," he said, "obviously is under a great strain, and the court will not tolerate such outbreaks as this. If this happens again, I shall clear the court of spectators."

There was no sound in the chamber as Beth continued her testimony. Her fists clenched, her cheeks flaming, she stumbled repeatedly as she related how Leon Graham had abused and threatened her, how he had forced her to wear provocative attire and heavy cosmetics, and how he had compelled her to give in to his advances repeatedly.

"He treated me like a prostitute," she said, her voice choking, "and I felt that I had indeed become one. I had no pride, no dignity, and I felt degraded. I drank more liquor than was good for me. It was the only way I could keep going and fulfill his insatiable demands on me."

She was so overcome that Judge von Thalman called a halt and offered her a glass of water.

She regained her composure, and her attorney took advantage of the respite to ask her, "Was there any indication that the end of your ordeal was in sight?"

"No, sir, there was none," she replied. "I had no hope of ever winning release. I saw myself being forced to spend weeks and even months as his sexual captive. His demands were becoming stranger and more outrageous, and I abandoned all hope for the future." She looked plaintively at the judge. "Must I go into detail about his demands?"

"Certainly not," Ernst von Thalman told her firmly.

Her voice gathering strength, Beth told how she had found a pair of pistols used as wall decorations and had discovered that the weapons were loaded. Then, showing no feeling, she explained that she had shot him when he had returned to make outrageous sexual demands once again.

It was very quiet in the courtroom, and Glenn Chapman said, "I have no further questions. Your witness, Mr. Prosecutor."

Amos Gallagher, looking disconcerted, spread his hands. "I'll pass," he said.

"You may step down, Mrs. Martin," the judge said, compassion on his face.

Beth was so exhausted that a bailiff had to assist her down from the witness stand and help her back to her seat at the defense table. She desperately wanted to look at Rob to gauge the effect of her story on him, but she was so tired, so drained, that she could not make the effort. Perhaps, she decided, she was too afraid of his disapproval to face him.

Chapman surprised the spectators by recalling Kale Salton to the witness stand. It was evident from her expression that she, too, was surprised, but she retained her composure.

"Miss Salton," Chapman said, "you've heard Mrs. Martin's testimony. Does her experience parallel your own?"

The witness sat erect in the chair. "Beth Martin's experience was exactly like mine. There was only one significant difference. I went there voluntarily and was paid for my efforts. Mrs. Martin was forced to be there and really *was* a prisoner."

She was excused from the stand, and Chapman said simply, "The defense rests."

Judge von Thalman called for a recess. A cordon of

marshals immediately surrounded the defense table in order to shield Beth from the press and curious spectators. A white-faced, shaken Rob Martin came forward toward the defense table, and after he identified himself, the marshals admitted him through their cordon. He approached his wife and stood silently, looking down at her. Their eyes locked and held, and she smiled wanly.

"Hello, Beth," he said lamely.

They had no privacy, but Beth had grown accustomed to living in the equivalent of a fishbowl. "Why don't you sit down?" she asked, and gestured toward a chair opposite her.

He sat and propped his elbows on the table, then forced himself to speak. "Your ordeal," he said, "was even worse than I'd imagined it. But you showed real character in telling the whole story to the court."

Her weariness was reflected in her eyes and her voice. "I didn't have . . . too much choice, did I?" she asked.

He shook his head. Conscious of so many strangers, he felt inhibited. "I just want you to know," he said, "that I wish you the best of luck in the outcome of the trial."

"Thank you, Rob." She might have been speaking to a stranger.

He opened his mouth to say something more, changed his mind, and instead jumped to his feet and made his way back to his own seat. He was so perturbed that he did not see General and Mrs. Blake.

Lee understood, however. "This has to be as rough for Rob as it is for Beth herself," he said.

Eulalia explained to Kale Salton. "Rob," she said, "is Beth's husband."

The young woman's violet eyes narrowed as she studied Rob Martin at length, without comment.

Attorney Chapman came to the Blakes and leaned

toward them. "The picture has changed," he said softly. "Beth's testimony had a tremendous impact on the court, and I think we stand better than a fighting chance now, thanks to you, Miss Salton."

"Regardless of the outcome," Lee said, "we're in your debt, Miss Salton."

"Like hell you are," she replied huskily. "It's good enough for me that the reputation of that bastard Graham is ruined."

The pounding of a gavel signaled the return of Judge von Thalman to the courtroom, and the trial was resumed. Prosecutor Gallagher asked for recognition. "If it pleases the court," he said, "I want to withdraw the charges against the defendant."

Ernst von Thalman pounded his gavel. "Thank you, Mr. Gallagher," he said. "You saved me the trouble of requesting such a withdrawal. Will the defendant please rise and approach the bench?"

Beth Martin stood and moved forward slowly, her fists clenched, then stood at the base of the dais as she looked up at the black-robed judge, whom she had known all her life.

"A basic law that applies to all humanity," Judge von Thalman said, "has been observed in this country since the days the first settlers came here from England. It is a very simple law, as first expounded by Moses in the Ten Commandments: 'Thou shalt not kill.' At the same time, however, Americans have always observed another law. It was paramount throughout colonial times, and it still has existed as this nation has expanded from a few Eastern Seaboard colonies to a great land extending from the Atlantic to the Pacific oceans. I refer to the right of self-defense. When an American is attacked, he replies in kind to defend his home, his person, and his honor. That right is inherent, a basic standard in our society.

"Had you been my wife or my daughter, Mrs. Martin," Judge von Thalman continued, "I wouldn't have expected your conduct to have been any different than it was. Your rights as a woman and as an American citizen were violated; you were shamefully treated, and you acted as best you could in defense of your own honor. This court finds you guilty of killing Leon Graham, Mrs. Martin. . . ."

The judge paused, and gasps were heard in all parts of the courtroom.

"However, because of the special circumstances, you are exonerated of all wrongdoing, and I hereby order you set free, with full rights of citizenship restored to you at once."

There was pandemonium in the courtroom. Beth was in a daze. She exchanged ecstatic hugs and kisses with her father and stepmother, then hugged Attorney Chapman.

The marshals again drew a tight cordon around her and moved her to an anteroom. There, with Lee and Eulalia flanking her, she was able to greet well-wishers.

The first to be admitted were Chet and Clara Lou Harris. "We're here to offer you more than our congratulations," Chet said. "We owe you our most sincere apologies, and we hope that you'll accept them."

"Of course," Beth replied.

Clara Lou's face was tortured. "We feel that the whole terrible nightmare was our fault," she said. "You would have suffered none of the pain and embarrassment if we had not introduced you to Leon. But we had no idea he was depraved."

"You can hardly blame yourselves," Beth replied. "No one knew the type of person he really was."

"Clara Lou," Eulalia said, "Lee and I are taking a private dining room at the hotel for a celebratory dinner this evening, and we hope that you and Chet will be there."

Clara Lou and her husband exchanged a quick glance. "Are you quite sure you want us?" Chet asked diffidently.

"Naturally," Lee said. "You're hardly to blame for the sins of your nephew!"

The next to appear was Susanna Brentwood, who fell on Beth with loud, glad cries. "You have no idea how happy I am for you," she said. "I sweated bullets for you until the verdict was announced."

"I was none too easy in my own mind," Beth admitted. Then, after a moment's hesitation, she said, "Did you get a good story for your newspaper, Sue?"

"Not really," Susanna replied, looking unhappy. "The fact of the matter is that I had to wire the *Herald* to say I couldn't write the story after all. I explained that since you're my husband's first cousin, I was unable to be objective."

Beth grinned at her. "Sue, I'll give you an exclusive interview, and I'll answer any and all questions."

"You really will?" the excited Susanna cried. "How wonderful! That will save my professional reputation."

Before Beth could reply, Kale Salton came forward, both hands outstretched. " 'Hello, wench'!" she said, imitating the hated mynah bird.

" 'Hello, wench!' " Beth replied in the same tone.

As others watched them in wonder, the two young women laughed uproariously and embraced.

At this juncture Rob Martin came hesitantly into the

room and stopped short when he saw the merriment. At last Beth saw him, and hiding her lack of ease behind a mask of laughter, she sobered sufficiently to present him to Kale.

Rob shook the young woman's hand warmly. "I owe you thanks," he said. "If it weren't for your testimony, the Lord alone knows what might have happened to Beth."

Kale smiled but made no reply, her violet eyes boring into him, searching and analyzing. He felt uncomfortable beneath her intense scrutiny.

Lee and Eulalia Blake greeted their son-in-law warmly, and Rob realized there was no opportunity for him to spend even a moment alone with his wife. Instead, he exchanged congratulations with the Blakes and inquired of Eulalia about Toby's whereabouts and activities.

"You'll be joining us for supper this evening, I hope," Lee said. "We're planning to make it quite a celebration."

Rob had hoped he could dine alone with Beth. They had so much to discuss, so many misunderstandings and jealousies to be cleared away in order to set their marriage on the right path again. He realized, however, that this was not the time for sober considerations. Beth's life and freedom had been in jeopardy, and both had been preserved. So the prevailing mood was one of jubilant hysteria, and he knew he would have to attend the dinner and join in the festivities.

There was one thing he felt he could not explain to the Blakes, much less to Beth: He had left the Sierra Nevada at the worst of all possible times. He and his crews were encountering one of the most difficult stretches of terrain in the entire route that the railroad would follow from Sacramento to the East, and he had to be present before any new track could be laid. Only because of the urgent importance of Beth's trial had he left the mountains in the first place. Now that she had been exonerated, it was his duty to return as quickly as possible.

Certainly this was not the moment to reveal that with his wife's future no longer in doubt, he was obligated to return without delay to the mountains. He could only hope to make his position clear to Beth before he left.

Millicent Randall and her cousin, Jim, gained admission to the room, and Rob presented them to his wife.

"I'm so pleased for your sake—and for Rob's," Millicent said. "I know how difficult these past weeks must have been for you both, and I wish you every happiness."

Thanking her, Beth studied her surreptitiously. She recalled Rob describing Millicent Randall as plain, but the young woman was anything but ordinary-looking. Millicent's sincerity generated a vitality that made her attractive in an unusual way.

Other well-wishers clamored for Beth's attention, and she was forced to devote time to them. When she next took note of Millicent, the young woman was standing in the far corner of the room in animated conversation with Rob. Something in the attitude of the couple gripped her. Both appeared deeply absorbed, and it was plain there was a bond between them.

Kale Salton materialized at Beth's elbow. "Chummy, aren't they?" she said.

Beth only nodded.

"You're lucky the judge let you off," Kale said in the same low tone. "Your husband and that girl wouldn't

waste any time if you'd been shipped off to a peniten-
tiary for years."

Beth forced a laugh. "It isn't that bad. And I trust Rob
completely."

Kale looked at her pityingly. "There's a chemistry at
work," she said bluntly, "between the lady and your husband. Whether she realizes it or not, she's attracted to
him. As for him, he's a man, and, Beth, there isn't a man
alive I'd trust as far as I could throw him. You don't
know them the way I do. They're all liars and cheats,
every last one of them."

Beth was in no position to argue with someone with
Kale's experience. The thought entered her mind, however, that if she felt jealous of Rob based on such flimsy
evidence, he must be suffering the tortures of the
damned after hearing her testimony. She wanted to go
to Rob immediately and explain that Graham had meant
less than nothing to her.

But there was no way she could speak to him alone; a
score of people were clamoring for her attention. Almost
wistfully, she watched him across the room as he continued talking with Millicent.

Toby Holt concluded that his work in Dakota was finished, at least for the present. He had faithfully followed
the directive given by General Grant and had visited at
least forty towns and villages of the Sioux, trying to persuade them to make peace with the United States. The
time had come for him to return to Montana and to
place himself at the disposal of Colonel Andy Brentwood. If war broke out this summer between the Indians and the whites despite Toby's mission, then the
troops would have to be called out, and Toby would go
with them. No doubt by now, he reflected, Andy's regi-

ment had been augmented by the troops sent him by
Grant and Blake, and there would be no way the Indians could win this unfortunate war.

There were matters still to be settled. First, there was
the question of the whereabouts of Tall Stone and Ma
Hastings. Shortly after Ralph Hastings disappeared,
Toby had ridden off by himself to the vicinity of Five
Rocks. His plan was to take advantage of his knowledge
that Tall Stone and his braves would be there, and he
was going to approach the site just so far, then beat a
hasty retreat, hoping the Indians would give chase.
Then he could get them where he would have the advantage, namely in a small valley while he was in the
heights, and he would put an end once and for all to the
plots against him and Gentle Doe.

But the site at Five Rocks was desolate, as barren as
the rest of the Badlands. Toby saw that Indians had
indeed been encamped there, and he saw from the
tracks of a horse that this was the direction Ralph
Hastings had taken after he had left their camp. There
was blood on the ground, and Toby realized what
Hastings had done: He had given up his own life to save
Toby and Gentle Doe.

Solemn, bewildered, Toby rode back to the campsite
where he had left the Indian woman. He told her what
he had learned, and she looked down at the ground for
some time.

"I do not know why Ralph Hastings gave up his life
for us," she said at last. "But he was a very brave man."

Now there was the question of what Toby should do
with Gentle Doe. The time was approaching when they
would have to part. He refused to dodge the issue. It
never occurred to him that he could simply ride off and
abandon Gentle Doe. He waited until they were eating

their supper of fish, wild onions, and corn, and then he launched into the matter.

"My work in Dakota is finished," he said to her, speaking in the language of the Sioux. "I have done that which the general in Washington commanded me to do, and I can do no more."

Gentle Doe made no reply, but from the way that she lowered her head, Toby knew that she had heard. He fell silent, too, giving her an opportunity to respond before he spoke again.

At last she raised her head and smiled at him, and when she addressed him, her voice was calm. "I have known from the beginning," she said, "that we would not spend the rest of our days traveling to the towns of the Sioux in Dakota. When do you leave?"

"Soon," he said, "but first we must settle your future."

"There is nothing to be settled," she replied firmly. "Do not concern yourself with me."

He raised an eyebrow. "If I left you to your own devices, what would you do, and where would you go?"

She shrugged. "I could find a home for myself in many towns of my people."

"I think not," he replied firmly. "It would not be so easy for Gentle Doe."

"Why not?" she demanded, displaying emotion for the first time.

"You have been with me for many months," Toby said, "as I have visited the towns of the Sioux and have spoken to their chiefs and medicine men and their warriors. All who have seen you have known that you accompanied me. The leaders of the Sioux nation have not yet accepted the advice that I have given them. They still might go to war against the United States. That would make me their enemy, and because of me, you, too, would be their foe."

She knew he spoke the truth, and she fell silent.

Accustomed to her ways, Toby knew he had to ride roughshod over them. "You," he said, "will ride with me to Montana. I will place you in the care of Colonel Brentwood, the commander of the Eleventh Cavalry, and his troops will watch over you. You have served the United States, and now it is time for her soldiers to offer you their protection. You will have a warm place to live during the winter months that lie ahead, and you'll be provided with food and shelter."

"But you will not be in Montana with me," she said in a small voice.

He met her gaze. "I expect," he said, "that I will be in Montana only for a short time. Eventually I must travel across the high mountains to Oregon, where my wife waits for me and where our baby is already born."

Gentle Doe sighed faintly. "I have known from the beginning that the day would come when you would return to your own squaw and would wish to look upon your child. It is right that you do this."

She was releasing him gracefully, and Toby inclined his head in thanks to her.

"I have always known," she said, "that you have not given me your heart. You have loved only one woman, she who is your lawful squaw. You have slept with me only because I tempted you, and you are a man, so you have been unable to resist temptation. I say this only in truth, not in anger. I expect nothing from you in return, and I am thankful that you think enough of me to plan for my future in Montana. So be it." She folded her arms across her breasts and looked into the campfire, her face resembling carved stone. "I am content."

She was sincere, Toby knew, and he was relieved.

With Gentle Doe's future settled, he lost no time in setting out for Montana with her. They traveled rapidly, covering a minimum of thirty miles per day, and as they left the Black Hills behind them and headed into the eerie wilderness of the Dakota Badlands, the weather was cooler and the landscape was bleak and forlorn.

There was no game in the Badlands, and Toby had to rely on jerky and dried corn. For her part, Gentle Doe remained unchanged; she was tranquil, serving Toby when it came to tending a campfire or making a soup, and she was always cheerful, though more silent than usual.

They rode deeper into the Badlands, and one day, in midmorning, Toby halted suddenly, dismounted, and examined the ground carefully.

Gentle Doe also dismounted, looking at him questioningly. Toby pointed silently to tracks in the foliage underfoot, and the young woman dropped to one knee beside him and studied the tracks in silence for a time.

"A large party of warriors has passed this way recently," Toby said. "A far larger party than that which lay in ambush for us at Five Rocks."

Gentle Doe continued to study the tracks. "There were three parties, not one," she said. "There were Sioux, there were also Blackfoot, and there were Cheyenne."

Toby, who was usually adept at reading such signs, looked at her, raising an eyebrow.

Her reply was simple. "These," she said, pointing to the ground, "are the hoofprints made by many different kinds of horses. Some have been made by the horses of the Blackfoot, which are larger than Sioux animals, and some must have been made by the horses of the

Cheyenne, which are very small and more adept at living in the mountains."

Toby shuddered when he realized that the braves of the three Indian nations had banded together. He could guess what the purpose of their union might be: war.

He decided to take no chances, and keeping a sharp watch for tracks, he made a detour to the south. He halted for the night near the base of a cliff, from the top of which he could look down on all sides at anyone who might be approaching. Leaving their horses at the base of the cliff, they climbed up to the heights. They lighted no fire for their evening meal. Instead, they ate their jerked beef and parched corn dry, without benefit of warm soup.

It grew darker as they ate, and the couple noticed campfires burning in a valley off to their right, below them. Toby felt increasingly uneasy. He counted more than a dozen large fires and knew that a substantial number of warriors was attending the gathering of Indian nations below.

The fires were too far away for Toby to make out the identities of any individuals. But the significance of the gathering was all too painfully obvious. It meant that his own attempt to persuade the Sioux to forego their alliance with the Blackfoot and Cheyenne and to maintain peace had ended in failure. Thunder Cloud had no doubt managed to play upon the war fever of the Indians, and the nations had chosen after all to form an alliance that could have only one purpose: to go to war against the white men.

Soon, if United States troops did not take action, the farms and ranches of settlers in Dakota, Montana, and Wyoming would be attacked. Men, women, and children would be killed and scalped, cattle would be stolen, and homes and barns would be plundered and put to the torch.

Gentle Doe also understood the meaning of the gathering. She realized that the months that she and Toby had traveled from one end of Dakota to the other talking to the Sioux had been spent in vain. She appeared on the verge of tears.

Her reaction was so at variance with her customary restraint that Toby put an arm around her shoulders to console her. This, added to the unsettling certainty that the nations were taking to the warpath, robbed him of his vigilance. Ordinarily he would have realized that the Indians, gathering for a major conclave, would have posted sentries in the hills surrounding their major campsite, and he would have been on the lookout for them. The momentary dulling of his caution permitted the hulking Sioux warrior to draw close to the campsite that Toby and Gentle Doe had established for the night.

Tall Stone himself was the leader of a patrol of Sioux scouts. Having left Ma Hastings to meet her fate on the Dakota prairie, he had returned to his village and was overjoyed to learn that his people had finally decided to go on the warpath. Now rich booty would be his, including the scalps of many white settlers.

Having seen horses near the rocky heights, Tall Stone had decided to investigate, telling his men to continue on their patrol without him.

He climbed up the steep slope of the cliff, and when he reached the top, he crept to where the intruders were sitting. Staring out from behind a rocky crag, he recognized Gentle Doe, and a sense of wild excitement surged within him. The gods whom he worshipped were proving their omnipotence to him by delivering into his hands the woman who had spurned him.

So this white man was Toby Holt, Tall Stone thought,
the man he once believed he had killed. He had made a
mistake before; he would not fail now. He reached for
the tomahawk hanging from his belt, felt the sharp cutting edge of the blade, and grimly took a firm grip on
the handle.

Gentle Doe was the first to become aware of the in-
truder. Reacting instinctively, she threw herself across
Toby's body. At the same moment the tomahawk left
Tall Stone's hand. His aim was true, and the deadly
weapon found its target, inflicting a crushing blow on
Gentle Doe's back.

Toby reacted immediately. He pulled his six-shooter
from his holster and fired a bullet into the Indian's heart.
Tall Stone died instantly and fell to the ground as the
shot thundered through the hills.

Toby dropped to the ground beside Gentle Doe and
gathered her in his arms. He saw at a glance that she
had suffered a mortal wound. She had given her own life
for his, and the realization devastated him.

Gentle Doe had not lost consciousness. In spite of her
pain, she managed to smile up at him. "Do not grieve
for me," she whispered. "The gods are very wise."

Cradling her in his arms, he could make no reply.

Her smile remained steady. "Soon," she whispered,
"you will return to your own squaw and baby. Rather
than allow me to live in loneliness and grief, my gods
have summoned me and will provide a sanctuary for me
in the hunting grounds where my ancestors dwell." She
was finding it increasingly difficult to speak.

"Save your breath," he told her. "I'm going to save
you."

She shook her head. "No," she replied, speaking so
softly that he found it hard to hear her. "It is too late. I

have known only happiness with you. I have but one request. . . ."

"Ask it," he said huskily.

Her strength ebbing rapidly, she was too weak to reply in words, but Toby sensed from her expression that she wanted him to kiss her.

He bent lower, and his lips touched hers. For an instant she responded, warmth in her lips, and then, all at once, she went limp.

Toby refused to abandon her body to the coyotes or to the Indians, who might dishonor her in death. Moving swiftly, aware that his shot had alerted the camp below of his presence, he carried her down the rocky slope and lashed her body to her mare. He then quickly gathered his belongings from the heights for a swift departure. He could not tarry to mourn.

Before he sped on his way, Toby's glance rested for an instant on the body of Tall Stone.

This was the wilderness, a primitive land. Pausing for a moment, Toby drew his knife, scalped the Sioux warrior, and unmindful of the bloodstains on his buckskin trousers, stuffed the scalp into his belt. Then he descended from the slope, mounted his horse, and galloped toward Montana, leading the horse with Gentle Doe's corpse behind him.

The party in the private dining room at the Palace Hotel continued to gain momentum as the evening progressed. General Blake made a short speech, in which he thanked the many friends who were present for their support of his daughter. Defense Attorney Chapman also made a brief address, in which he gave full credit for the outcome of the trial to Kale Salton. Kale was loudly cheered.

A highlight of the party was the sudden, unexpected appearance of Judge and Mrs. von Thalman. The judge enveloped Beth in a bear hug and told her, "In all my years on the bench, nothing has ever given me as much pleasure as I had when I exonerated you of wrongdoing."

Beth returned his warm embrace, then looked around the crowded, noisy room. One good thing had grown out of her ordeal: her reconciliation with her father and her stepmother. She knew now that she had been infantile and selfish in opposing Lee Blake's remarriage. Catching her stepmother's eye, Beth ran to her and hugged her fiercely. Eulalia held Beth just as tightly.

"I don't quite know how to tell you this," Beth said awkwardly, "but it was your support and Papa's that enabled me to survive. You believed in me when I could no longer believe in myself."

"We believe in you," Eulalia replied softly, emotionally, "because we know you for what you are. But, dear, don't dwell on the past."

"That's right!" Kale Salton, who had overheard the exchange, added emphatically. "There's nothing to be gained by reliving your miserable experience with Graham. Put him out of your mind and concentrate on your future."

Beth's eyes automatically flicked across the table to her husband, who was deeply engrossed in conversation with Millicent Randall and her cousin Jim, whom Rob had invited to the party.

Kale studied him again, her violet eyes narrowed, her full mouth pursed. Curious about their conversation, she eavesdropped.

"Jim and I," Millicent said, "have just reached a momentous decision—momentous for us, that is. We've decided we're going to settle in the West."

"Really?" Rob had no idea why he felt so pleased.

"A great many factors went into our decision," Millicent continued. "We have no family back East. In fact, we have no ties at all, other than at the Conservatory of Music in Baltimore. But I'm far enough advanced as a flutist that I don't need instruction any longer, and I can continue my studies myself."

Rob nodded, listening intently.

"Fortunately," Jim said, "we have sufficient funds to live wherever we please. So we're free to do what we choose."

"You'll buy a house here in San Francisco perhaps?" Rob asked.

Millicent looked at Jim, then shook her head. "San Francisco certainly is pretty," she said, "and Portland is very attractive, too. But after Baltimore, we've had our fill of cities. The real charm of the West lies in the open spaces, the rolling hills, and the towering white peaks. I think we're going to buy a ranch somewhere."

"Millicent mentioned to you my business meeting in town," Jim said. "It was with a real estate man who has properties for sale in Nevada, Utah, and Idaho."

"Do you understand ranch life?" Rob asked.

Jim smiled. "Not really. In fact, we don't know any more than do most people who migrate to the West and settle on ranches. But we'll learn, and it will be so good for me to be occupied again. You have no idea how badly I've floundered since I lost my eye in the war and was retired from the regular army. Owning a ranch will give me a new lease on life."

Rob nodded and then cocked his head to one side.

"What about you, Millicent?" he asked. "Won't you be lonely on a ranch?"

She shook her head. "I think not," she said. "The murder of my fiancé has been such a blow that I welcome solitude—at least for now. As to being lonely, I'll have my flute and my music. And with the completion of the railroad, I'll certainly be able to travel to San Francisco every now and then to attend concerts."

Rob absorbed what she had told him. "Have you picked a site for your ranch?"

"Not yet," Jim said. "But we're going to look at some of the spots the real estate man talked to me about. We intend to take our wagon and some supplies and leave for the Nevada Territory in a few days."

"Be careful," Rob told the cousins. "Life can be pretty rough there."

"I know," Millicent said, smiling, remembering some of their adventures in the West, "but Jim can take care of himself. Come to think of it, so can I."

Indeed she could, Kale thought. Millicent Randall struck her as being very competent indeed. She appeared to be gentle, sweet, and contemplative, a woman wrapped up in her music. But Kale felt certain she was capable of meeting any crisis.

It might be wise, Kale reflected, to have a few words with Beth on the subject of her husband and his interest in the young lady musician from Baltimore. But this was neither the time nor the place for such a discussion. Kale bided her time, accepted another glass of champagne, and clinked glasses merrily with Glenn Chapman.

It was an unusual experience for Kale to be accepted socially, not only by leading citizens of San Francisco but also by their wives. The trial of Beth Martin had served her well, enabling her to rise in San Francisco society and to find a relatively secure place for herself there. For the moment, at least, she was not being treated as an outcast by the ladies, nor did the men eye her speculatively. Her advice and testimony had won Beth's case, and Kale realized that she, too, had profited greatly from her new friendship.

Rob Martin tugged at the fob at his waistcoat pocket, glanced at his nickel-plated watch, and then told Beth that he wanted a word with her in private. They rose simultaneously from the table, murmuring apologies, and made their way together from the private dining room to an antechamber.

Watching them, Kale realized that it was the first time she had see them together all evening.

When they reached the anteroom, Rob closed the door, shutting out the sounds of laughter and conversation. He turned to Beth and, not knowing how to break his news to her, said abruptly, "I've got to go."

She was stunned. "What do you mean?"

"I've got to get back to work," he said.

"I suppose so," Beth said dispiritedly.

He raised his voice unconsciously, speaking defensively. "I stole the time to come down here to the city for your trial," he said. "There was a conflict between duty to my wife and duty to my work, and my wife won."

Beth laughed shakily. "I'm glad of that," she said.

Rob said, "Now, I've got to get back. I'm needed for the laying of the track in the mountains. Be patient with me, Beth. If all goes well I'll be back within a few weeks' time, at the most. I can't say precisely, but it shouldn't be more than four weeks at the outside."

She nodded, swallowing hard. "When must you leave?"

"Right now," he replied. "Tonight. I've delayed as long as I can. I'll have to ride all night and all day tomorrow in order to reach our advance camp by the following day."

"I see." She was very subdued.

"I'm sorry, Beth," Rob said. "Truly I am. I don't mean to dampen the celebration. But it can't be helped."

"Of course it can't." She made an attempt to rally.

"At least," he said, trying to speak heartily, "I'll be returning to work with an uncluttered mind. I thank the Lord your name has been cleared."

She wanted to pound his chest, to cry at the top of her voice that exoneration was not enough. She longed to be treated as his wife, to spend her nights and days with him, to have him make love to her and demonstrate that the experience with Leon Graham had not come between them. But so much unpleasantness, innuendo, and suspicion had separated them that she stood tongue-tied, rooted to the spot.

"When I'm finished," he said, "do you want to meet me here in San Francisco, or are you going back to Fort Vancouver with your father and Eulalia?"

Beth wanted to assert her independence. "You'll be able to reach San Francisco far more quickly than Fort Vancouver," she said, "so I'll meet you here."

He raised an eyebrow and had to choke back a desire to say that staying on alone in the city had caused her enough trouble in the first place. "Will you keep your quarters at the hotel?" he asked, hoping the question sounded innocuous.

Beth shook her head. "Kale Salton has asked me to pay her a visit," she said. "She has a lovely house on Powell Street, and I think that's where I'll go."

He was startled. "But she's a—a prostitute!"

"Her morals aren't transferable," Beth replied stubbornly, determined to show her husband that if he had a life of his own, so did she. "I owe her my freedom, and perhaps my life itself. I'm grateful to her. As far as I'm concerned, she's a wonderful person."

"But, damn it, Beth—" Rob began, then stopped. She saw him struggle with his irritation and concern, then, sadly, watched the flame go out of his eyes. He said coldly, "If that's what you want."

She had hoped to provoke him into some strong action—either refusing to return to the mountains or, at the very least, forbidding her to stay with Kale—but instead he had acquiesced, as though where she stayed and what she did were matters of indifference to him.

She was afraid then that the marriage was finished, but she showed no sign of her apprehension. Outwardly composed, she faced her husband with just a glint of defiance in her eyes.

The confrontation was as uncomfortable and painful for Rob as for her. "I can't delay any longer," he said. "I must be on my way."

"Of course," Beth replied, and raised her face to his.

Rob placed his hands lightly on her shoulders and kissed her. The lips that brushed hers were those of a stranger.

Then he was gone.

Beth stood alone in the anteroom, her fists clenched, shaking her head as she fought back tears. Finally, she walked dry-eyed into the dining room, where the dinner party was still in progress.

Kale Salton saw that she was white-faced and tense, however, and hastened to join her before she could reach her place at the table. "What's wrong?"

"Rob has gone back to his work in the mountains," she said. "He claims he's urgently needed there."

"That," Kale said emphatically, "is rubbish! His wife needed him right here. If he had a brain in his head, he would have stayed with you tonight and loved you as you've never been loved before!"

"He didn't see things that way," Beth replied bleakly. "He'll come for me next month."

"By next month," Kale replied harshly, "you may not want him."

Beth looked surprised and shocked.

"Beth," Kale told her bluntly, "you may not know it, but you're the most famous woman in the United States, at least for the moment. Your testimony and your release by the court are in every newspaper in America. A lot of men are going to find you very interesting."

Beth smiled somewhat ruefully. She did not quite see the situation in that light. "I don't want anyone except Rob," she said.

"You've been whirled around so hard that you don't know what you want," Kale said sympathetically. "Put the whole problem out of your mind for now. You're free, and that's good enough for the present. Tomorrow you're going to sleep until noon and then have breakfast in bed. Then we're going on a shopping spree, and we'll decide whether we'll go to the theater or a concert tomorrow night. In a couple of days we'll have a little chat about Rob Martin, and then you can decide where you're going to go from here in your marriage, or if you're going anywhere."

The young officer who served as assistant adjutant of the Eleventh Cavalry tapped at the office door of the regimental commander of Fort Shaw in Montana, then burst into the room before Colonel Andy Brentwood had a chance to speak. "Excuse me, sir," the agitated lieutenant said.

Andy looked up, startled.

"Captain Toby Holt just showed up at the fort, riding hell-bent-for-leather. He looks like he's been dragged through a swamp. He has a dead body with him wrapped in a blanket, and he swore he'd put a bullet through the forehead of any man who touches it!"

Andy was on his feet. "Where is he now?"

"The last I saw of him, he was tethering his horses and was on his way here, sir. He—"

The door opened, and the lieutenant had no chance to complete his statement.

Toby Holt stood in the doorway, weaving slightly from side to side. He was unshaven, his clothes were rumpled and filthy, and mud was caked on his boots. There were deep smudges of exhaustion beneath his red-rimmed eyes, and he appeared on the verge of collapse.

"Andy," he said tensely, his voice hoarse, "I've ridden here straight through from Dakota to bring you some vital news!"

Andy stared at him. "How could you possibly ride straight through from Dakota?" he demanded.

Toby spoke matter-of-factly. "I changed horses at the houses of settlers on the way here. When they heard my news, they cooperated. I'm sorry to have to tell you this, Andy, but our effort to prevent a war with the Indians has failed." He went on to describe the conclave of Sioux, Blackfoot, and Cheyenne he had seen in the Badlands of Dakota.

"Lieutenant," Andy snapped, "notify all battalions and independent companies—including all the new troops that have arrived to augment the regiment—to be ready to take the field in full battle gear at dawn tomorrow morning. And I want all unit commanders and the regimental staff to report here for a meeting in one hour's time."

"Yes, sir," the lieutenant said as he saluted and hastily departed.

"When did you leave Dakota?" Andy asked.

Toby pondered for a moment, then shrugged wearily. "I'm not sure," he said. "The days and nights run together. But I'm sure I got here before the tribes started killing, burning, and looting. From the looks of their encampment, they must have had more than two thousand braves gathered, and they'll wait until their whole force is assembled. I estimate they'll be at least three thousand strong when they go into the field. To be on the safe side, I estimate they can put about thirty-five hundred warriors into combat. By marching promptly, I reckon you'll be able to reach them before they do any appreciable damage."

Andy perched on one edge of the desk. "What's this about you carrying a body into the fort with you?"

A dark shadow passed across Toby's face, and his voice was grim. "I brought Gentle Doe of the Sioux here for burial," he said. "She not only worked and traveled with me for many weeks in an attempt to preserve the peace, but she sacrificed her life for me." He sketched briefly the circumstances of Gentle Doe's death.

"I want a coffin," Toby said, "and a plot in the fort's cemetery. I think it would be fitting, too, if a chaplain presided."

Andy was afraid his friend would collapse from fatigue. "Leave the details to me," he said. "I'll attend to them."

An hour later, Toby stood in the Fort Shaw cemetery before an open grave. In front of it was a pine coffin draped with an American flag, and an honor guard stood at attention as the chaplain intoned the service:

"I am the resurrection and the life, saith the Lord. He that believeth in me, though he were dead, yet shall he live. And whosoever liveth and believeth in me, shall never die. I know that my redeemer liveth, and that He shall stand at the latter day upon the earth. And though this body be destroyed, yet shall I see God, whom I shall see for myself and mine eyes shall behold, and not as a stranger. We brought nothing into this world, and it is certain we can carry nothing out. The Lord gave, and the Lord hath taken away; blessed be the name of the Lord."

Toby swayed from side to side, scarcely hearing the familiar words the chaplain was saying.

At last the flag was removed and folded, the coffin was lowered into the grave, and a thirteen-gun salute broke the silence.

Toby reached down, picked up a handful of loose dirt, and threw it into the grave. "Thank you, Gentle Doe," he said softly.

As he turned away from the grave, Andy materialized beside him. "I'm taking you home with me," he said, "and putting you to bed. You'll be needed tomorrow to ride with the scouts and seek out the Indians for us. That means you're going to need a long sleep and a hefty meal before we go into the field."

Toby did not protest. "What news is there of Clarissa?" he asked.

"I had a letter from Susanna just this morning," Andy

replied. "She's on the Pacific Coast, and she recently saw Clarissa and your new son."

Tired as he was, Toby beamed.

"Yes, a baby boy. And both mother and son are doing fine. They were staying at Fort Vancouver with General and Mrs. Blake, but Susanna writes that they've moved to the ranch in Oregon, now that school's let out for Cindy and Hank." Knowing his friend had enough on his mind, Andy decided to mention nothing about the trial of Beth Martin.

Toby was elated. He would wire Clarissa in the morning. Now, however, having honored Gentle Doe in death, he was ready to sleep. Then the next day he would be prepared for the war with the Indians that he had tried so hard to prevent.

XI

The Eleventh Cavalry's special battalion of scouts was both an elite and motley group. Some of its members were full-blooded Indians, most of them from the Arapaho and Cheyenne nations, who had chosen to cast their lot with the United States. Some were half-breeds, men who had been rejected by the Sioux and the Blackfoot and had found their welcome in the ranks of those whom the Indians regarded as their foes. Some were white, wilderness-hardened trappers and hunters, who had achieved familiarity with the mountains and valleys of the West.

Divided into two troops, each comprising fifty men and each commanded by a captain, they made up the very soul of the Eleventh Cavalry. They knew what was expected of them as scouts and as soldiers, and above all, they respected no man solely because of his rank or status.

Toby Holt had been called to active military duty by Colonel Brentwood and had been granted the brevet—or temporary—rank of major. He had been given command

of the scouts, and the members of the battalion cheered
when the news was broken to them. They knew Toby,
admired and trusted him, just as he knew them. Together they formed a team that the scouts believed to be
invincible.

Leading the battalion, Major Toby Holt was meticu-
lous in his observations, scouring the terrain for any clue
to the whereabouts of the enemy. They spread out over
a wide area as they rode, several miles in advance of the
main body of the augmented Eleventh Cavalry regiment. Always on the alert, they crossed from Montana
into Dakota, then headed into the Badlands, scouring
the terrain for any sign of the foe who was threatening
the Western territories.

The original meeting place of the Indians that Toby
and Gentle Doe had encountered had been moved,
probably because of the arrival of many more warriors. The camps of the Sioux, the Blackfoot, and the
Cheyenne would now no doubt be located in a spot that
afforded them the greatest security and protection. But
in moving their camp from the original meeting place,
the Indians had successfully covered their tracks, no
mean feat for a large body of warriors. By splitting up
into small groups, apparently heading in all different
directions, the Indians successfully eluded any pursuers.

"The Indians," Toby told his men when they halted
beside a small river to water their horses, "are good at
self-concealment. There's nobody who can hide more effectively. But one thing is sure. There's no way on earth
that they can hide three thousand men—maybe more. It
can't be done. Sooner or later we'll find them . . . or
they'll find us."

Riding easily, comfortably, the scouts covered considerable territory each day. Toby was familiar with the

tricks necessary for a successful operation. The first requisite was that the horses had to be rested and never overworked, and he did not push the battalion beyond its limits. Thanks to ample game, the men also ate well. They had plenty of time for sleep, as well, and after they had been in the field for ten days, they were as fresh as they had been when they had first left Fort Shaw.

It would be wrong to claim that they found the enemy. On the morning of the scouts' twelfth day after leaving the fort, a large force of Blackfoot, commanded by their chief, Red Elk, found them.

The scouts were riding cautiously through a rugged, wooded patch in a basinlike valley of the Black Hills. The trail was wide, but it was surrounded by wooded slopes, and it was impossible to see if any Indians were concealed on the heights. As the scouts were beginning to ascend the trail leading up the slope, out of the valley, a hail of arrows suddenly descended on them from the heights above. The unit reacted instantly and went into battle formation, the men on the flanks moving in toward the center.

"Fire at will!" Toby shouted, and soon rifles began to crack as the scouts spotted braves through the screen of trees.

The barrage of arrows from the concealed Indians on the heights was so thick that Toby realized his unit was badly outnumbered. Fighting off his growing sense of alarm, Toby knew he would suffer many needless casualties if he tried to force his way forward through the woods and out of the valley. Two of his men had already fallen from their horses, Indian arrows sticking from their chests, and Toby instantly ordered the scouts

to fall back. At once, the unit retreated down the side of
the hill and returned to the floor of the valley.

Too late Toby realized he had maneuvered the battalion into a dangerous position. The slope directly in
front of them, which they had just abandoned, was steep
and wooded, as were those to the left and right. This
meant that all three could hide attackers and would be
difficult to defend. To the rear there was also rugged
terrain, which would inhibit a further withdrawal. This
meant the two troops would be obliged to hold their
present positions; if they tried to move, they would face
greater hazards.

As Toby pondered the dilemma, the Blackfoot, ably
led by Red Elk, were quick to take advantage of the situation. The braves spread out to occupy the heights to
the left and the right of the defenders, which would enable them to attack simultaneously from three sides.

Toby's heart sank as war whoops echoed from the
three slopes, indicating that the Indians were massing
for an attack. He could blame no one but himself for his
battalion's predicament, but he knew that if he did not
panic, he might still snatch victory from defeat.

Toby's mind had always responded swiftly and coolly
in times of crisis. He had always managed to keep his
head, and his analytical abilities, rather than becoming
impaired, invariably had been sharpened. But today,
inexplicably, his mind refused to function, though he
recognized the problems that faced him and his men
and knew that he bore the brunt of responsibility for ex-
tricating the battalion from its predicament.

He saw the two scout captains watching, waiting for
his orders, but he remained blank, and no orders came.
Never had he been in such a tight spot.

As the hoarse war cries of the Blackfoot sounded

shrilly, their rapidly growing volume and cadence indicating they would launch an all-out attack at any moment, Toby tried to regain his equilibrium by wondering, deliberately, how his father would have reacted to the situation in which he found himself.

Whip Holt's reputation had been that of a magician. It had been said many times that he had never been outsmarted or outmaneuvered by Indians. Toby had been advised on countless occasions by his father on what needed to be done when engaged in combat with Indians, and the son had been able to absorb more of Whip Holt's philosophy than had anyone else.

Suddenly, as the Indians prepared their assault and the scouts waited for instructions, Toby heard the unmistakable drawl of his father's voice, and the cries of the Indians faded as the voice of Whip Holt gained strength and intensity.

"Son," Whip said, "anytime you get into a fight with Indians, always keep in mind that they're the best in the world on the offensive. They throw themselves heart and soul into an attack, and if you use conventional defenses, they're going to trim you every time."

Toby wiped beads of cold sweat from his forehead and listened intently. He recalled having heard his father speak such words in the past, but Toby believed he wasn't merely remembering what his father had told him through the years; he could swear he was actually *hearing* his father's words spoken aloud again, as though he were reaching out to him.

"Now," Whip said, "if you live long enough and you get involved in enough hassles with the Indians, there are bound to be times when you're going to find yourself in a bad fix. The Indians will take you by surprise because they're experts at it. They'll attack before you know what's happening to you, and then you're in for it."

Toby nodded soberly. That description certainly fitted his present situation all too perfectly.

"When that happens," Whip went on, "there's only one thing you can do, son: Dig in! Take a firm stand and don't budge a yard. If you pull back, the Indians will be sure they have you on the run, and they'll swarm all over you. Dig in! Match them shot for shot—and then some. For every arrow they fire at you, give them one, two—a dozen—bullets in return. Bullets are a heap more deadly than arrows. You and I know it, and it's your job to make blame good and certain that the Indians know it."

Toby began to breathe easier. The situation was clarifying now, and he began to see what he needed to do.

"Eventually, if you hurt the enemy badly enough, they'll pull back. That's when you change your tactics."

Toby nodded eagerly.

"That's the point where you go on the offensive yourself! The instant they stop attacking, you start. You'll have them on the run, and there's no way they can possibly stand up to you!"

Toby knew now what had to be done. "Thanks, Pa," he murmured. He could have sworn he heard the older man's familiar voice say distinctly, "Don't mention it, Son. It's like I always told you—think fast, shoot straight, and keep your powder dry." He chuckled, and his voice slowly faded away. The whole conversation, Toby realized, had occurred in just seconds.

Now the moment of decision was at hand, and Toby no longer hesitated. "Circle, dismount, and shield!" he called.

"Circle, dismount, and shield!" The two captains, who

had been waiting for instructions, bellowed the order, repeating it.

The scouts, all of them veterans of innumerable encounters with Indian tribes, performed the difficult maneuver creditably. They formed in a circle, the classic defensive posture when holding off an Indian attack, and dismounted, simultaneously forcing some of their superbly trained horses to lie down, while the other horses were rounded up by some of the men and brought into the center of the circle. Taking up positions on the ground behind the reclining horses, the scouts used the animals as shields.

"Fire at will, boys!" Toby called. "Give them a lead bath!"

The circle erupted in gunfire, the scouts responding eagerly to the order, as he had known they would, demonstrating their superb skill as marksmen.

The order had been timed to perfection. As the warriors swooped down the three hills toward the valley, gesticulating and whooping, only occasionally firing their arrows, they were met with a steady drumfire of bullets. The carnage was frightful.

Husky braves, their faces hideous with war paint, screamed as they threw their hands above their heads and dropped to the ground. Horses stumbled and fell, riders collided, and the sweep was checked. But the Blackfoot were ferocious; and the battle was far from ended. Still the warriors came, in spite of their heavy casualties.

Toby's men were outnumbered by at least three or four to one, but those odds no longer mattered. Their superior weapons were equalizing the odds. Firing steadily, repeatedly, Toby brought down four warriors. Suddenly he saw his greatest chance.

Leading a wild charge down the hill at the head of a band of screaming warriors was Red Elk, the principal chief of the Blackfoot and a fighting man renowned throughout the West. Toby squinted down the barrel of his rifle at the chieftain wearing an elaborate feathered headdress and a beaded cloak of leather, which flew in the wind from his shoulders. Then he squeezed the trigger firmly, evenly, and in the next instant Red Elk fell heavily to the ground and rolled partway downhill. There he stopped. His arms flung wide, his body twisted grotesquely, he stared with sightless eyes at the blue sky above the Black Hills.

The loss of their leader threw the Blackfoot into confusion, and their attack faltered. They halted and began to regroup.

Toby took advantage of the opportunity. Leaping to his feet and tugging at his stallion's reins, he shouted, "Remount and into battle formation!"

The two captains repeated his order, and the scouts reacted swiftly. Within moments the entire battalion—with the exception of several men who had been wounded—were on their feet, in the saddle, and moving into battle formation, awaiting the command to advance.

"Charge!" Toby roared.

"Charge!" the captains repeated, and the battalion swept forward in a broad swath, ascending the hills.

The scouts fired repeatedly as they rode. They knew the tide of battle had turned in their favor, and they pressed their advantage. Their rush carried them into the midst of the enemy.

Unlike the bulk of the Eleventh Cavalry, who would have required an order to change weapons, the scouts needed no such instruction and acted on their own initiative. Dropping their rifles into the leather slings at-

ached to their saddles, they drew their sabers and
began slashing to the left and right.

Had Red Elk still been alive, he might have rallied his
braves and enabled them to resist this new, vicious surge
by their foes. But without him his warriors were lost.
Each Blackfoot was on his own, cut off from his fellows,
and was being subjected to a merciless onslaught by a
saber-wielding demon.

Swinging his own saber with expertise, Toby saw that
his men were not only inflicting severe casualties but
were also creating a panic in the ranks of the Indians.

The Blackfoot began to take flight. They tried to escape the sabers of their opponents and flee uphill.

"Spread out!" Toby roared. "Keep showing them your
steel!"

The scouts spread out, their sabers glinting in the sun-
light, as they rode with precision up the slopes in pursuit of the Blackfoot. Their maneuver was a classic
cavalry move, and they executed it perfectly. This assault created still more terror among the warriors. They
dug their heels into the flanks of their swift horses, urg-
ing the beasts to greater and yet greater speed in an effort to escape.

Toby restrained his men. They had turned what might
have been a humiliating defeat into a significant victory,
with few scouts lost and many Indians killed. But Toby
knew how quickly the tide of battle could turn. Therefore, rather than risk the lives of his men, he called off
the pursuit.

Having made contact with the enemy, Toby was now
in a position to instruct the bulk of the Eleventh Cavalry
on what Colonel Andy Brentwood most wanted to know,
the location of the main body of Indian troops. Clearly,
the Blackfoot were fleeing in the direction where most of

their comrades were encamped, and it would be a
simple matter for the main force of the Eleventh
Cavalry to follow them, once Toby brought the information he had gleaned to Andy Brentwood.

The bloodlust of the scouts was aroused, and they
would have preferred to kill every warrior within reach.
But their discipline held, and they obeyed Toby's order,
reluctantly abandoning their chase and keeping their
formations, pulling toward the rear through the narrow
valley.

Toby, riding at the head of the formation as he started
off in the direction of the regiment's main body, had
good cause to feel pleased with himself. What he didn't
know—and had no way of finding out—was whether he
had remembered his father's words from times past or
whether he had actually heard the voice of Whip Holt
speaking to him at the start of the battle. To say that his
father had been with him, had been beside him, and had
spoken to him anew, defied all logic and common sense.
Never a follower of the occult, Toby did not believe that
spirits of the departed returned from the dead in order
to advise and guide the living. That was too much for
him.

All the same, he had not only heard his father's voice
but had also felt his father's physical presence beside
him. He realized that if a skeptic demanded to know
how he had determined that his father was actually near
him, he would be unable to answer that question to his
own satisfaction or anyone else's. In the heat of battle,
particularly at a moment of great crisis, he supposed his
imagination could have been playing tricks on him. Pondering on the strange occurrence as he rode at the head
of the column of scouts through the Black Hills, Toby at
last came to a hard and fast conclusion: It did not mat-

ter whether he had simply recalled words of advice his father had given him over the years or whether Whip Holt had actually materialized beside him. The one thing that mattered was that his father's views were still sound and still applicable to the problems of today. Whip Holt had known no peer, with the possible exception of Kit Carson, in his dealings with Indians, and his opinions remained valid, even though times were changing.

When the scouts rejoined the augmented regiment, the troops continued to move forward through the Black Hills. Toby fell in beside the regimental commander and made his report as they rode. Andy Brentwood listened intently, and when Toby had finished his recital, the colonel asked, "Would you estimate that you defeated the better part of the Blackfoot force?"

Toby laughed dryly. "Far from it," he said. "From what I gleaned visiting the towns and villages in Dakota, the Blackfoot are able to muster at least one thousand braves. The force we whipped this morning was no more than one-third of that size."

"In other words," Colonel Brentwood said crisply, "we still have six hundred or more Blackfoot to beat, approximately that same number of Cheyenne, and one thousand to fifteen hundred Sioux."

Toby weighed the estimates carefully. "I guess those figures are pretty accurate, Andy," he said.

The colonel sighed. "Then I've got my work cut out for me, that's for sure," he replied. "Even with the extra men that General Blake sent me, I can't put more than one thousand men into the field, and that's an optimistic figure."

"Based on my experience with the Blackfoot this morning," Toby said, "you have enough to win a victory."

"I don't have much choice," Andy replied grimly.

Every man in the Eleventh Cavalry was important. The scouts, having fought a full-fledged battle that morning, were exhausted, but they shook off their fatigue, and with Toby again in the lead, they once more rode out ahead of the main body, seeking the enemy.

Their efforts proved futile. For two days and two nights the scouts searched the Dakota countryside in vain. They found a spot where an enormous body of Indians had been camped, but for some reason the camp had been abandoned, the Indians again scattering in all directions.

Toby made a great effort to understand what was happening. "As I see it," he said to the captains of the two troops of scouts, "the Blackfoot became discouraged after they lost Red Elk. It's possible that the pessimism of the Blackfoot was contagious and was picked up by the Sioux and the Cheyenne."

"Do you really believe, Major, that three of the toughest, meanest tribes on the entire continent of North America would quit without fighting a major battle?" one of his captains asked.

Toby shrugged. "I don't know what to believe," he replied. "There isn't much question but that the loss of Red Elk was a major blow, and the Blackfoot will need to recover from it. Chief Big Knife of the Cheyenne is undoubtedly a warrior of courage, but I'm not forgetting that he's the junior partner in the alliance, so he's bound to be cautious. What the Indians will do really boils down to the decision of one man, Thunder Cloud of the Sioux. He'll lose no chance to throw us out of the Dakota Territory. At the same time, however, he's a wise, shrewd operator, who's had enough contact with our weapons to know that our rifles are infinitely more powerful than the bows and arrows that his Sioux warriors carry. How he'll react is anybody's guess."

In order to search more effectively for the enemy, the scouts spread out over an area of several miles, with Toby maintaining his position in the center of the loose formation. The battalion left the Black Hills behind and descended into the vast plains of Dakota, with the troops increasingly mystified by the absence of the Indians.

At last two scouts, riding on the extreme right wing of the battalion, notified Toby that they had sighted a large gathering of Indian braves ahead. He immediately sent word to Colonel Brentwood and then rode to judge the gathering for himself.

Sunset was approaching by the time he reached the observation post in the tall grass. Squatting with the two scouts, having left his horse with theirs to the rear, he peered at the gathering.

"Near as I can make out," one of the scouts said, "there's at least one thousand warriors in that city they've set up yonder—maybe even more."

Toby peered at the sea of tepees and counted the large number of campfires. He could see that more than one nation was represented at the camp, and he suspected that each of the three allies had a considerable body of men there. But, like his scouts, he was mystified and had no idea what could be motivating the Indians. It made no sense that they had retreated to the prairie when it would have been much easier for them to make a stand against the Eleventh Cavalry in the hills. It made even less sense that the braves of three different nations had chosen to stay together instead of dispersing promptly to their own towns and villages. Apparently something out of the ordinary was brewing.

Retracing his steps to the place where he had left his stallion, Toby mounted and set out at a gallop for the main body of cavalry, which was on the move some miles behind the scouts. When he joined the regiment, he told Andy Brentwood about locating the elusive body of Indians.

The colonel frowned. "What do you suppose is behind their retreat to the prairie?"

Toby shrugged. "I'm not much good at guessing games," he said, "but I feel this much. The braves still have their horses and their weapons, and they're not going to surrender without giving us a fight."

The augmented regiment continued its march long past its normal supper hour, and the colonel finally called a halt late in the evening beside the bank of a river. The campfires of the Indians were visible in the distance, and several officers on his staff questioned the wisdom of halting within sight of the enemy.

Andy nevertheless ordered campfires lighted so a hot supper could be prepared for the men. "The Indians use scouts just as we do," he said, "so they're bound to know we're in the neighborhood. It's impossible to keep the approach of a large body of men secret in terrain this flat. I couldn't ask the men to fight on empty stomachs at the end of a long day's march, so they may as well eat a decent, hot meal and get a good night's rest . . . if we're allowed a night's peace."

There was little rest for Toby that night. He moved forward with his scouts to positions as close as he dared to the Indian encampment, then took turns with the men of his battalion keeping watch on the foe. The night passed slowly.

In the morning the Indians seemed undisturbed by the proximity of the cavalry. Campfires were built up, and then the braves proceeded to cook large amounts of meat. It was obvious from the quantity of meat that they prepared that they had encountered a large herd of buffalo.

Toby and his men, eating cold field rations of jerked meat and baked beans, determined that all three of the allied Indian tribes were represented in the camp, and this information was forwarded to Colonel Brentwood. The regiment, Toby knew, was preparing for any emergency, and at the first signs that the Indians were mobilizing, Colonel Brentwood would order an immediate attack. But that moment did not come.

Instead, to the astonishment of Toby and his scouts, a small group that consisted of older warriors from all three of the Indian nations was formed. While they waited for the appearance of someone to lead them, two Sioux warriors produced a pole to which a large square of white cloth was tied.

This was enough to convince Toby that the Indians intended to ask for a truce so they could parley with the commander of the regiment. He hastily retreated to the Eleventh Cavalry bivouac, where he relayed the information to Andy Brentwood.

Andy, who had intended to give an order to attack soon but had been deterred by the confusing lack of activity in the Indian camp, smiled at his old friend. "What do you think?" he demanded.

Toby shrugged. "In my experience," he said, "an Indian who talks doesn't attack. I reckon we'd better find out."

They moved to a better vantage point and watched the slow advance of the procession across the prairie. Toby had borrowed a spyglass from one of the staff officers, and through it he studied the approaching Indians. "Most of them," he said, "appear to be members of an escort—a bodyguard. They're all heavily armed. They're carrying every weapon in their arsenal, bows and arrows, lances and tomahawks.

"Thunder Cloud, the principal chieftain of the Sioux, is riding directly behind the warrior who's carrying the flag of truce. Big Knife of the Cheyenne is riding directly behind him, and so is another man who appears to be in his forties, who's wearing the war paint of the Blackfoot. I assume he's the new chieftain they've elected to replace Red Elk, but I don't recognize him."

"Let's meet them halfway, Toby, and see what's on their minds," Andy said.

The lieutenant colonel who was second in command of the Eleventh Cavalry intervened. "I suggest, sir," he said, "that several aides accompany you, and an armed honor guard, too. There are a lot of savages in their delegation, and I don't trust them as far as I can throw them."

"Oh, I don't trust them," Andy replied calmly, "but Major Holt and I can look after ourselves."

Toby addressed those who were remaining behind. "Keep watch on my left hand, gentlemen," he said. "If I take a bandanna from my pocket and drop it to the ground, that means serious trouble is brewing. In that case, don't hesitate. Send your fastest battalion galloping across the prairie in a full charge. We're going to be in a vulnerable spot, but don't do a blame thing unless I give you the signal."

He and Andy mounted their horses and started forward across the prairie. Both wore their swords, carried pistols in the holsters at their sides, and had fully loaded rifles laid across their saddles.

From a distance they could see Thunder Cloud's lips

moving, and they realized from the way the other Indians in the party were staring at them that the Sioux chieftain was explaining their ranks and identities. Toby guessed that he was recognized as the leader of the cavalry scouts who had won a victory over the Blackfoot.

The Indian escort halted, and Thunder Cloud moved forward, with Big Knife of the Cheyenne and the new leader of the Blackfoot falling in behind him. Each raised a hand in a stiff-armed greeting.

Andy Brentwood and Toby returned the gesture, but both remained silent, waiting for the Indians to speak first.

Thunder Cloud's full, resonant voice was sorrowful. "I cannot call those my brothers," he said, speaking in his own tongue, "who killed Red Elk of the Blackfoot and so many of the warriors who followed him."

Toby, looking intently at Thunder Cloud, spoke in the language of the Sioux. "We cannot call those our brothers who ravage our land, who burn our farms and ranches, kill and scalp our people."

Andy spoke immediately, as though he and Toby had rehearsed the scene. "You know us, Thunder Cloud," he said, "just as we know you. When you and your people decide to live beside our people as good neighbors, we will grant peace. The same is true of the Cheyenne and of the Blackfoot. We have offered peace to many Indian nations, and they have accepted it. We have given them vast lands where they hunt, fish, and live in freedom."

Toby was quick to pick up the refrain. "When you choose the arrow and the tomahawk in preference to the pipe of peace," he said, "then you become our enemy, and we will make war against you, just as you have made war against us. We will use our powerful firesticks against you. For every soldier you kill, ten of your braves will be killed in his place. I visited your villages this winter and spring, Thunder Cloud, and everywhere my message was the same. Make a treaty of friendship with us, because if you go to war against us, you cannot win."

Andy Brentwood now resumed. "The soldiers you see behind us at this moment are fewer in number than the braves of your nations gathered here on the prairie. But if I give the order for them to fight, they will vanquish you. Not because they are stronger or wiser or more courageous or better warriors. No! Because their weapons make them invincible!"

There was a wry gleam in Thunder Cloud's eyes, and his voice was dry as he responded. "We have listened to the words of Brentwood and the words of Holt. But we have not needed those words to make up our minds. We knew what we intended to do when we rode forward to-day to meet you."

Andy tensed, and Toby also felt uneasy as they waited for the chief to continue.

"You have demanded that we sign treaties of peace with your government," Thunder Cloud said flatly. "So be it. We are here now, and we are ready to put our marks on the papers that you will present to us."

Colonel Brentwood stared at him incredulously, and even Toby, after a lifetime of training in impassivity when dealing with Indians, found it hard to hide his feelings. He, rather than Andy, was the first to find his voice. "Does Thunder Cloud tell us," he said, "that the Sioux, the Blackfoot, and the Cheyenne are willing to become the friends of the United States and her people?"

Thunder Cloud's reply was harsh and unexpected.

"The Indian nations," he declared, "will never be the friends of those who steal their hunting grounds and deprive them of the food they need to live. But the arrows and lances, the tomahawks and knives, that our braves use cannot compete with the thundersticks of your soldiers. One man who has been trained in the use of a rifle is the equal of ten braves."

He was being realistic, Toby thought. Perhaps an all-out, definitive battle was not inevitable, after all.

"We will make a treaty with the United States," Thunder Cloud said. There was a grudging, resigned quality to his statement.

Thunder Cloud's manner put both Andy and Toby on their guard. "We will sign a peace for all time," said Andy forcibly.

Thunder Cloud permitted no expression to cross his face. "For all time," he echoed, without conviction. "And we of the Indian nations will trade our animal skins for your horses, your cloth—and your firesticks."

Andy and Toby looked at each other. It was plain that the Indians were only buying time. When they acquired firearms of their own and learned to use them, the threat of war in the West would be renewed.

Andy, however, had no choice. He could not insist on fighting a battle against foes who were willing to sign a treaty. Therefore, he was obliged to accept the peace that Thunder Cloud offered him.

His only recourse was to notify his superiors in Washington of the scheme devised by the Indians. If the War Department could be convinced that the peace was illusory, that full-scale hostilities would break out as soon as the Indian nations had guns, then the goverment could devise a policy of keeping firearms out of their hands. Only in that way would a permanent peace be assured.

"I accept the peace offer of the tribes," Andy said, and smiled.

Thunder Cloud returned a smile as cold as Andy's. They reminded Toby of two free-for-all fighters who circled each other warily, each seeking an advantage before the start of a bout.

The regimental adjutant was summoned, and he prepared four documents, one for each of the three nations and for the United States. Colonel Brentwood signed them, the chieftains did the same, and Toby Holt affixed his signature as a witness.

The formalities duly observed, the two forces drew apart, with the Indians separating as they went back to their encampment on the prairie, from there heading for their towns and villages throughout the Plains. The augmented regiment marched back to Fort Shaw in Montana.

Andy Brentwood and Toby Holt knew they had bought a temporary peace that would last only two or three years, but they were satisfied they had done the best they could. At least no lives had been lost, and settlers were free to continue to move into Dakota, Montana, and Wyoming. Also, considerable progress could be made on the northern railroad line across the continent.

"When we get back to the fort," Andy said thoughtfully, "we'll write separate reports to the War Department, and we'll both stress the temporary nature of the peace that has been established. Then what are your plans, Toby?"

"I assume you're going to release me from active service—"

"Of course," Andy interrupted. "You'll be demobilized immediately."

"I'm going to head for the ranch in Oregon as fast as my horse will carry me," Toby replied, grinning. "My baby is more than two months old now, and I want to see him and my wife."

Andy laughed. "Then you can act as your own messenger and carry copies of our reports to the Army of the West. You can do more to convince General Blake orally than we can do on paper that the peace we've arranged is temporary and shaky."

"I'll convince him, never fear," Toby replied firmly.

After wiring Clarissa from Fort Shaw that he was on his way home at long last, Toby traveled swiftly. He crossed the Continental Divide in the Rocky Mountains in a few days, taking only short rests on the heights for himself and his horse. The summer weather was mild, and he quickly traversed Idaho, then the much larger stretch of Washington before nearing the Pacific and heading south to Oregon. He stopped only briefly at Fort Vancouver to drop off Andy's report, and finding that General Blake and his mother were away on a tour of nearby army posts, Toby gave the report to the general's second in command.

Toby and his horse crossed the Columbia River by ferry. When he was on the Oregon side of the river, he remounted and rode toward the ranch outside Portland. It was then that his personal dilemma came to him in full force.

Should he confess to Clarissa that he had engaged in an affair with Gentle Doe? Granted, he had fought with all his strength against his desire, but he had lost the struggle. No matter how he looked at what had happened, he had been unfaithful to his wife.

What made his decision so difficult, so painful, was

the knowledge that his marriage to Clarissa was still very new and that there had been little time for him to prove to her how much he loved her. In the beginning there had been doubts, questions, suspicions about his reasons for marrying her, and Toby realized Clarissa would be very sensitive to anything that indicated less than wholehearted love for her.

Toby knew he loved Clarissa, that he had always loved her, even when he was in the midst of his affair with Gentle Doe. But if he couldn't explain to himself how, in the light of this feeling, he had given in to his desires and had slept with Gentle Doe, he had no idea how he could explain the mystery to his wife.

Was it really necessary that he try? Gentle Doe was dead. No one on earth knew for certain that he had had an affair with her. To be sure, the residents of various Indian communities had taken it for granted that Gentle Doe had been his woman, but they would never be in a position to tell his wife that.

If he kept quiet, Clarissa would never learn of his affair. It was tempting to argue that he would be wise to refrain from mentioning the matter to her. They not only loved each other, but their lives had been complicated by the birth of their son. A confession might relieve his feeling of guilt but was certain to make Clarissa unhappy. His marriage was precious, and he wanted to take no chance of destroying it.

By the time he reached familiar countryside near the ranch, his mind was made up. He would bury the past and live for the future.

The ranch soon spread out before him. With more than a thousand acres of fine pastures and grazing land for the horses that were raised here, the ranch was an enduring testament to Whip Holt, who, with Eulalia, had made his home there for so many years after arriving in Oregon. A ranch hand saw Toby when he stopped to open a gate at the far end of the property, and soon thereafter Stalking Horse rode up to him at a gallop, a broad smile of welcome wreathing his lined face. They greeted each other joyfully.

"Every year," Stalking Horse said, "you look more like your father."

Toby was flattered. "Clarissa is here?" he asked.

The elderly Indian nodded. "You bet!" he said, chuckling. "She makes everybody work hard. Work in fields, work in barns, work in house, especially in kitchen. Your young wife is like your mother. Everybody works, everybody keeps busy."

Clarissa would be delighted she had been compared to his mother. Toby took a deep breath. "You've seen my son, Stalking Horse," he said. "Is he all right?"

The Indian nodded solemnly. "Fine baby," he said. "A big boy. Soon I will teach him to ride a pony." Suddenly he gestured toward the large main house in the distance. "You go now," he said. "Don't keep your wife waiting."

Toby rode on, habit taking him to the rear of the sprawling ranch house. Mr. Blake, who had been outside with some of the hands, now spotted his master and bounded toward him, barking excitedly. Toby dismounted and bent to hug his dog, who licked his face repeatedly.

"Good to see you, boy," Toby said, rising. He handed his horse over to one of the stable boys, then continued on toward the house. As he approached the kitchen, the door burst open, and Clarissa emerged. She was running, her arms outstretched in greeting, her long red hair flying behind her, her smile ecstatic.

He caught her in his arms, and they embraced eagerly, breathlessly. Their lips met, and they kissed hungrily. Her presence overwhelmed him, and he knew from her taut embrace that she felt as he did.

At last they drew apart, although his arms continued to encircle her small waist.

"Let's—go inside, darling," Clarissa said breathlessly. "Every hired hand on the property is watching us."

Toby laughed, then kissed her soundly again before he gave in to her request. "You look wonderful," he told her, one arm continuing to encircle her.

"That's how I feel," she said, "particularly now that you're here." She searched his face carefully. "You're tired, Toby."

He shrugged. "It's nothing a few nights in my own bed with you beside me won't cure," he replied. "How's my son?"

"I just fed him and put him to bed," Clarissa replied. "He's probably still awake. Come along."

He followed her down the corridor to a room adjacent to their own bedchamber. There, staring up at him solemnly from his bassinet, was a diaper-clad creature with fair hair and pale blue eyes.

Returning the gaze, Toby felt uncomfortable. "Good Lord, boy—you're so little!" he muttered.

Clarissa reacted indignantly. "Little?" she demanded. "He's huge. He weighs over ten pounds! Dr. Martin said he looked like a Holt from the moment he was born, and he's right." She stooped down and picked up the infant. "Don't you agree?"

"I reckon," he muttered, and involuntarily took an alarmed half-step backward as she thrust the baby at him. Then he took the child in his arms, holding him as though afraid he would break in two, and stared down at him in fright.

Clarissa had to curb a desire to giggle. "Here's the father I've been telling you about," she said. "Say hello to Papa."

Toby stared down at the baby, unable to look elsewhere. "Have you given him the name we once agreed upon?"

"Of course. He's Timothy Holt. Tim. In naming him that, we go back to the first Holts in America."

"Hello, Tim," Toby said, smiling. "Glad to know you. I reckon we'll become a heap better acquainted as time goes on."

The muscles around the baby's mouth twitched slightly.

Toby was electrified. "He smiled at me, Clarissa!" he cried. "He actually smiled at me!" Pointing, he waggled a finger in the direction of his son.

Tim Holt further endeared himself to his father by reaching up and grasping Toby's finger. The man looked ecstatically at the tiny hand that encircled his finger. "Well, now," he muttered. "Well, now."

Clarissa laughed happily.

Toby's joy was boundless. "He'll soon be big enough to take riding lessons on the smallest pony I can find for him," he said, "and I know a sergeant in ordnance at Fort Vancouver who'll make a tiny pistol for him, a replica of a Colt six-shooter, that will actually shoot real bullets. He can't start too young to learn about firearms."

She rescued the infant from his proud father's grasp. "Since you're not going to be giving him any riding or shooting lessons today," she said, "maybe you'll let me put him back to bed instead."

"By all means," Toby replied sheepishly, and after his wife replaced the baby in his bassinet, Toby followed her into the kitchen.

"I thank heaven you're home for more reasons than one, believe me," Clarissa said. "Cindy and Hank Purcell are spending their summer vacation here with me on the ranch. They've gone out riding and will be home soon, and they've been pestering me until I've gone half out of my mind wanting to know when you'd arrive."

Toby was amused. "And how are they both making out?" he asked. "Did they have a good year in school? Did they get along with each other?"

His wife nodded. "They've gotten along splendidly! Your mother and the general were able to go off to San Francisco without the slightest concern for the welfare of the children, and now that the trial is ended, they're able to make a tour of the army posts under General Blake's command."

Toby looked at her blankly. "I don't understand," he said. "Why have they been in San Francisco? What trial?"

Clarissa looked at him, and comprehension dawned slowly. "Oh, dear," she said. "It hadn't occurred to me that you don't know, but, of course, you wouldn't. Sit down, Toby."

He sank into a chair and listened in wonder as she related the story of what had befallen Beth Martin.

Toby hardly stirred in his chair, and when she was done, he rose, went to a cupboard, and poured himself a drink of whiskey. "What a nightmare!" he said. "I feel so sorry for Beth—and for Rob."

"Me, too," Clarissa replied. "I just hope they can get together again."

Toby was alarmed. "They're not together now?"

She shook her head. "Rob is up in the Sierra Nevada laying track for the central route for the transcontinental railroad. Beth has decided to wait for him in San Francisco rather than come back here or go to Fort Vancouver. According to your mother, she's staying with her new friend, Kale Salton, the woman whose testimony turned the case around."

He was on the verge of commenting that Beth had showed less than good judgment when she accepted the hospitality of a prostitute. But he knew so little about the case that he kept his opinion to himself. Besides, his own past was far from spotless. He was reminded again of his affair with Gentle Doe, and a wave of guilt swept over him.

Just then, the baby began crying, and Clarissa said, "I guess Tim is hungry."

"I thought you just fed him a little while ago," Toby protested.

Clarissa smiled, walked over to where Toby was sitting, and kissed him. Her husband had a great deal to learn about his son. "At his age," Clarissa said as she headed out of the room, "Tim spends most of his days eating and sleeping."

Toby was left alone, but not for long. His sister and Hank came into the room. Cindy took one look at him, shrieked gleefully, and threw herself at him, hugging him ferociously.

Hank stood back shyly, although it was obvious from the sheen in his eyes that he regarded Toby as his hero.

The youngsters jabbered simultaneously. This appeared to be a common occurrence because when Clarissa returned to the kitchen to begin supper, she ordered them to speak one at a time. Both were eager to learn details of Toby's adventures in Dakota.

He had to oblige them, but he spent little time telling them about the visits he had paid to the towns and villages of the Sioux. Gentle Doe had accompanied him on those journeys, and he felt uncomfortable recalling that period in Clarissa's presence.

Instead, he concentrated on later developments and found them especially interested in his account of the battle that had taken place between the battalion of scouts and the larger force of Blackfoot warriors. The adolescents regarded his account of the meeting that he and Andy Brentwood had held with the chieftains as anticlimactic.

Hank sounded a trifle scornful. "You don't expect the Indians to keep their word, do you, Toby? They'll tear up their peace treaty and go to war again the minute they think they can win."

"Colonel Brentwood and I bought time for Dakota and Montana, and nothing else," Toby agreed. "There's no doubt in my mind that war with the Indian nations is inevitable. We're going to try and hammer that fact home to the War Department. You understand it right off, Hank, because you're a Westerner. People who have never lived on the frontier don't really understand."

"All I know, Toby," Hank replied vehemently, "is that the only good Sioux is a dead Sioux!"

Again Toby thought of Gentle Doe. But thinking of her in the presence of his wife was too much for him, and he suffered such discomfort that he made a great effort to put the Indian woman out of his mind.

His discomfort lasted well into the dinner hour. Clarissa celebrated his return by preparing his favorite meal:

fresh vegetable soup, broiled steak, baked potatoes, and apple pie.

Toby ate heartily enough, but his guilt had flared anew. He began to doubt the wisdom of his decision to make no mention of the past.

After dinner, Cindy and Hank cleared the table, helped do the dishes, and tidied up the kitchen. Then they were so eager to stay in Toby's company that Clarissa had to remind them that she and her husband had had little time alone together since he had come home.

"But we haven't seen much of Toby, either!" exclaimed Cindy.

Hank demonstrated a greater maturity, however, and responded before Clarissa or Toby could intervene. "I guess your brother and his wife won't exactly be pining away for us if we go off to our rooms," he said. "After all, they've been separated for a mighty long time."

His words were too much for Cindy, who turned scarlet, jumped to her feet, and fled from the kitchen. Hank quickly followed her, apologizing and telling her that he had not intended to embarrass her.

Toby and Clarissa grinned at each other. "I can see that with those two around life here is never dull," he commented.

She nodded. "Why don't you take your coffee into the parlor, and I'll join you there as soon as I fetch the baby? It's time to feed him again."

"I can see that Master Tim Holt is a highly privileged person around this house," he replied as he picked up his coffee cup and carried it from the kitchen to the parlor.

Once he was alone again, his smile faded. He had been wrong in deciding to keep silent about the past.

The single most important element in life, as his father had told him repeatedly, was truth. Plain, unvarnished, simple truth.

By keeping silent about what had happened between him and Gentle Doe he was committing a lie of omission. He could not live with himself, much less with Clarissa, unless he told her the entire story and let her make her own judgment. She was not only his wife but also the mother of his son, and she deserved his loyalty, just as he expected loyalty from her.

When Clarissa came into the parlor carrying Tim, Toby, who was standing at the window, turned slowly to face her. "There's something I've got to tell you," he said as gently as he could.

When she saw his face and heard his voice, she braced herself.

Toby told her the story of his relationship with Gentle Doe, omitting nothing, from the time of his first meeting with her, until her burial at Fort Shaw. He refused to evade, rationalize, or make excuses, and he ended on the same, firm, solemn note on which he had started his recital.

"I want you to understand one thing, Clarissa. I never loved Gentle Doe. I took her because she was a woman who made herself available to me, and I was a man. I loved you, I love you still, I've never stopped loving you, and I hope you can find it in your heart to forgive me so that you and little Tim and I can go on together."

Clarissa stared at him, so stunned that she could not reply. She had been looking forward to his homecoming for so long now that his news shocked her all the more. Why did he have to tell her this when she so wanted everything to be perfect, when she wanted more than anything else an affirmation of his love for her?

Pulling herself together, she finally replied, "I don't rightly know what to say to you, Toby." Her voice was choked, and her tone was cold, distant. "I'm not having hysterics, and I'm not saying any of the mean things that would hurt you because I'd regret them, and once they're out, there's no taking them back."

He nodded slowly, his fists clenched.

"I can't tell you now how I'll feel or what I want," she said, taking a deep breath. "I need time to digest what you've told me. I've got to sleep on it. I'm not putting a noose around your neck or trying to punish you, but I need time to think, to decide what's best for me, and what's best for my baby—our baby."

He took a step toward her, about to speak.

"Don't say anything," she said. "Not right now. Let me be by myself, for tonight at least. Maybe tomorrow, or the next day, I'll know what to do."

Carrying Tim, she rose slowly to her feet and left the room.

Toby, torn between hope and despair, didn't know what to think of his chances of recovering his wife's love and respect. Time, it had been said, was a great healer, and Clarissa could certainly have all the time she needed to work the problem out. But what if she was unable to do that, what if their marriage was always going to be shadowed by suspicions and doubts? Toby, who had rejoiced when he found the one person he could love with his whole heart, now found himself feeling very much alone.

He sighed deeply, then left the parlor and walked out of the house. In the growing darkness he could make out the numerous ranch buildings in the distance and could hear the snorting, shuffling sounds of the horses in the nearest paddock. For now, there would be no answers to

his questions. He would have to wait until Clarissa was
ready. In the meantime, he would attend to the affairs of
his ranch. Only in that way would he be able to find
peace of mind in the weeks to come.

★ WAGONS WEST ★

A series of unforgettable books that trace the lives of a dauntless band of pioneering men, women, and children as they brave the hazards of an untamed land in their trek across America. This legendary caravan of people forge a new link in the wilderness. They are Americans from the North and the South, alongside immigrants, Blacks, and Indians, who wage fierce daily battles for survival on this uncompromising journey—each to their private destinies as they fulfill their greatest dreams.

☐	24408	**INDEPENDENCE! #1**	$3.95
☐	26162	**NEBRASKA! #2**	$4.50
☐	24229	**WYOMING! #3**	$3.95
☐	24088	**OREGON! #4**	$3.95
☐	26070	**TEXAS! #5**	$4.50
☐	24655	**CALIFORNIA! #6**	$3.95
☐	24694	**COLORADO! #7**	$3.95
☐	26069	**NEVADA! #8**	$4.50
☐	26163	**WASHINGTON! #9**	$4.50
☐	22925	**MONTANA! #10**	$3.95
☐	26184	**DAKOTA! #11**	$4.50
☐	23921	**UTAH! #12**	$3.95
☐	26071	**IDAHO! #13**	$4.50
☐	24584	**MISSOURI! #14**	$3.95
☐	24976	**MISSISSIPPI! #15**	$3.95
☐	25247	**LOUISIANA! #16**	$3.95

Prices and availability subject to change without notice.

Buy them at your local bookstore or use this handy coupon:

Bantam Books, Inc., Dept. LE, 414 East Golf Road, Des Plaines, Ill. 60016

Please send me the books I have checked above. I am enclosing $_____ (please add $1.50 to cover postage and handling). Send check or money order —no cash or C.O.D.'s please.

Mr/Mrs/Miss_____

Address _____

City _____ State/Zip _____

LE—7/86

Please allow four to six weeks for delivery. This offer expires 1/87.

Special Offer
Buy a Bantam Book
for only 50¢.

Now you can have an up-to-date listing of Bantam's hundreds of titles plus take advantage of our unique and exciting bonus book offer. A special offer which gives you the opportunity to purchase a Bantam book for only 50¢. Here's how!

By ordering any five books at the regular price per order, you can also choose any other single book listed (up to a $4.95 value) for just 50¢. Some restrictions do apply, but for further details why not send for Bantam's listing of titles today!

Just send us your name and address and we will send you a catalog!